Taken by Fate

NEW YORK TIMES BESTSELLING AUTHOR

SHANNON MAYER

Copyright

Taken by Fate

Copyright © Shannon Mayer 2022

All rights reserved

Published by Hijinks Ink Publishing

www.shannonmayer.com

Dedication

To Christine Bell
& Denise Grover Swank,
without whom this
book wouldn't be in your hands.

ONE

Sienna

IT'S BEEN FIFTEEN YEARS since the Veil between us and *them* fell.

Fifteen years since humans realized we were no longer at the top of the food chain in the most literal of senses.

The thin, iron handcuffs pinching my wrists were chained to the next girl in front of me, and because she had to keep walking, so did I.

I had to remind myself that I let them catch me. That this was where I needed to be to find Jordan. He'd been taken in the last raid over on fifth street, during the hours that I was dancing. I couldn't let him go without a fight. Without trying to get him back.

He was the closest thing to a little brother that I had, and the fact that he'd been stolen out from under me . . . my guts tensed and I tried not to think about it.

Four lines of women, all shackled together. I was in the third line to the right, trying to see past the bodies ahead of me.

"Why are we stopped?"

"Who knows?"

"Maybe they'll let us go?"

A laugh answered that question.

Another time I might have laughed with them. I'd always enjoyed gallows humor. This time, though, the gallows were a little too close for comfort.

For just a moment the rain eased off, almost to a drizzle, but the sound of water falling caught my ear. I turned my head to the line of girls on my right, shuffling along the same as us. All shades of hair, all under thirty by the looks of it.

But it was the brunette closest to me that I locked my eyes on. She didn't even look up as her bladder emptied, soaking the filthy, white dress she wore. Her knees trembled as the smell of urine, strong even in the muck and rain, filled the air.

"Chin up," I said softly, "nothing is set in stone. I'll bet that a lot of us end up just as maids."

That was my hope. Become a maid to the shifters, and then I'd find Jordan and we'd make our escape. At least I'd been able to figure out that much—I knew which part of the territories he'd been taken to.

The girl's dark eyes swept my way, the tears in them spilling over. "My older brother sold me to pay off his gambling debt. My mom couldn't stop him with the new rules. I shouldn't be here. I can't . . .I can't do this."

A bolt of fury shot through me at her words. What had this world come to? Since the Veil had fallen and the "Others" had taken control, life for us humans had been in a slow, downward spiral. These past couple of years, though?

A straight nosedive.

As much as I'd love to blame that all on the Others, turned out humans were just as monstrous as the creatures that hunted us. Brothers selling sisters, husbands sacrificing wives, brokers auctioning people like cattle, to the highest bidder.

But I wasn't here to change the world. I was here to find my friend and get us both the fuck back home.

I blew out a slow, shaky breath and laid my hand on the girl's lower back, giving her what little comfort I could.

"I'm sorry, honey. I really am. But you will be okay, I'm sure of it. You'll be fine." Of course I had no belief in such assurances. Not really.

Not with all the stories that came out of the territories. Blood and death. Torture and rape.

You couldn't really call that a fairy tale waiting to happen, no matter what the powers that be tried to convince the General populace.

"I'm sure your brother—"

"He doesn't care about me. And my mom didn't even try that hard. I'm one less mouth to feed." She wrung her hands together, over and over, her cuffs clinking.

Jesus, and I thought I had it bad. At least my parents had the decency to die on me before they saw me here, like this. Chained up and being sent to the auction pens like an animal.

The sound of retching ahead of us echoed down the line, a cascade effect as other girls were triggered by the sight and noise.

"Shite," I hissed the word and grit my teeth, looking away. This was not the time to show weakness.

I'd been assured by one of the pen guards who frequented the bar I danced at that the next shipment was going to the werewolves. The shifters. It was their turn for new girls and boys.

Which meant it was my one shot to get to Jordan.

I had a boat lined up to meet us, two months from the day I went into the territories. I touched the beaded bracelet on my wrist. I'd started with sixty beads. I'd remove one a day to keep myself on track. If I couldn't find Jordan by the last day. . .I'd have to leave without him.

But I refused to even consider that as a possibility.

Ahead of me, the young brunette trembled so hard that her body rattled the chains connecting her to the girl in front of her, and to me behind. Still, she shuffled along. A tug on my own chains got me moving forward, but the brown-eyed girl needed a lifeline.

I could be that for her, for at least a few minutes.

"Hey. My name is Sienna. What's your name?"

"Hannah." She hiccupped a sob. "You really think a lot of us will be maids? I don't want to go with the wolves. Or the blood. . .suckers." Her voice lowered and she shook her head rapidly, as if straight denial would save her.

Our four groups kept on shuffling along through the mud made from thousands of feet being pushed into the pens since our treaty with the Alpha Territories over a decade before.

That treaty was simple. Our side offered human sacrifices in exchange for relative peace from those that could destroy us if they chose. They could come replenish their supply as needed from the mainland, so long as they didn't create chaos by swooping in and creating terror and mayhem on the streets.

Vampires, werewolves, fae, demon and the fallen were not allowed to roam freely here.

Supposedly.

A shudder rippled through me. "I think you'll have a shot at being with the fae, or maybe even the winged guys. You're very pretty, and beauty is highly prized there." At least, from what I understood. To be fair, I didn't know a lot about the pens—people who went in didn't come back to tell the tales—but Hannah didn't have to know that. And she also didn't have to know that we were all going to the wolves. No point in adding to her panic.

The crack of thunder above our heads was followed by a brilliant flash of lightning that cast the lines of girls into stark relief on the shoreline pens.

"How did you get here?" Hannah asked through her hiccupping sobs. "You have an accent. Where are you from?"

I smiled, though it felt odd when I wanted to have my own little breakdown. Because reality was setting in.

Two months.

I had two months to find Jordan and get us both out.

"My parents died not long after the Veil fell and the world went to shit. I was in an orphanage in London for close to ten years before they said I was on my own. I've just been . . .making my way across North America ever since."

Always there was a pull to keep moving, to keep going. I didn't stay in any city long. Just long enough to make some money dancing so me and Jordan could move again.

Lather, rinse, repeat.

Staying in one spot was a fool's errand and a good way to draw attention to you. Especially at my age. A few more years and I'd be outside the range of what Collectors were looking for.

"Were you looking for a safe place?" Hannah asked.

"Looking for something, I guess." I shrugged and forced a smile to my lips.

A something I couldn't define, but I felt it inside of me, whispering that I was closer every day. Whispering that there was someone out there looking for me, as hard as I was looking for them. Fanciful thinking, I know.

I blinked and made myself smile at Hannah. "I was here in Seattle, trying to find an old school friend," that part was true, too, "Rose. That's her name. We were in the orphanage together back in London. Anyway, I got caught up in one of the Collectors' sweeps of the downtown area."

That last part was not quite true. I'd gotten very good at avoiding the sweeps, but this time I let them catch me. For Jordan.

"Oh. So you really have bad luck, then, huh?"

I choked out a laugh. "Oh, honey, you have no idea."

Perhaps it was my laugh that turned my luck that day, calling down the wrath of some unknown god by my lack of humility. Because I believed I could outsmart the supernaturals that had claimed our world as their own. Maybe if I'd been more sober, more demure, I wouldn't have ended up facing my worst nightmare.

A hand clamped down on my arm, and I spun to face a large, portly man, his gut hanging out from beneath a too-small shirt that was bursting at the seams under a thick pelt vest that was also too small. As it was, he looked like a sausage stuffed too tight and growing long mold.

The fur trim on his vest along with a patch emblazoned with the head of a wolf marked him as a liaison for the shifters. I had to fight the sigh of relief.

Closer and closer—it wouldn't be long before I was with Jordan.

"You, in this pen over here," he growled, roughly uncuffing me.

Above us, the thunder barked like a junkyard dog, booming out a warning, the lightning sparked, and the skies opened up. A sudden torrent of rain fell as if someone upended a bucket on our heads.

The northwest was known for its shitty weather, but this was a bit much. I held a hand up to the sky and flipped off the clouds. I mean, at this rate, there very well could be some other race up there just jerking us around.

Not that we didn't have enough as it was.

Fae.

Werewolves.

Angels.

Demons.

And the worst of them all, in my opinion? Vampires. They had been at the front of the lines when the war started after the Veil fell.

Not that the war lasted long.

No, not long at all.

The combined might of the five races, their magic, and control over the elements had put us, humans, in our place in a matter of weeks.

The world governments and NATO had begged for a plea bargain, and this was what we'd been given.

An exchange system—a few lives sacrificed to spare the majority.

I lifted my hand to the chain-link fence that surrounded us. A perfectly round pen that held twenty-five women.

"Oye now, listen up! We got one pen for sex. One pen for food. One pen for slaves. And the last. . . the last you did not want to be in." The fat vested man laughed. "Always the same. Chum. You don't want to be in that last pen."

Chum.

My heart lurched. "Fuck me," I whispered. I hadn't known that was an option.

The portly one walked around the cages, speaking loud enough to be heard over the thunder and rain. "Twenty-five women will go onto the same boat as the rest of you. But instead of setting foot onto the Empire Territories, they will be cast into the ocean over the deep of the Pacific Ocean."

"What, why?" A woman in the pen across from us wailed. "Why would they throw us over board? Why not just send us back home if we're of no use?"

More laughter from the fat man. "Food for the supernatural creatures of the deep my dear. They have appetites too, you know—another part of the bargain. Just one that nobody likes to make public, you got it? No telling our secrets." His laugh rolled around us. "Ah, I forgot none of you will be able to tell anyone our secrets!"

Horror flickered through me and it was a struggle to stay on my feet. I thought I'd be made a servant at best. A concubine or part of a harem at worse. I had a plan in place for that possibility. Peeing myself would look like child's play compared to what I was prepared to do to make myself undesirable. Now though? That had all changed because of one. Single. Word.

Chum.

Chum hadn't even been on my list of 'what-could-happen-if-you-go-after-Jordan'. Because no one came back from the pens to tell the tales.

I clutched at the fence and breathed through the oncoming panic, focusing on the sense in my head that this was the right thing to do. I had to go after Jordan. He needed me.

A soft, melodic voice from one of the other women began to rise around us as the rain rolled down over our bodies, slicking hair, skin, and clothes alike.

I wrapped my arms around me for a little warmth and let the haunting tune give me a moment of peace as it echoed across the stinking pens.

"One hundred women brought to the pens
One hundred cast the dice
Not all will leave alive, but all give sacrifice
To keep the peace

9

To stop the flow of blood
One hundred women, our tears that flood
Each phase that comes, your turn is soon,
A thousand tears, for the fullest moon."

"Get that singer over here," a booming voice cracked over the storm around us. "The bidders want entertainment."

And just like that, one of us was saved. For the moment, at least. Because she played the game right. She'd charmed them.

"Double shite," I muttered. Unless the bidders wanted a girl with a mouth full of English cursing and an affinity for finding trouble, I was in deep.

It never occurred to me that I'd have to come up with a damn talent like singing when I'd let the Collectors take me. I'd figured they get a look, realize I was far from the beauties they wanted, and I'd be a maid to a pack of barking boys. Easy peasy.

Before I could go much further down that line of thought, someone tugged on my shirt. I turned to see Hannah behind me, her brown eyes wide and shocky, her skin as pale as cream. Without even considering that I barely knew her, I threw my arms around her and held her tight—maybe needing the contact as much as she did in that moment. Her slight body shook hard against mine, and she buried her face against my shoulder.

"I'm so afraid. Sienna, what can we do? I can't even swim! Never mind sing, or . . ."

The other women around us watched as I did my best to soothe her. "I know. All of us are in the same boat, honey. All we can do now is make the best of it."

"The best of it?" a growling voice snapped from across the pen. "There is no best of it you stupid girl.

A woman who was probably younger than she looked approached us. Her once-blonde hair was tangled and knotted and a chunk had been pulled out from the side of her head, leaving a raw-looking bald spot She limped heavily on her right leg.

"This place is death, even if you don't get tossed into the ocean as passage."

Hannah blinked. "As passage?"

"That's the price the boat pays, to bring the rest of the girls to the Territories. Chum. You heard the fat boy over there." She smiled, showing off amazingly white, even teeth that stood out in stark relief against her dirty face. "But you think if you don't go into the ocean, you'll live long? The werewolves, they have their games. Hunting the humans they take. The fae look at us like bugs, insects to be squashed or stuffed into jars if we are interesting enough to bother studying."

Her voice gained power as the women around us went silent, listening to her.

"And the angels? They are no better than their demon cousins. Light and dark, two kinds of demons that only want to destroy your soul, leaving your body to rot." She lifted a hand to me and pointed to my hair, daring to snag a long strand of it. "But it's the vampires that be the worst. We all know that. They drink our blood. They fuck us senseless. And then, when they are tired of us, they feed us to their pets. Abominations of their own making.

Dragon-like creatures they call Hunters. More like devourers, I say. Hunting implies that us prey have a fighting chance to get away."

My hands were cold now, the rain pelting down was turning icy, but it barely registered as the woman's words sunk deep into my heart, shaking what confidence I had left.

"How do you even know this? You haven't been there. Or you wouldn't be here." I pointed out and a few of the other woman murmured their agreement.

The woman snorted. "My man was one of the port guards. He knows. He knows the stories, and he whispered them to me."

"How'd you end up here then?" A redhead with bright blue eyes said. "If you've been fucking a port guard why aren't you safe?"

The blonde's lips pursed. "Because he decided he wanted to be rid of me and an unwanted child." She smoothed her top over a slightly bulging little belly. "Easiest way, I suppose."

Beside me, Hannah shook so hard she dropped to her knees.

"I . . .I'm not strong enough. I can't do this, Sienna. I can't. My mother told me . . .that there is always a way out."

Her words didn't make sense. I turned toward her as she lifted a hand to her hair. My brain struggled to process her words as she tugged a pin from her brown locks. Long, slender, and shaved to a deadly point.

Her eyes met mine. "Be brave for us both, Sienna."

In one, swift motion, she drove the pointed hairpin into the side of her throat. She gurgled, toppling to one side before pulling the pin free. Blood spurted from the wound as I dropped to my knees next to her.

"Hannah, no!" I pressed my hands to her throat, but it was too late. She'd severed an artery, and her hot blood slicked my icy hands.

A series of screams went up around me as Hannah's eyes met mine one last time, her mouth moving without sound.

Be brave. Be brave. Be brave.

I saw the moment she died, the light flickering out of her dark brown eyes, the pupils fading in the strangest of ways. As though a cloud had slid over her vision as her soul left her.

"Get off 'er!"

Rough, calloused hands grabbed me by the shoulder, and I was flung away from Hannah, into the mud and piss and shit of the pens.

I turned on my hands and knees to see the Pen Wardens drag Hannah out by her ankle.

"One for the chum, that's easy enough," the one dragging her barked.

I closed my eyes and fought back the tears. Not because Hannah didn't deserve my grief, but...she was right. I had to be brave for both of us.

Both me and Jordan.

I could almost hear his voice now, building me up the way he always did.

"If anyone can do it, you can, Ceecee."

I dug my hands into the mud to push myself up, and there under my palm was something narrow, hard, metallic. I clenched my hand around what could only be the hairpin that Hannah had snuck past the guards.

Of course no weapons were allowed, but she'd gotten this through.

Pulling it carefully out of the mud, I wiped it on my shirt, cleaning the worst of the filth and Hannah's blood off it. The golden hairpin had a butterfly etched into the thickest part.

"Head toward the light, butterfly girl," I whispered as I reached back and twisted up the thick mass of my hair and slid the pin through it.

A weapon, however small, might give me the edge I needed. And perhaps it would give Hannah's horrible death some sort of meaning if I managed to stay alive, find Jordan and escape.

"Oye, all of yous. Line up." Moldy Sausage Man with the furred vest was back.

A tiny bit of hope flared. He looked exactly as you'd expect someone working for the werewolf clans would look if his clothing and the distinct smell of wet dogs emanating from him were any indication.

It had to be the wolves bidding on us then.

Hold tight, Ceecee. Almost there.

I was on my feet in a flash and fell into line with the others. This was not the moment to tip my hand that I was different from the other women. That I had a purpose. That I had a reason to be there. It would come, I just had to be patient. I let a slow breath out and took a step, then another as my turn came.

Portly boy held his hand up. "Name, age, any talents?"

Now, I should have known better, but the fear and shock made me . . .impertinent.

"Is this the Miss America contest? I didn't bring my bikini." I fake gasped and put a hand to my mouth. "Goodness, whatever will I do?"

For being such a big man, he moved fast. His hand snaked out and he clapped me on the side of the head, quite literally ringing my bell.

"Name, age, talents. Now, unless you want to go straight into the chum bin with your little friend over there."

He grabbed my head and twisted it so I had no choice but to look at poor Hannah, crumpled in a heap in between the pens.

Her glazed eyes stared back at me.

For just a moment I saw Jordan there instead, crumpled, his eyes lifeless.

No, no I refused to believe he was gone.

"Sienna, twenty-one." I paused, struggling to find something I was good at. Sure, dancing was on that short list, but what would werewolves want?

"I'm...um, good with animals?"

He let out a snort of disgust before shoving me along. "Follow the others. Good fucking luck with a talent like that."

That was it. No other direction.

And then, I was pushed down a narrow path between pens of weeping women. I bowed my head, a mixture of outrage and sorrow racing through me. The tears leaking from my eyes were hot, scalding my cold skin as I trudged up a low set of stairs and stood on a platform. I tried to see into the gallery of seats before us but floodlights along the floor blazed to life, effectively blinding us to anyone or anything else besides each other.

"They took men to the wolves last month, so it'll be us women now to the same pack."

"How can you be sure?"

I looked around to see the woman who'd claimed to be sleeping with one of the guards.

"Because Robbie told me so," she replied with a smirk, once more touching her belly. "Best he could do for me. They like breeders over in the wolf packs."

I looked at her belly, and a cold swell of unease gripped me. Was Robbie the kind of man who actually wanted to help his baby mama, or was he the kind to try and get rid of her in a more permanent sense?

The women in front of me shifted from foot to foot in the silence. The frantic whispers started, but I could hear the low murmur of male voices in the audience and the creaking of chairs from below.

The bidders.

The werewolves.

They could see us, but we couldn't see them.

Heart pounding, I strained to get a look at them.

"Can anyone see them?" I asked.

Someone shushed me, but a fresh and all-encompassing sense of dread swept through me. I had to see the bidders.

I carefully worked my way through the rows of women, not that anyone tried to stop me.

No one wanted to be on that front row.

Except idiot me.

I stopped at the edge of the platform and stared out into the inky darkness, desperation clawing at my throat. If I could just get a look at them, maybe this awful terror would subside a little. Just when I thought I couldn't take it another second, one of *them* stepped forward into the light. My mouth opened and closed soundlessly as I stared down at a man I'd seen all too often in my dreams.

Eyes the color of dark chocolate, hair as black as midnight, a face that could surely have been carved into stone by Michelangelo himself...

In every dream I'd had of him, I'd run. He'd always caught me, his hands around my throat, his anger palpable, even in my sleep.

Worse than all of that . . .

Fangs, gleaming in the light like polished pearls, sharpened and honed for murder just peeking past the bottom of his top lip.

"Oh, fuck," I whispered.

Any hope I'd had evaporated as horror rolled through me. Not only was I being sold off to the most sadistic creatures in all of the Empire of Magic. Now I knew that the monster of my nightmares had been brought to life.

And I couldn't escape him by waking up.

TWO

Dominic

HER HAIR WAS MATTED and so filthy it could have been any color. Her body hidden under a ragged dress that looked as if it had once been a sack, was lush and curvy, nothing like what was currently trending in the kingdom. Those thoughts faded as her eyes locked on mine and her mouth dropped open in a soft 'O'.

Eyes of gold, liquid honey that drew me in.

"Oh fuck," she whispered, her husky voice driving deep into me like a spike to the chest.

My heart rate skyrocketed and I held my breath to literally stop it in its tracks. My fangs dropped of their own volition as if I were a teenager again, unable to control myself. I tore my gaze away in just a split second, but it was enough to burn her into my mind.

A bell tolled, signaling the start of the auction, and the honey-eyed girl was shoved to the back of the group of women. Gone from sight, but certainly not forgotten.

What the actual fuck had just happened?

Had Anthony spiked my drink with something? I whipped around to look at him, but he was chatting with Raven, a vampire who currently ruled the Seattle area.

Anthony, Earl of DuMont, represented everything that was wrong with our territory—the pomp and circumstance, the excess and extravagant entertainment. Even knowing we'd be tromping through mud, shit, and piss to get to here, Anthony wore shiny, leather unsealed boots, velvet pants, a silk coat with an ascot at his throat, and a bright blue cloak. I'd pay good money to see him sitting on a horse, about to go to battle, while rain poured from the sky. I bet he'd piss his pants before the first bugle sounded.

As he ended his conversation and moved to join me, his foot slipped and he reached out for Raven's arm to right himself. I rolled my eyes in disgust. Vampires were supposed to be fast. Graceful. It had been fifteen years since the Veil had fallen, unmasking the supernatural creatures that ruled the world in secret for so long. Fifteen years since we'd gone from hiding to living in the open, and those fifteen years had made my brethren lax, none more so than Anthony.

"This should be fun," he said when he finally picked his way through the dreck to take his seat beside me.

I let out a non-committal grunt by way of reply.

In my opinion, this place was a perfect example of the changes that had not been in our favor since the falling of the veil. Before, we'd come to the mainland to find food and servants, but we'd been more discreet. We'd chosen the best and taken them away without anyone knowing. Now, we and the other supernatural factions made no secret of using humans as food, servants, and entertainment. Rather often, simultaneously.

I hated the market and view of humanity at its lowest. I hated the stench and the filth. I hated the pleading and crying, for reasons I didn't want to explore. It would take an hour to get the mud out of the cracks and crevices of my leather boots, a task I would be doing myself, not a human servant. A warrior depended on his equipment to be in top-notch condition, and boots were an essential part.

I hadn't wanted to make this trip, and I definitely didn't want to spend time with Anthony. We'd arrived the day before, and last night he'd insisted I join him for dinner with his friends. I'd turned him down, and he'd pulled out the responsibility card in his sniveling tone.

"I thought your purpose was to guard me, General. Are you shirking your duties?"

I very nearly pointed out that I was there to guard the shipment, not him, but I kept my mouth shut and joined his "soiree" as he'd called it, eating the rich food, which included a series of women for dessert.

Anthony and his companions liked to fuck their food, but that had never been my style, and Anthony knew it. So I'd drank the wine spiced with human blood and I watched the debauchery around me with thinly veiled disgust. I finished off my wine, then got up to leave. Studying maps of the sea, determining where a threat might attack on our return trip home seemed like a better use of my time.

As I'd strode for the door, I'd felt Anthony's eyes on me. With his dick in the woman on his lap and his fangs in the vein on her neck, he looked to be in ecstasy. I couldn't help wondering if part of his joy was watching me leave.

I was Dominic Blackthorne, General of the Crown Prince's army and bastard son to King Stirling. Men like Anthony would not let me forget that I would never be legitimate. We had never been friends, and never would be, but I had to wonder what game he was playing. Because if there was one thing I knew about the man, he was always scheming and looking for his next step up in the ladder of our society.

When he'd made their last trip to procure humans, the ship had been raided on the return voyage. All the humans had been taken and four of my guards had been killed—a feat in and of itself for anyone not supernatural. Anthony had returned to court with a tale of the danger he'd faced but with no actual visuals on the killers, as he'd been hiding in his room. His only clue was that he was sure he'd heard animalistic growling. Which of course not so subtly pointed at our werewolf neighbors and added fuel to an already tense situation.

He'd demanded I accompany him on this trip to protect his life—of all the people he could have asked for, it surprised me when my name had even been mentioned.

I'd agreed to join the next trip, not to protect Earl Dumont's life as he'd like to believe, but to make certain I didn't lose any more of my troops—and to see if those responsible would attack again.

While it was possible that the werewolves were behind the incident, I doubted it. My money was on Vanators. The vampire hunters had been on the rise in the last fifteen years. Still, they didn't tend to attack by ship, instead preferring the cover of darkness on land. And why had they stopped? If their forces were strong enough to kill four of my men, why not take everyone on the ship out, Anthony included?

There were too many unknowns to suit me, and I was left with an overall feeling of unease. The same feeling that I'd had before every battle in my life.

A war was coming, even if I was the only one who could feel the rumbling under my feet.

Dragging myself back to the present, I focused on the dais before me.

Despite it being their turn, the werewolves had forgone this shipment, which meant it was now ours. As emissaries of the Crown Prince, Anthony and I were alone in the front row. Behind us were a dozen or more of the vampires who opted not to inhabit the Empire and stayed on the mainland interspersed among humans. They acted as go betweens for the King and the human government.

I nodded at a few that I recognized, and they tipped their heads in return, even as my mind ticked back to the girl with the golden eyes.

I was going to have to get laid when I got home. I knew it had been a while, but I'd been busy, and sex had been the last thing on my mind. Apparently, my dry spell needed watering if I was so hard up that a ragged street rat caught my attention. I snorted at myself and adjusted my dick as it stirred to life.

The manager of the auctions had learned his lesson the hard way to keep the supernaturals apart, and the vampires were often given the best of the best due to our deep pockets. From the looks of the women I'd seen in the pens, though, I had serious doubts that had happened today.

Perhaps that was why the werewolves forfeited their turn?

Once we were seated, the auctioneer nodded toward Anthony and then addressed the crowd.

"You all know how this works. We'll introduce the first specimen, let her show her wares, then you bid."

And then it began.

I refused to wonder who would end up buying the honey-eyed woman. Perhaps Raven. He liked his women on the exotic side.

I'd been to auctions before, before they segregated the supernaturals, but it had been at least five years, and it looked like nothing had changed.

Someone grabbed a woman from the side of the stage and tugged her to the front. She resisted, flailing her arms and letting out little shrieks as she fought back, which only made the vampires around me excited. They missed the thrill of the chase, and they lapped her fear like kittens drank warm milk.

The auction attendants dragged her to the center of the small platform that served as a stage.

Terror filled her brown eyes and her heart beat louder than the rest of the women. Faster. Closer.

Anthony's eyes burned bright and he licked his lower lip, his tongue playing with the tip of one fang.

Before he even made a bid, I knew he'd try to purchase her. And he'd use her first, before he put her back with the group, before the ship reached landfall. That was, if he didn't kill her. It wouldn't have been the first time. But I suspected he'd be more careful on this trip since I was along.

Which again begged the question, why had he really asked for me to come on this trip?

He was purchasing her for the kingdom, and Anthony liked to pay for as little as possible from his own pocket. He wouldn't want to reimburse the King for a dead human.

"What's your name?" the auctioneer asked the woman as two other workers held her forearms to keep her from running.

She stared wide-eyed into the crowd, blinking in the light shining upon her. She didn't answer.

"Okay then," the auctioneer grunted. "We'll just call you Daisy." He turned his attention to the audience. "Daisy looks to be in her early to mid-twenties but she appears to have given birth to at least one child. Could be good for any breeding programs ya might have going on."

"Let me go!" The woman tried to pull loose from the two men, to no avail.

The auctioneer walked over to her. "Her body strength appears to be subpar, so you won't get much manual labor out of her, but she *is* a looker." He grabbed her chin and held her face up so we could see, her long brunette hair hanging like a curtain down her back. Then, he grabbed the top of her tunic and ripped it down the middle. Both men pulled off the remnants then held her arms as she tried to cover her naked breasts.

"She's got nice tits," the auctioneer continued. "So she'd be good for fuckin' or food. Or perhaps you'd like her for both."

Anthony was practically salivating, but he remained quiet as others started to make their bids.

"Two hundred," a man called out.

"Three hundred."

The bidding continued and then began to slow. The auctioneer called out, "Do I hear twelve hundred? Going once, going—"

"Thirteen hundred," Anthony said in a clear voice that sounded as smug as he looked.

"Fourteen," a low voice behind us called. That was Raven.

Anthony opened his mouth to continue bidding, but I grabbed his arm and squeezed in warning.

"No more," I muttered through gritted teeth.

His gaze flattened in fury and he opened his mouth to defy me, but something in my expression must've stopped him because he swallowed hard and nodded.

"Fine, then. I was thinking we could have shared her on the long journey home."

The asshole had no concept of what constituted a long journey. "It's only two days to cross, Anthony. And we're not to touch the females until they're claimed, after the Harvest Games are complete."

His brow lifted. "The Harvest Games haven't started yet."

"A technicality, as you well know. The women are not to be touched. Understood?" I stared him down until he looked away.

"Spoilsport."

Our conversation over his attempted misuse of royal funds would wait until we were on the ship and away from outside ears.

The auctioneer handed Daisy off then brought out the next woman. Her name was Becky and she was a hairdresser.

"Amelia was saying we need someone who can do updos for the other girls," Anthony mused. "Especially in light of the Harvest Games coming up. This one would be useful."

I looked away, already bored of this conversation and unfathomably irritated by the name of what once had simply been called the Testing. If the kingdom was devolving with opulence, the annual Harvest Games was the biggest one of them all. Mocking the humans once more, as if a woman fighting for a place in our world had any chance at true freedom.

Anthony bid on Becky, and won her.

A parade of women crossed the stage, almost every single one of them exposed so the purchaser knew what they were getting. Some tried to cover themselves, their hands splayed wide, but some stood proud with their chins up and their skin pebbling with the cold.

Rather than pay attention, I let my mind wander from the return trip. If it had been the Vanators that had attacked, were they working with another supernatural group? Perhaps they had joined forces with the werewolves in order to fool us?

The vampires were at the top of the hierarchy, and everyone coveted our place. We negotiated on behalf of all the territories with the humans. Whoever it was that had come after the boat had equipment that would have taken a large budget to obtain. It could have been the Shifters to the east of our kingdom, the tensions there were rife with animosity just waiting to spill over.

Finally—thankfully—only one woman was left.

The girl with the golden eyes.

Two men dragged her out and my blood stirred again in a way I didn't like. They didn't bother trying to remove her clothes as they led her to the front of the stage. Her eyes flashed with pure fire as she stared them down. Her hands curled into fists, and I tried not to laugh at her defiance.

That is, until one of the handlers grabbed at her shirt, and her curled fists flew.

Right into his nose.

The blood spray was immediate and the portly man in the wolf pelt vest howled, spinning away from her. More than a few vampires let out soft sighs at the scent of fresh blood. All were old enough to control themselves, but still . . .

"Fucking whore!" The portly man caught himself and stood, blood dripping down his lips. "I'll kill you!"

She didn't run and I couldn't help but arch a brow as she lifted both fists. "Go ahead and try."

Anthony rose from his seat patting a kerchief under his nose as if the blood offended him. I put a hand on his shoulder and shoved him back hard enough into his seat that he bounced.

"You'll miss the show. I rather would like to see if she stops him," I said.

Behind me, Raven laughed. "A bet, old friend?"

"Sure," I said with a clipped nod. "What are the stakes?"

Raven stepped up beside me. "If she loses, I'll take her and she'll become my maid. If she wins, you purchase her for the Harvest Games. Can you imagine the stir a firecracker like that would make with the Duchess trying to turn her into a lady?"

"This is a waste of time," Anthony grumbled. "This one is chum at best. Just look at her."

I narrowed my eyes, trying to figure out why he thought so, before turning my attention back to Raven.

"I'll take that bet, friend," I said with a grim smile. The chance of her actually beating a guard who outweighed her by at least a hundred pounds was slim, but for some reason, I had the sense she was stronger than she looked.

I held a hand out and Raven grasped it hard.

"Done."

The pen warden circled around the woman and she mirrored his movements, never taking her eyes off him.

"She's fought before," Raven murmured. "Damn, I might not get my maid after all."

He wasn't wrong. I'd seen enough fighters to recognize the grace in her movements, the way she kept her feet from lifting off the ground, instead sliding them along.

She wasn't as lithesome as some of the women who had been sold to fill harems of the lesser nobles. She also wasn't as sturdy as the women who had been purchased for manual labor. Her breasts were full and her hips rounded, made for midnight sins that never saw the light of day. Her dark auburn hair was a matted mess precariously held up by a golden pin. Narrowed eyes glittered with a fiery anger that was so clearly alive in her, despite her situation.

Maybe that was what intrigued me.

The guard lunged at her then, open-handed as if to smack her in the head. She ducked, and as his back turned to her, she struck, hard.

"Ouch." Raven winced. "She knows where the kidneys are. Perhaps I do not need a maid all that badly. I do so love to grab their plump asses, and I suspect that one might not be so. . . allowing."

"Backing out already?" I laughed at him. "Coward."

"You there," Raven grabbed one of the auction attendants, "what is the girl's name?"

She hesitated and then looked over her sheet, "Sienna."

Anthony rolled his eyes. "We do not need any more women, and if you were so bored, why did you not stay for the festivities last night?"

I very carefully reached over and put my hand on Anthony's shoulder as the girl—Sienna—moved around the pen warden, blow by blow driving him to his knees.

"Anthony," I purred his name and the earl's gaze dropped to my mouth. I slowly slid my hand up to his neck and then, with a speed that had him still thinking he wasn't in danger, tightened my hold. "Question me again, and I'll tear your head off and throw you out with the chum. Understood?"

He looked astounded, not that I blamed him. Typically, I kept myself in check.

But not today.

Not now.

I shoved Anthony back hard enough to send him sliding through the mud until he came to a stop against the bottom of the stage. Trembling, he touched at his throat.

"How dare you?"

I looked up just in time to see that the guard had finally landed a blow on the girl, straight to the stomach. She doubled over and when he lifted his filthy boot to kick her while she was down, I stood.

"Stop." I let the command roll out of me, not using just my voice, but also tapping into the control every vampire had on humans.

The guard froze, and the girl forced herself to her feet. She paused for the scantest of moments before kicking him in the balls with all her might.

Laughter rolled through the crowd as the fat man fell over, wheezing. Sienna stood, visibly shaking but still . . .defiant.

Interesting.

"Well," the auctioneer cleared his throat. "I don't suppose any of you would like to open the bid?"

Raven snorted. "She won, Dom, thanks to your interference. If I didn't know better, I'd think you'd wanted her to win."

My jaw clenched. "I was merely wagering for sport."

"Anyone? Or should I just send her to the chum pens?"

A vision of her thrashing through the waves as her blood spilled out, her golden eyes dying in front of me . . .fuck me. I should just walk away.

Her eyes trapped mine. Fire and anger burning hot in them.

Defiant.

Wild.

Everything in me tightened. I wanted to fuck her. Even worse than that? I admired her.

"One hundred," I called out.

"Are you insane?" Anthony choked as he crawled to his feet. "We've already spent our allotted money, and she's not worth it."

"A bet's a bet," I replied.

"Do I hear one-fifty?" the auctioneer asked, smiling at Raven who shook his head.

I looked at Anthony, took two strides and put my boot on his hand, holding him in the mud.

"Today is not the day, Earl."

"Sold to the General! Thank you everyone, your wares will be delivered to you..."

The sound of the auctioneer faded as the girl took a step toward me, her body humming with energy that fairly drew my cock to life.

This was a mistake.

I should have left the girl to Raven.

"Let's consider her a present for the Duchess." I ground my heel into Anthony's fingers. "Understood?"

Anthony glared up at me, but then nodded. "Of course. Whatever you want, General."

What I wanted was to grab the girl and throw her up against the wall, burying my cock and my fangs into her over, and over.

Instead, I turned away from the stage doing all I could to not look back, forcing myself to keep on moving.

"Raven. You owe me a drink for taking that one off your hands."

But it would take far more than a drink to forget those eyes.

Damn me, what had I done?

THREE

Sienna

"IT'S TIME TO GET ready, Miss. The Duchess will be coming by for inspection in less than an hour, and we've much to do to prepare." My maid's soft voice tugged at me.

Two and a half days spread between a boat and a ride in a blacked-out carriage and I still didn't understand just how the fuck I'd ended up here.

Here.

In the vampire territories, instead of in the shifter territories. As if my half-baked rescue mission hadn't already been complicated enough.

Hang on, Jordan. Just hang on.

The water sloshed around me in the tub as I lifted a hand to touch my face. The fat guard hadn't hit me anywhere anyone could see at least. My stomach still ached and a large bruise had spread across my belly.

I let my heavy eyelids drift open and nodded to my maid. The frustration I'd managed to tamp down for a solid twenty minutes roared back to life. We'd been dropped off late the night before, each been given a room, a maid, and instructions to rest.

Other than that, I had no idea just what I was doing here. I was meant to be a maid and yet I'd been given one instead.

A bossy one at that.

"Yes. Of course. Just give me a minute? The bath is heaven after being filthy for so long."

The young woman who'd introduced herself as Bethany hesitated and then nodded. "I've got to get some bits and bobs for your hair, in any case. I'll be right back."

She scurried away and I watched her go, wishing I could go with her...wishing I could *be* her.

Bollocks, what a cock up this was.

How was I going to get to Jordan now? I put a hand to my head and settled back into the perfumed water.

Where to even start? I plucked at my bracelet, undid it and dropped another bead off. Three days gone. Fifty-seven to go.

The two of us were both going to die out in these territories if I didn't figure out something fast. Maybe I could ask Bethany about becoming a maid? That would give me the ability to move around more freely.

I snorted to myself. Aspirations to be a maid now?

The last time I'd even thought about a profession of choice, I'd have been six years old. Clueless and happy, like the rest of the human population. Oh-so confident we were at the top of the food chain. Oh-so comfortable in our innate superiority, so much so that it wasn't even a topic of conversation.

As a little girl I'd spent hours in front of the mirror, daydreaming of becoming a ballerina one day, with a crisp, white tutu and cotton candy-colored slippers. Spending my nights leaping through the air while the orchestra played, and the violins sang, and the audience cheered. I'd even taken some lessons here and there.

But that was before the Veil had come down.

And now, maid to a thicket of vampires was what I wanted more than anything else.

Not that things had been all that terrible for me so far, if I was being honest.

In fact, they'd been pretty okay given the whole watching-a-new-friend-commit-suicide-with-a-hair-pin-to-escape-our-shared-destiny-and-then-being-sold-to-a-vampire thing a couple days before. When we'd been loaded onto the massive, wooden ship that looked like it had belonged to Blackbeard in a previous life, I'd half-wondered if I'd die of scurvy or some equally archaic malady on the trip. But, aside from having to wash with a basin and a sponge, and the repeat meal of a rather uninspired chicken soup (please let it have been chicken and not some other white meat), I had to admit, I'd been treated decently. I mean, it wasn't the Princess Cruise line or anything, but I'd been given three squares a day, a decent cot to sleep in and a room of my own. More importantly, I'd gotten off the ship with the same number of holes in my body as when I'd gotten on, and the ones I did have had remained unmolested.

I was logging that as a win after the way the one who purchased me stared me down. The General, they'd called him. His gaze had been like a physical touch. I shivered in spite of myself, my hands drifting over my body before I realized what I was doing and snatched them away.

The truth was, the ride on that bloody pirate ship had been the calm before the storm. But the calm was almost over now and, all too soon, I'd be headed straight into the maelstrom.

The General's face was etched into my mind. Nightmares, he'd haunted them for so long, to see him in the flesh . . .my breath came in little gasps thinking about how he'd looked at me. At the bulge in his pants. Would he fuck me before he killed me, or after?

I sucked in a breath and dipped my head beneath the water for a long moment before coming up for air, doing my damnedest not to imagine what my future held... Not to wonder if I was going to be able to get me and Jordan out of this mess.

And still, I couldn't stop thinking about the dreams. More like premonitions, it now seemed. When I'd seen his face at the auction, it had been a total mindfuck. How? How could I have known him without ever having known him? Once the Veil had fallen and the truth of what was possible in this world came to light, nothing should have surprised me anymore, but I couldn't wrap my head around it.

What did it all mean?

"Hurry, Miss!" Bethany called as she came bustling back into the bathroom, blue eyes wide. "She's running ahead of schedule and will be here in twenty minutes!"

I stood reluctantly, the chill in the air making my skin break out into goosebumps as the water sluiced off of me.

"I know you aren't supposed to divulge much," although that hadn't stopped me from asking so far, and I wasn't one to break a trend, "but can you just tell me who 'she' is, Bethany? I know you said the Duchess, but what is her role here? What is my role here? I just want to be a maid!"

She held out a fluffy, crimson towel and I stepped out of the massive, porcelain tub and allowed her to wrap me in it.

Amazing what being rounded up, kept in a pen, and treated like a pig that hadn't won a ribbon at the county fair could do for a girl's modesty. At some point, I'd apparently stopped giving a shit who saw me naked unless there was a chance they planned to eat me.

Thoughts of the General floated back into my consciousness again. How could it be that the very man I'd dreamed about so many times before had been there, standing before me?

Wisps of those dreams flashed through my mind even now...

Dark eyes as he hunted me down, chasing me through the forests of my imagination. His hands grabbing at me, pinning my arms. Bruising me as he manhandled me, as my clothes tore and . . .chills swept up and down my arms.

"Oh, you're all goosebumpy again! Here, let's use another towel. This one is warmed," Bethany snatched the first towel off and threw the fresh one around me.

I barely felt the heat. Because seeing my nightmare in the flesh had been a kick to the gut that I'd not recovered from.

Then there was the man beside him, who had sent a different kind of tremor through me. Eyes the color of onyx that I hoped I'd never have to look into again. There had been a cruelty to them I couldn't escape, no matter that I'd pushed my way to the back of the crowd to hide from him as the auction started.

Not that it helped me in the end.

Thank Christ he hadn't been the one to bid on me. It had been the other one...the man from my dreams, with the deep, mesmerizing baritone. Not silky, like his counterpart, but gruff.

Raspy.

I shivered and shoved the memory aside, turning my focus back to Bethany. My dreams had been a warning, and I was going to heed them. No matter how it might have seemed at the end, the General wasn't there to help me—he was there to kill me.

To eat me.

What I needed to focus on now was gathering information. Even a little bit would help calm my nerves. This whole push/pull, from misery and filth to the palace and finery I'd been ushered into within a very few short hours was surely designed to make me dizzy with anxiety and fear. Fear of the unknown. Fear of what was coming.

Assholes.

All that did was piss me off, which was good. Anger felt a whole lot better than terror. I knew that much from experience.

"Please, Bethany. I'm flying blind, here," I whispered, hoping to play on the maid's sympathies. "Anything at all you could tell me..."

Bethany rubbed my skin briskly with the warm towel and then wrapped it around me tight before leaning in.

"Duchess Evangeline," she whispered. "She is your everything, Miss. She'll make sure you're taken care of, she'll be your mentor..." The younger girl swallowed hard and looked away. "As best she can be, at least. And she'll make sure you have the best possible chance of —"

"Fifteen minutes!" a voice called through the closed door.

"Damn it! She's going to be cross with me if you're looking a mess." Bethany whipped the towel off me and started furiously drying my hair. "Sienna, if you promise to work with me and get ready fast, I promise I'll tell you more later. Deal?"

Flush with the promise of more information, I nodded and snatched the towel from her. "I'll do the hair, you grab my clothes."

For the next fifteen minutes, we worked together toward a common goal: turning me from a sea hag into a passable-looking young woman. When I stepped out of the bathroom and into the dressing room to peer into the full-length mirror with only sixty seconds to spare, I had to admit, we'd done fairly well.

Bethany had dressed me in an emerald green confection that six-year-old Sienna would've blown a gasket over. It had a sweetheart neckline and nipped in sharply at the waist...a waist that looked impossibly narrow due to the corset that she'd stuffed me into and tied shut with one knee in my back. I smoothed one hand over the silky ruffles and lifted the other to my hair.

I'd managed to wrangle it into a passably fashionable—if somewhat damp—knot that Bethany had tucked tiny sprigs of flowers into. The deep auburn color looked even richer against the green of my dress, and I found myself wishing that life was normal again. That this was me, going to the prom I'd never had, to meet a boy I'd never kissed, and have a magical night that would never happen.

But as I turned my head, the light caught the golden butterfly pin I'd slid into my hair and my whole body tensed.

Poor Hannah. She'd not chosen to get into those pens. At least I could blame myself for ending up here.

This was no fucking prom. I was nothing more than an extra in the most macabre horror movie ever made.

In a word?

Expendable.

Which meant there was no more time for foolish daydreams about proms, or becoming a maid. I had one job and one job only, to find a way to Jordan, and from there to the boat. And I had fifty-seven days to do it.

Once I'd figured that out, I'd move to the next step.

No problem at all.

I fisted my hands at my side and turned to face Bethany, who was fussing with the bow on my bustle.

"Am I going to pass muster?" I asked through suddenly numb lips.

"You are," she said with a satisfied nod. She frowned and snapped her fingers. "Almost forgot."

She rushed back into the bathroom and returned a moment later, a beach stone pendant on a leather thong. "You'll need this."

I bent my head low and let her fasten the clasp, gasping as the cool, clear stone settled between my breasts.

"Need it?" I asked, staring down at it. Granted, it was lovely, giving off an almost ethereal glow. Despite that, though, I wanted to rip it off my neck. Because it strangely felt too much like the chains I'd been wearing in the pen. "Why?"

Bethany wet her lips and opened her mouth to answer when the door swung open.

An older woman wearing a black and white maid's cap like Bethany's stuck her head in and hissed, "Let's move it! The Duchess awaits the girls in the north parlor. Quick, quick!"

"We've got to go, right away. The last thing you want to do is start off making a bad impression," Bethany said, grabbing my hand and half-dragging me out of the room and down the wide, marble hallway.

Fear gripped my heart as we jogged hand in hand, darting past the older maid toward a wide set of open doors at the end of the hall.

"Please, Bethany, you've got to give me something, here. Anything. Is she looking us over like Christmas hens and the plumpest, prettiest bird winds up on the menu tonight?"

Bethany didn't answer, she just ran faster, urging me along with her.

"I'm begging you. The anticipation is killing me," I gasped, my slippered feet sliding along the marble as the open doors loomed just yards away, now. "I seriously think I'm going to explode if someone doesn't tell me something. Am I going to die tonight in that room? Because if I am, I want to at least, you know, prepare a little. Say a few prayers to some gods that might still be listening. Something."

Bethany skidded to a stop and wheeled me around to face her. Blue eyes flashed fire as she glared up at me, her plump cheeks high with color. "Damn it, Sienna, mind your mouth! You will survive the night well and fine if you would just—"

She broke off a second later, cheeks turning pale as the sound of the doors slamming shut echoed down the cavernous hallway.

I shot a glance at the massive doors, then back to Bethany, who let out a groan and shook her head.

"Bloody hell. Now we're late!"

FOUR

Sienna

"S-SO WHAT DOES THAT mean?" I asked, blinking at the doors, unsure of why Bethany was so upset. "We can't go in? Because that's fine by me. We can go back to the dressing room area, maybe play some cards or something until—"

The slap was a shock, and if it wasn't for the resounding crack that shattered the silence, I'd have almost thought I imagined it. But then my cheek started to throb.

"Did you just hit me?" I demanded incredulously as I stared down at Bethany. Damn, she was fast.

I towered over her by a good four inches, but she didn't back down.

"I did it for your own good, you nitwit. If you don't get into the parlor, you don't get to meet the Duchess face to face. If you don't get to meet the Duchess face to face, you don't have a chance to earn her favor. And if you don't earn her favor?" She shook her head slowly. "You're as good as dead."

It took a moment for the words to sink in, but when they did, I swayed on my feet like I'd been struck a second time.

No matter how bad things had gotten, through the death of my parents and the veil coming down, losing Jordan . . .one thing had remained constant.

In order to protect and save my friend, I had to stay alive.

Bethany must've read that truth in my face because she tipped her head in a clipped nod.

"All right, then. Follow my lead, stop with the jokes, and get your head on straight. You speak when you're spoken to and not before. And for gods' sake, don't ask any questions. They no more have to answer to you than you would have to answer to a cockroach, and they have little patience for impertinence. Understood?"

I swallowed hard and nodded. Maybe it was my fear, or maybe my defense mechanism triggered attempts at humor had won her over a little, but for whatever reason, I knew in my gut that Bethany was truly trying to help me in what little way she could manage.

It was exactly the dose of hope I needed. Everything was terrible, and the unknown yawned before me like a gaping maw of doom, but I had a friend. It was a start in the right direction.

Her hand snaked out faster than a viper as she smacked my other cheek.

"What in the fresh hell was that for?" I demanded, glaring at her.

She shrugged. "Sorry about that, but one red cheek looks like a rash. Two looks like a charming flush on your pale skin." She gave me a quick once-over, smoothed my skirts, and took my hand again. "Remember, follow my lead," she mumbled as she tugged me toward the doors.

She rapped hard on the heavy mahogany and then stood back.

Waiting.

The sting in my cheeks was forgotten as the doors swung open.

Two dozen heads turned our way and the low chatter in the room went silent.

A regal woman dressed in all black Victorian garb stepped forward. Her cheekbones were so high and sculpted, they could've cut glass. Her lush lips were painted a deep ruby red. But it was her eyes that had me mesmerized. They were like silver chips of ice, standing out in sharp relief against her dark skin. My stomach did a flip as her brow caved into a thunderous frown.

"What is the meaning of this?" she demanded, voice like a whip-crack.

"My apologies for our tardiness, Your Grace," Bethany murmured in a rush. "You know how clumsy I can be. I tripped over my skirts and Miss Sienna, here, was kind enough to tend to me and check for swelling and all that. I humbly implore you not to punish her for my carelessness." She dipped into a deep curtsy, and squeezed my icy hand with her warm one, indicating I should do the same.

I bent one knee and mimicked the young maid's motions, my head spinning.

Had she seriously just risked her own well-being for mine? She barely knew me. Moreover, if she was to be punished because of me, I'd never forgive myself.

I needed to stay alive for many reasons, but I wasn't about to let someone else take the heat for my actions.

I straightened, opening my mouth to spill the beans, and then snapped it shut when the heel of Bethany's boot stomped on my toe. Apparently, on top of being a shockingly violent harridan, she was also a mind reader.

I swallowed a muffled curse as the Duchess swept gracefully toward us, every rise of an elegant foot revealing a splash of her red-bottomed stilettos. She stopped just a few feet away.

"Rise, child," she murmured with a sigh, the anger in her dark eyes fading to something I could only interpret as affection as she locked gazes with Bethany. "Your clumsy nature will be the end of you. I fear that someday, you'll go to air out a room, open a window, sneeze, and tumble out of it to meet your death. And then what of me, child? Who will make my cocoa exactly as I like it?"

Bethany released my hand and curtsied again.

"I know it, Your Grace. I vow to be more careful in the future."

The Duchess inclined her regal head and her crimson lips tipped into a glimmer of a smile. "You do that. And go speak to the nurse about your . . . ankle."

Interesting. She knew it had been a cover.

Bethany stepped back and spared me a glance and a surreptitious wink before bustling off, faking a limp. It took everything I had not to run after her.

"Sienna, is it, then?" the Duchess asked, studying me intently, as if I was a butterfly under a sheet of glass.

"Yes . . . Your Grace."

She clicked her tongue and tipped her head. "You're a curious one, aren't you? A challenge." She began to circle me as she continued. "Not as lean as some, but it suits you. The gods have gilded this flower, it seems. Back when I cared about the male gaze, I'd have killed for hair that color." She completed her trip and stopped in front of me, her face close enough that our noses almost touched.

I tried not to panic, but it was all I could do to keep from crumpling when she opened her mouth, fangs flashing.

She pressed her lips to my ear, and when she finally spoke, her voice was barely a whisper. "I'll give you a second chance because Bethany clearly saw something in you she thought was worth saving. But my heart isn't as soft as hers. Two strikes and you're out, no matter who purchased you. Understood?"

"Yes, Your Grace," I said, forcing the words past the knot in my throat.

With that, she stepped back and smiled.

"Shall we get on with it, then, ladies?"

My pulse still raced as she turned to face the room at large. It was only then that I even really took note of the others present. All young women, some a little older than me, but most around my age. All dressed to the nines. Every single one of them looked hella-relieved that they were standing in a pack on one side of the room and not separated from the rest of the herd like yours truly.

"Form a line."

The girls did so in a hurry and then stood, backs straight, staring straight ahead.

"Sienna, go stand over there," the Duchess commanded, pointing to the space beside a waifish blonde girl wearing a white gown as if she were headed to her own wedding and got sidetracked.

I did as instructed and then watched, motionless, as the Duchess strolled up and down the line.

"This may not be the life you imagined, but as women, we have to work with the hands we're dealt. Your time here can be as easy or as difficult as you choose to make it," she said, slowing to a stop and regarding the group as a whole. "The palace can be a wonderful place if you play your cards right. You'll make friends, indulge in fine food and wine. We also have some of the most beautiful land in the Empire, and you are welcome to explore it in your free time, so long as you stay on this side of the eastern bridge. The rest of your time will be spent preparing for and engaging in the Harvest Games. The winners will enjoy a life most could only dream of. The losers...well, suffice it to say, that you don't want to be one. For the next eight weeks, until the blood moon, you will be on display."

Eight weeks?

I did the math in my head as fast as I could. Fifty-six days. The first bit of luck finally turned my way. Long enough that the boat would be coming for Jordan and I the day after the Harvest Games was done.

Fecking perfect.

I turned my attention back to the Duchess.

"Your one and only task is to impress. Use your face, your form, your charms, your character...whatever you have at your disposal. Each of you was given a pendant. They are to be worn at all times. The gem within starts out clear and changes color, quite like a human mood ring might, except this gem senses bloodlust. The more you are desired and wanted by the men here in the palace, the better your chances of being selected by one of them to partner with. It is to be worn at all times and is something that I convinced the men to agree to by telling them it would be a useful tool for them to gauge their competition for each female. But, truth be told, they're not meant to help them. They're meant to help *you*."

She scanned the faces before her and continued, her expression somber, her voice ringing with sincerity.

"The first week will be an orientation, of sorts, as you grow accustomed to our ways and the behavior we expect in court. In the following seven weeks, the competition will get serious. As unimportant as an event may seem, make no mistake. Any time you are in the presence of the men, including tonight, it is an opportunity for you to secure the interest of one who might be able to help your cause. If your gemstone isn't changing color as the days pass, it is an indication that you need to work harder. The more often the gem is infused with the men's lust, the longer the color will remain. The longer and darker the color of the gemstones, the more freedoms and better treatment you will enjoy. If you retain only one thing I say today, let it be this; A clear gemstone by the end of the games means certain death."

A murmur passed down the line as girls gasped and shifted, each casting furtive glances at their own necklaces and one another's. Some were already slightly darker than others, even if just by a few shades, causing an even bigger ruckus.

"Worry not," the Duchess said with a sweep of her hand. "Despite our efforts to keep you out of sight until the feast tonight, some of you were spotted by a number of the men when you entered the palace. There will be plenty of time to even the playing field. That said, there's no time like the present, so I suggest you turn those worried frowns upside down, girls. We're due to meet the gentlemen in the Great Hall. It's time for dinner."

Perfect.

Just the sentiment I wanted to hear from a vampire...

Ring the dinner bell, the humans are on their way!

FIVE

Dominic

I FUCKING HATED THESE dinners with the passion of a thousand burning suns. Trussed up like one of the human's godsdamned Christmas birds, as far as I was concerned, in my overly tight leather tunic and soft pants that wouldn't stop an arrow even if it missed. My youngest brother insisted the nice clothes were necessary for dining with him.

So why was I going, when I'd avoided every dinner of this size for several years? Turned down every offer? Flat out refused the mere suggestion I attend?

Maybe I was curious if a certain human would be there. Curious, that was all, to see what she did with the Duchess bringing her to heel. To see what she looked like without rags hiding her body.

My lips quirked. I wondered if anyone would have a broken nose.

That had been the deciding factor when my squire had begun the process of begging me to get into the bathtub, explaining that the younger prince threatened to beat him if he didn't get me cleaned up and at the dinner. My brother was far too kind to follow through on that threat, but here I was anyway. As much for the auburn-haired spitfire as for Will.

"Listen, brother, you must understand that if you aren't there, people will think that we're fighting, or that you're trying to stage a coup against Edmund. You know we can't have that."

William, younger than me by forty years, and shorter by several inches, clapped a hand hard against my back. Even now, he liked to see if he could goad me into a fight. To see if he could throw me off balance. We got along better than it looked to some.

Edmund, on the other hand, was a whole other ball of wax. I shoved him from my mind as I leveled a side glare at my younger sibling.

"The King would no more believe it than any of our people, Will."

His deep, blue eyes narrowed, but there was humor in them. "Then tell me brother, why did you come? Don't get me wrong, I actually enjoy these dinners far more when I can watch you squirm as the royal wenches try to get you off under the table, but . . .it's not like you to give in so easily. How long has it been? Two years since you last came to one of the functions?"

"Three," I corrected.

I certainly was not going to mention the redhead with the golden eyes. "I want to keep an eye on DuMont. He's a prick and I think he might have something to do with the attack on the shipment last month."

William, youngest prince of the Vampire Kingdom and second in line to the throne, grabbed my arm. "Are you fucking kidding me? Anthony? I mean . . .An-phony?"

My lips twitched at the terrible nickname. "An-phony. Yes. I threatened him heavily, I hope he remembers."

"He's not smart enough to pull off an attack," Will murmured.

I brushed his hand off my arm. "I am looking into it. He survived a raid that took out four of my best guards. Men I'd trained myself, men who wouldn't go down easy. DuMont couldn't fight his way out of a wet paper bag." One of the few rather human sayings I'd always wanted to use, and DuMont was the perfect idiot to apply it to.

Will stared at me, his jaw working hard, but he said nothing. "You're sure? I mean, I know he's a complete moron and totally under Edmund's thrall but . . ."

"No, I'm not sure it was his doing, which is why I haven't brought any charges against him." I lowered my voice. "I don't want to upset the King. He does not need to have this on his plate. If I must, I'll just kill Anthony in private and feed his remains to the Hunters."

No, I did not call the King "Father". To me, he'd always been the King. I doubted that would ever change. The King had an . . .indiscretion . . . that had produced me, nearly a hundred years after Edmund, the Crown Prince, had been born. Not that I'd been raised in the castle, but I'd known who my blood came from and why—there were no secrets in my world. My mother had raised me on her own in a cabin on the edge of the forest, and I'd trained to be a part of the army from the time I'd been old enough to be a squire.

I made a mental note to go visit my mother. It had been too long since I'd checked on her. Even as it was, it had been long enough that I would get a serious tongue lashing.

I grimaced. On that thought, perhaps I would wait a little longer.

I motioned for Will to go ahead of me, stepping into the dining hall first, as was his due as an actual recognized prince of the realm.

I didn't really give a shit about titles or prestige, though there were many enough who didn't believe that I'd not wanted to fight for the throne. And I could have. I could have called a challenge and killed Edmund when I'd come of age, and taken the crown for myself.

Despite Edmund's sadistic behavior, I never did.

Not because he would make a good king one day, not by a long shot in the dead of night. And not because I couldn't beat him.

I clapped my hand on my younger brother's back, making him stumble a few steps, which drew laughter from the crowd. He did a slow spin, waving. "Welcome, all!"

I did not kill Edmund because of Will.

Not that Will knew that. He could never know the truth. If he did, I had no doubt he would challenge Edmund. And then Edmund would murder the only royal worth protecting.

The glitter of the room drew my attention, finally, and I did a visual sweep, looking for anything out of place. Because, while I might not challenge Edmund, there were others who were close enough in the bloodline that they could. And then there were others that thought Will was a threat to Edmund—which was ridiculous.

But an assassination attempt on Will's life in order to protect Edmund's position wouldn't be out of the question.

My eyes caught on the back of an emerald green dress, bare shoulders, and a neatly woven bundle of auburn hair. Tiny sprigs of blooming ivy were woven through the strands and I had the strangest urge to bend close and smell them.

A stronger urge to tear the dress off her body and lick my way down to her pussy.

Sienna.

"What the actual fuck?" I muttered, stunned by the strength of my need, even as I struggled to pull my gaze from her back.

"Hungry?" A tiny hand pressed against my chest, turning my gaze down to the petite woman with the heart-shaped face in front of me. "Wow, you're big. Is *all* of you that big?"

Her hand clenched, digging into my skin, her mouth making a perfect 'O' as I stared down at her.

"Eloquent," I said as I brushed her hand off, wondering how the hell this woman had gotten so close without me noticing. Had I been staring at the redhead *that* hard?

"Big boy, could I give you a ride?" she whispered as she leaned in again, this time with both hands. Her perfume was subtle, her big doe eyes would be a draw for many a man here, the dress fit her slim figure and I knew in an abstract way she was beautiful.

And still...

I blinked and had to force my gaze away from Sienna. And found myself staring at Will, who was staring right at me, head tilted in curiosity.

Fuck, I did not need this right now.

"Got a new friend, huh?" Will jerked his chin toward the brunette still standing far too close to me, weaving her arms around my waist. Gods, they were getting brassy.

"You want her?" I pried her hands off—again.

"Not really my type." Will smirked as I found her arms snaking once more around me, like a damn octopus.

I lifted my hand and snapped my fingers. My aunt, the Duchess of Stillwater and manager of the Harvest Games, saw me and glided forward. Her silvery eyes latched onto the girl who all but shriveled under her gaze.

"Leave him. We do not throw ourselves at the men, Holly." Tone sharp, she didn't have to give the girl more than that. The girl's pendant was clear, not a drop of color in it.

And if I'd been standing closer to Sienna? Hers would have been saturated with color, clearly labelling her as a desirable fuck.

No, that couldn't happen. I needed to maintain my distance until I had a chance to relieve myself with someone else.

"General," the Duchess tucked her arm into mine and drew me away from Will. "Lovely to have you here. I would like a word with you, though."

Will laughed. "Good luck, brother."

I stopped myself from rolling my eyes. Barely. "Duchess, what can I help you with?"

"Dance with an old lady, and let us discuss your recent purchase. I find it . . . interesting."

I kept my expression impassive as I took her arm.

"What purchase is that?" I pulled her carefully around me, moving through the steps of a waltz—vampire created, of course, not the insipid human version—spinning her lightly and then letting her set the pace as she preferred.

Her laugh was sharp, but she kept her voice low between us. "The girl. Why in the name of the blood moon would you buy that one? She is nothing like the current style. And fiery too! Not the demure lady that your father and brother have asked to be brought in."

The upside of being so much taller than her was that I could pull her close and keep her from seeing my face. Normally, I wouldn't have worried about what my face gave off in terms of emotion but in this case, less was better.

Lucky for me, I could think on my feet. A necessary skill in battle.

"She was cheap. I thought it would be interesting to see how someone so obviously not at the level of the other girls would fair. I have to have some entertainment, don't I?" I spun with her, moving my feet as I would in a fight, knowing full well that the Duchess's words could be as wicked as any weapon. "You know she broke the nose of one of the guards?"

This dance was as much a battle as any involving armor, weapons, and bloodshed.

"Hmm." The Duchess tapped her hand against my shoulder. "True, that could be curious to see. If her passion could be directed correctly, she could change the course of the games. So you believe her a dark horse, of sorts, a come from behind winner, if you will?"

Not one given to flights of fancy, the words 'come from behind' sent off a wave of images that tumbled rapidly through me, catching me fully off guard.

The honey-eyed girl on all fours, naked, looking over her shoulder at me as her hair hung to the side, bite marks on her neck, pale skin glimmering with a sheen of sweat, her fists tangled in the black satin sheets as she pushed her ass back toward me, her hips soft in my hands as I slid my cock into her pussy, feeling her convulse around my length.

Moans sliding from her throat as she begged for more.

I had to swallow a groan as I stiffened in more than one way, fighting to banish the images.

"Duchess, let her sink, if you must. Take it out of my wages if you are so concerned, or hand her back to the boat captain and feed her to the waves. It was nothing but a momentary impulse that I acted on, perhaps rashly. A bet between Raven and I, one that I lost." Stepping away from her, I took her hand, bowing over it. "Now please, worry not, and try to enjoy the rest of your evening, won't you?"

Without waiting for a reply, I turned and left her on the dance floor.

Thank gods for the longer tight leather tunic or every vampire in the room would think I had a hard-on for the Duchess. Thoughts of the girl on her hands and knees would not leave me and I struggled to breathe around the growing tension under my skin.

The sensation of her body under my hand was impossibly real.

Fuck. I had to get laid. And soon.

I made my way to the head table, sat next to my brother, and poured myself a glass of spiced blood-rum, snapped it back, and poured another. The alcohol wouldn't affect me much, but the blood helped soothe me and dampen the other need that clawed at my cock.

Eventually, the chatter around began to slowly penetrate through the pounding of my heart.

"We are so blessed to have Edmund. Not only to purge us of the bloodworms, but to now be dealing with the werewolves?"

"Truly, he will make a grand king one day."

"Long live King Stirling."

Words, just words and I could barely comprehend them.

This...this was not me. When did I lose track of my surroundings?

Never. It had never happened.

Perhaps I'd been poisoned?

That thought was not a new one. I'd considered it briefly at the auction pens as well.

I twisted around to look for DuMont. Motherfucker was sitting not too far from us, a girl on his lap, his hands clearly under her skirt. He didn't look my way. Just because he was busy now, that didn't mean he couldn't have slipped me something, or had someone else do so. A massive, one time draught that felled me would've looked far too suspect and caused chaos, but perhaps a slow death, by sips, wouldn't raise suspicions.

I stared at the glass in my hand. Even if I knew I was grasping at straws, it was all I had to blame these disturbing sensations on.

Scrubbing a hand over my jaw, I stared down at the food on my plate and pushed it away.

Just in case.

Irritation flared anew and when the discussion turned to the Oracle and her latest news, I couldn't help the snort that escaped me.

"You have a thought, General?" Teresa, Duchess of the Southwind Estates, leaned so I could see straight down her cleavage, all the way to her belly, if I'd been so inclined. Her black hair was braided up into a straight-up crown and interspersed with jewels. Not overly subtle.

"I think that the Oracle is highly overrated, and preys on the whims of an ailing and weakened king," I said. "I do not take her words as gospel, as so many do. I take facts and reports from my men far more than her . . .incantations and gossip."

A slow intake of breath around the table said it all.

I'd taken it one step too far.

Yet, on my right, Will slowly nodded. "Yes, I've often thought that, too. She gives him false hope, but as long as we know that it is nothing but false hope, is it truly all that bad? Like giving a dying man a last drink. A comfort. I know that what she is saying is nothing but nonsense."

A few hands tapped on the table in agreement as a series of performers spilled into the room. Acrobats, all human. At one time, we'd had acrobats from the fae realm, but after the last war with them, we'd agreed to have no more slaves from the land of Fairy. Pity, the humans were so breakable when they fell from the heights.

A series of long poles, two inches in diameter, were placed to touch the ceiling and floor and the acrobats—though I doubted they were trained at all—tried to swing about them, did a few flips.

Fell, as predicted.

Cried as they were carried off stage with broken and twisted limbs.

"They'd be better off as clowns," I said as I took in the scene, my eyes drifting to my right.

The glitter of a green dress, the curve of a soft hip, and I snapped my eyes back to my plate, anger surging through me.

Maybe I should kill her myself.

Except I could so easily see my fingers wrapped around her neck, tugging her to me as I bruised her mouth with a kiss that left us both panting. Need coursed through me and I struggled to breathe normally.

Something was definitely wrong with me.

"Will," I said. "I am—" I couldn't say unwell, he'd never believe it. "I need to look into something."

He looked up at me as I stood. "Already?" He turned toward the rest of the table with a wide grin. "Who had fifteen minutes? I think you might win the pool!"

A low spin of laughter rippled by but I didn't give a single shit about their betting, even if it was on me. Just another game to entertain themselves rather than look at the state of our world.

I made myself keep my eyes on him. "You know how much I enjoy these soirees, a true bright spot in my life that I'm not sure I could ever live without. But duty calls." I gave him a choppy salute to go with the heavy sarcasm, and turned to leave.

Will stopped me with a hand on my wrist. "I wish to speak with you before you go, General. In private."

Another night, that wouldn't have bothered me, but seeing as I wanted nothing more than to escape to my rooms and have a very long cold shower, his need to talk was unwelcome.

"Can it wait?"

Another row of breath sucked in sharply past fangs all down the table. It was a ruse, everyone knew my relationship with my brother was not one of power struggles. But I think the other royals wanted it to be.

Drama. Like our previous hunting grounds of the ton in Old England, they thrived on it.

Will lifted both hands into the air, a smile ghosting over his lips. "I suppose it can. But soon, brother. I await our meeting with baited breath."

I bowed at the waist, hand over my heart, matching his formality. "As you wish, my Prince."

There, let the little bloodsucking drama queens chew on that.

The dining hall was abuzz with chatter, the smell of human fear, and even some desire. The Duchess caught my eye as I strode for the door, arching her eyebrow at me.

I didn't so much as blink. The doors were the way out.

"General."

I ground to a halt and turned to face DuMont.

"Tony," I said, deliberately shortening his name. A trick of the Duchess's that I stole from time to time to put people in their places.

The Earl's sharp face puckered up as if he'd sipped dead blood. "Anthony," he corrected.

I stared him down, towering over him, not giving him his name. "What do you want?"

His lips twitched at my lack of respect. "I'm being asked to answer for the extra funds spent at the auction. I suggest you confess to Edmund that it was you who purchased the last girl. She was six hundred, if I remember correctly. For a nothing." The people to either side of him watched with eyes wide, and ears tuned tight to the conversation.

I smiled and took a step toward the Earl, knowing this was an attempt at punishment for what happened at the auction. He tried to take a step back but there was a table behind him. He squeaked and paled as I let the anger that burned deep in my belly roll upward, filling my eyes with the calm that came before I killed.

"*Tony*," I said softly. "You know very well she was only one hundred, and it was you who overspent the majority of the funds. It would've been even more had I allowed you to purchase Daisy. So either you confess your excess, or I will ask to go on the next gathering of the shipment. And that little discussion we had at the pens? You remember that, don't you?"

Now, a smarter man would have clearly understood the implied threat that I'd wait until we were out on the ocean and kill him without witnesses. The human captain and crew who were paid handsomely for their services wouldn't so much as blink. And I could easily blame any number of things for the Earl's death.

The fantasy was almost as good as the girl on all fours, her round ass begging for my teeth and my cock.

Almost.

It took him far too long before his eyes widened with shock. "You dare threaten me?"

The vampires around us could clearly hear the conversation by the way the gasps rippled.

I put my hand carefully to the crook of the Earl's neck. "Why in the world would I need to threaten you, Tony? Unless of course you've been breaking the rules? Again?"

Another row of gasps from the others.

But Anthony, he just blinked stupidly up at me, a glaze of lust flowing over his eyes as I withdrew my hand. He liked his bedmates both under and on top of him, and made no bones about that fact.

And suddenly, I knew why he'd asked for my presence on the last shipment. The glaze in his eyes said it all. He'd wanted me.

I turned away, dismissing him. How I could have thought he'd have the brains to poison me made me doubt my own mental capabilities. At least, for a moment. That being said, I would need to keep an eye on the fool.

Especially if he was seeking to bed me. Fucking hell, that was the last thing I needed.

Out of the dining hall, I kept my stride up, eating the distance between me and my quarters on the third floor. Because the minute I was no longer dealing with Anthony, the redhead's body filled my mind in a way that I could not escape. I took the steps three at a time until I was at the top and bursting through the door to my quarters.

My young squire, Hobbin, looked up from cleaning Ares' bridle. "General?"

"Out." I pointed at the door and Hobbin ran for it. My leathers were not the easiest thing to get off but, in a matter of seconds, I had stripped everything off and strode to the showers, my cock hard against my belly, the tip already wet.

The girl was not going to win this round.

I flicked the cold water on and stepped under the stream, the icy droplets drawing a hiss out of me as they hit my overheated skin.

Seeing her in front of me, seeing her body push back toward me, begging me, a whispered plea to fuck her, over and over.

I put my hands against the tile of the wall, *refusing* to touch myself. "Fuck." I growled the word as I struggled to hold absolutely still, the water coursing over my body, the cold water a lover's touch I would not take. Not ever.

Desire was a tool used to control—as evidenced clearly by the Harvest Games and I would not succumb to the demands. Not even here in private. If I could not control myself, then I had lost.

Groaning, I bowed my head under the onslaught of desire, unable to stop seeing my hands fisted in her auburn hair, tipping her head to bare that golden kissed skin to me, burying my cock and my fangs in her at the same time, feeling her body tighten around me.

I fumbled with the lever, fighting to make the water colder and snapping off the handle in the process. "Jesus Christ!" I bellowed.

All while hating *her* for this moment. For making me *want* her. For making me see a *human* as anything but food. Need like this was a weakness for my enemies to exploit. I couldn't afford it, not in my life.

I would find someone to fuck. Break this cursed, self-imposed celibacy and get the image of her round ass and auburn hair out of my system for good.

But even as I stood there, the cold water icing my skin, my own mind and body fighting me, even as I finally felt the cold water cut through the need, I knew it was a lie.

A lie that could cost me everything if anyone ever found out.

SIX

Sienna

I TRIED NOT TO watch the General leave. It would do me no good to have my fear written plain on my face. And yet I breathed a sigh of relief as his presence faded.

"You are . . . acceptable, I suppose," the man on my right drew my attention back to him. "Though not the current style at all."

I lifted a single brow. "Current style?"

"Yes, well, the crown prince sets the tone of our beauty standards. He prefers his woman slim of hip, slim of bust, and dark of hair with . . .clean skin."

I couldn't help the laugh that escaped me. "You think freckles make me dirty?"

His frown deepened. "And quiet of mouth."

Oh dear, this was not going to go well for me. It took all I had to bite my tongue and lower my eyes, fluttering my lashes. "Of course, I will take that into consideration. Tell me, what are the kingdoms like? You must be well travelled, a man of your . . . stature?" I stood taller than him, and wondered if he'd pick up on my insult.

His frown eased a little as he continued to stare at my chest. "Yes, as one of the foremost merchants I do see the different territories. Do you have an interest in travel?"

The question was ridiculous. I was a captive and he wanted to know if I would like to travel? "Of course, I'd love to see all of this beautiful, exotic land," I said, forcing a smile as I thought back to the Duchess's words the day before. "As it stands, we're allowed to walk the grounds, but not beyond the eastern bridge. I can't help but wonder what's there..."

His frown was back, and before I could even backtrack and try a different tact, he was gone. And my pendant remained clear.

Fecking vampires.

A blonde girl, the one dressed in the faux wedding gown sidled up next to me. "This is not as easy as I'd thought it would be."

I shook my head and touched my glass to hers. "I'm Sienna."

"Holly."

We stood together a moment before she bumped her elbow into mine. "Which one do you fancy?"

I snorted softly. "None."

Her head whipped around. "You'd better find one, then," she said, her gaze tinged with fear.

"Believe me, I'm trying, Holly," I grimaced. "The thing is, I'm not their type. That's what the merchant there just said. I think you'll do well, and I'll just have to be grateful to be picked."

Yes, I did say the words even though I wanted to gag on them. I didn't give a shit about the Harvest Games. But I had to play the game and survive long enough . . . .

"Good luck, Sienna." Holly touched her glass to mine once more, a soft ring rolling off the crystal stemware. "You're going to need it I think."

She left me standing there, alone. I glanced around the room to watch the other girls making conversation and noted the similarity for the first time. Short or tall, black or white, blond or brunette, they were all on the slimmer side, with narrow hips and flat chests. Only a couple others had any curves at all.

Damn. If I couldn't get a vampire into a conversation, how in the hell was I going to find my way to the shifter territories? I needed to find at least one vampire who would talk to me. Someone young maybe? Less jaded?

A familiar face flickered in my mind and I pushed it away.

Nope. There had to be another path to Jordan that didn't involve engaging with the General.

But as time ticked by, I continued to stand alone. It seemed that I was indeed the underdog here, which wouldn't do at all. I needed to come up with a plan to get some attention, and fast.

It wasn't until midnight that the party began to break up. The men dispersed first, and then our maids came back to the room to lead us back to our quarters.

Bethany scurried across to me, her eyes going straight to my pendant. "Oh."

I touched it. "Right? I tried, Bethany, I did."

Her shoulders slumped and then she straightened up. "There's always tomorrow, right?"

"Right, of course. We have time." I smiled and slid my arm through hers as she led me away from the ballroom. "By the way, I was curious and meant to ask... what's over the bridge to the east? The one the Duchess says we aren't allowed to go beyond?"

Bethany slowed to a stop and pulled me along with her.

"Promise me you won't go there," she demanded, her voice shrill.

"Bethany, I—"

"Promise or I...I won't be your friend anymore," she finished feebly.

"Okay, calm down," I said, patting her hand. Her lower lip was shaking and I could tell by the look on her face that whatever was on the other side of the bridge, it was bad.

Like really, really bad.

"Do you swear it?"

"I swear," I replied, crossing my forefinger over my heart.

I didn't like lying to her. The fact was, I'd do whatever it took to find my friend, even if it meant crossing that bridge. But giving her the truth right now would help neither of us. I needed her to be invested in me staying alive. Having an ally here was crucial. But in a much less pragmatic way, I also valued her friendship. Late at night, when I couldn't suppress the fear and horror of my circumstances, thinking of that friendly face and her kind words was the only thing that got me through.

She narrowed her eyes at me and then nodded slowly. "Alright, then. Do yourself a favor and don't be asking questions like that anymore. Nothing good can come of it, I can promise you that."

When we were only a short ways from my room, I found myself pausing at one of the intersecting hallways. My heart began to pound and there was . . . I could only call it a *pull* in that direction.

I'd never been one to ignore my instincts, it was what had kept me alive. What had kept Jordan alive.

"What is this place?"

"Oh, that's the hall that leads to the soldiers' quarters," Bethany said. "Why?"

I shrugged. "Just curious about this symbol." I touched the emblem etched into the wall next to the hall. A pair of crossed swords with a shield behind them.

Bethany tugged my arm.

"You are far too curious for your own good. It's late. Tomorrow the Duchess will be hosting an archery competition as part of the games. It will give you girls a chance to mix and mingle some more with the men. You'd do well to look your best and try to impress," she warned softly. "Understood?"

I nodded gamely as Bethany continued chattering about everything she was going to do to help me win my way into the heart—or at least into the pants of—one of the bloodsuckers, but my mind was already far too preoccupied to pay her any mind.

Surely, the soldiers quarters contained everything I needed to forge a path to Werewolf Territory. Maps, compasses, not to mention, weapons. If I could just sneak my way in there...

When we were back in my room, I changed into my nightclothes, buoyed by my germ of a plan. Going forward, I had two immediate objectives:

Make myself desirable enough to not get cast aside or tossed to the Hunters before I had a chance to get to Jordan.

Figure out a way to sneak into the soldiers quarters without getting caught and fileted.

As far as rescue missions went, it wasn't exactly medal-worthy, but it was something. And from where I was sitting?

Something was a whole lot better than nothing.

SEVEN

Sienna

DESPITE FINALLY HAVING A clear path forward, I still wound up tossing and turning all night. Yet again, images of the dark, mysterious General kept pushing their way to the forefront of my mind, and it was irritating as hell.

"And you're sure you don't want to put a corset under the jacket?" Bethany asked for the second time as she surveyed me from head to toe.

"Oh, I'm sure," I shot back, sparing one last glance in the mirror. The royal blue pants and riding jacket fit me like a second skin and there was no point in trying to gild the lily here. I was thicker than most of the other girls, and no corset was going to hide that fact. I might as well embrace my differences and see if I could catch the eye of a man who appreciated some curves. Worst case, at least I'd be able to breathe while we were at this archery competition.

"So tell me exactly what's going to happen at this event?" The thought of being outdoors was far more appealing than spending the day inside, but my relief was tempered by concern. "This isn't some Gladiator bullshit where they give us bows and arrows, and then we have to like, kill each other until there's only one of us left or something, right?"

"No, no. Not at all," Bethany said shaking her head.

"Phew."

"The vampires are actually the ones given the bows," she said, her tone matter of fact, "and then you lot are set free in the woods so they can hunt you."

My brain went temporarily offline as I blinked at her.

For a second, we stared at each other in silence, and then a snort-laugh bubbled from her lips.

"You should see your face right now!" she cackled gleefully. "I can't believe you fell for that."

The panicked buzzing in my ears began to subside, but my heart was still pounding as I managed a thin smile at my "friend".

First the back to back slaps, and now this. Sweet, shy Bethany had really come out of her shell. I stared at her, half-wishing I could stuff her back into it, but also grudgingly impressed.

"Yeah, hilarious. Mock the vampire captive for sport. Lovely."

She hip-checked me with a wink. "Ever since you got here, you've had me in knots with worry. I've got to release the tension somehow, don't I?"

I grumbled under my breath, but couldn't find it in me to actually be angry. This was a weird place, and Bethany and I were in an even weirder circumstance. Both of us would probably rather be doing something else, somewhere far away from here. Whatever we had to do to muddle through our current situation was fine by me.

I cocked my head at her and asked the question I'd been wanting to ask since we'd first met. "How did you end up here?"

The smile slid from her lips, and she narrowed her eyes at me.

"Always the curious one, you. Maybe someday, if you get your act together, I'll tell you. No point in getting too close with a lass determined to get herself killed, now is there?"

Ouch.

"Tell me how you really feel, Bee," I said with a wince.

She sniggered indignantly but didn't protest the new nickname.

"A girl's got to protect her heart in a place like this." Turning, she glanced at the grandfather clock in the corner of the room and let out a gasp. "And look! Already causing trouble again! We've got to go, right now. If we're late once more, the Duchess might turn my little joke about your impending death into a prophecy."

On that note, she led me from the room through the winding castle hallways. When we finally exited, it was through a massive set of arched doors that had been flung open to let the sunshine in.

I sucked in a breath of cool, fresh air, and my roiling stomach settled some. As much as I didn't relish the thought of being surrounded by vampires under any conditions, it felt a whole lot less terrifying outdoors. Not that I could get away from them if they were chasing me in either case.

And on that note...

"I've been meaning to ask, and you did say you would answer some of my questions... So far, I haven't seen much in the way of superhuman powers. You hear stories and whatnot, but I'm sure a lot of that gets hyped in the media. Sort of like great whites during shark week," I said, keeping stride with Bee, who was moving over the cobbled stone at a steady clip and aggressively ignoring me. "And what about the blood thing? I don't see them tearing into people at the dinner table or having some blood host kneeling at their feet or anything."

I stumbled over a cracked stone and righted myself before breaking into a jog.

"Also, how fast are they, really? Like, twice as fast a human, or—"

Bee stopped so short I nearly plowed into her back. She wheeled around, smooth brow knit together in a frown. "If I answer you will you stop babbling and focus on the task at hand?"

"Yup," I shot back with a nod. "Absolutely."

"Fine. It's not media hype. The reason most don't have blood hosts at their feet is because the Duchess prefers to keep a civilized atmosphere, especially during the games. For the most part, the rest are amenable to that. What some do behind closed doors, however, is a whole other story," she said, her tone grim. "And as for abilities? Think of the strongest man you've ever seen, and multiply that times five. Then imagine he can move quicker than the eye can see—"

"Oh. Well, that's—"

"I'm not finished," Bee interjected. "Then, imagine he's close to invincible. As in, even if you managed to get the best of him and did everything exactly right, unless you find one of three ways to kill him and do it perfectly, he's just going to heal, like nothing happened. Then he's going to come after you again. And this time, he won't fail. Because anything you can do, he can do better. Escape is futile. The sooner you get your head around it and resign yourself to this fate, the better off you'll be, Sienna. Please..."

Her soft, pretty face was so full of concern that I wished I could tell her the truth. Instead, I nodded.

"Alright. I already told you, I promise I'll try. It's just all so new."

A trio of other young women rushed past us and Bee grabbed my arm, tugging me back into motion.

"What are the three ways?" I said, keeping my voice low.

Her jaw ticked lightly. "The true sun, not this fake cover they have up." She waved at the sky above us and I looked up.

The clouds were not moving and the sky was a perfect, painted blue. The longer I stared, the more unnerved I became. "It's not real?"

Bee gave a quick bob of her head. "They like everything to seem normal. The cover over their kingdom gives them proper nights and days in conjunction with the rest of the territories."

I tore my gaze away. A cover to allow vampires to roam in the sun. To pretend to be human. Fecking crazy. "The others?"

"Wood through the heart, that is true. Though it has to be a specific wood I believe. Beheading of course. And there was a fourth. Bloodworms. Though they were eradicated. So only three."

Shite, I needed to find whatever that wood was, and make myself a stake.

Bee kept on talking. "For today, let's just focus on finding you at least one admirer. Today, you'll pretend to be charming and sweet. And don't ask a lot of questions. Promise?"

"I'll do my best," I replied with a sigh. The information she'd given me though, it was a lot. And solid info to boot.

She made a beeline for a lush wall of shrubbery a dozen yards ahead with me in tow. I could hear the low drone of voices just moments before we stepped through a gap in the greenery and into a massive courtyard. To our left, a group of fifty or more male vampires milled around chatting. They were dressed in riding clothes, except for theirs', without exception, were black as night. To our right, the other girls were lined up like dolls, facing the Duchess expectantly as she smiled at them.

Bee yanked me over to the end of the line and scurried away to join the other maids who stood off to the side. I met the Duchess's gaze, trying not to squirm as she glanced down at the elegant, gold watch on her wrist. We must've made the cut because she tipped her head in a little nod of approval before shushing the other girls.

"I'm very excited about today's games," she said with a smile. "We'll be testing your skills with a bow. Now, let me be clear. You aren't expected to know how to shoot."

A low murmur of relief rolled through the group.

"You'll each have an instructor who will teach you everything you need to know ahead of time. At the day's end, we'll have a friendly competition. At the close of the festivities, an amazing prize will be awarded to the best archer."

"And the worst?" I blurted, unable to help myself. Bee's bleak assessment about the incredible power these creatures possessed had me a little shook.

"Will be forced to suffer the inevitable ridicule of her peers," she concluded with a solemn nod. "Do you think you can handle that, child?"

I nibbled on the inside of my lower lip as the heat of Bee's gaze just a few feet away made my cheeks sizzle.

No more questions. Roger that.

"I can, thank you."

"Splendid," she replied, clapping her hands together. "Now let's go ahead and select teams. Each of the gentlemen present have a colorful, patterned kerchief in their pocket. All you have to do is grab one from behind me," she gestured to the wooden display behind her, "and locate the man with its match. Come, come!" she encouraged, stepping aside.

The other girls rushed forward like a pack of rabid hyenas, yipping and giggling as they pawed through the silky cloth. It felt pointless to pick when there was no way of knowing which was good and which was bad, so I hung back. Better to just avoid the chaos and grab one at the end.

A loud hiss from the corner had me glancing over at Bee, who glared at me.

Alrighty, then...

I entered the melee, biting back a snarl when a booted foot stomped on my pinky toe. Without even looking, I reached for the nearest square of cloth and was just about to tug it down when my insides went cold. I turned to find a pair of inky, black eyes studying me intently from just a few yards away.

The one from the auction house who wore cruelty like a cape.

I turned back to the display and let the crimson and gold checked silk flutter from my fingers before selecting the next kerchief over. A pattern-less scrap in gun-metal gray. I pulled it down and stepped back into line.

Soon after, the rest of the girls joined me. The crimson kerchief still hung on the display, along with dozens of others.

"Gentlemen, if your cloth did not get selected, my condolences," Duchess Evangeline said with an apologetic smile. "Please enjoy refreshments in the garden for now. You may join the spectators in the stands once the competition begins. Those of you who were chosen, please come, find your match and make their acquaintance."

I shot a furtive glance back toward the men and nearly passed out with relief when I caught sight of the one with the black eyes heading toward the exit, jaw clenched in irritation.

I'd dodged a bullet, of that I was certain. The thought of spending an afternoon with that one was enough to make my hands go clammy.

"Well done," a raspy, familiar voice sounded from behind me. "You made a wise last minute change."

I turned to find the General standing in front of me, a gray kerchief—twin to mine—in hand.

"General," I croaked, cursing myself for celebrating too early. I'd dodged a bullet only to step into a missile's path. "I didn't expect to see you today. Shouldn't you be...doing whatever vampire Generals do somewhere?"

As soon as the words were out, I wanted to suck them back. Good thing Bee was out of earshot. She'd have probably cuffed me in the face again if she saw how charming I *wasn't* being.

The General tipped his head and, for a fleeting moment, his lips twitched into something I could almost make myself believe was a smile.

"I should be, yes. But given that my job is to protect the crown and its heirs, and the Duchess has decided it was wise to arm our captives while both the Crown Prince and second in line to the throne are within shooting range, I had no choice but to attend. Believe me, if I had an out, I'd have taken it."

I tried to calm my pounding heart and play the game I'd come to play. Truth be told, selecting the General's kerchief was actually the ideal outcome for me. If I wanted information about the soldiers quarters, who better to supply it?

All I had to do was make him like me enough to talk and possibly make my gemstone turn color, but *not* enough to want to keep me like some pet in his lair—assuming he had one of those.

And forget that his face has haunted your nightmares for years.
Right. That, too.

I had to stay focused on the present. And, right now, this man was my best chance at saving Jordan.

I managed a smile and met the General's gaze. "Well, then, I should thank the Duchess. I was hoping to get a chance to spend some time with you. I felt we had a...connection, of sorts." I swallowed hard, trying not to feel the truth of those words. If he only knew.

"Did you, now?" he asked, his tone dropping to a near whisper. "It seems as if you have made a connection with someone else here, as well." He jerked his chin toward my neck and I looked down with a start.

My pendant had turned pink.

But when?

How?

My mind skittered back to the man with the cruel eyes who had been staring at me a short while ago and I shuddered.

"No connection on my end, I can promise you that. I believe the man you were with at the auction has taken an...interest in me."

The General's dark brown eyes went flat as a pulse ticked in his jaw.

"The Earl Anthony DuMont. And has he? Well, he nearly got his wish because it was his silk that you touched first. I'd advise you to avoid him at all costs. He's not... let's just say he would not be a good choice."

I nodded, swallowing hard. At least my instincts were on point.

"I kind of figured. He sent my creep-o-meter needle off the charts. And anyway, my standards are crazy high these days. I'm holding out for a guy who has good credit, loves dogs, and doesn't want to eat me."

My little joke seemed to relieve some of the tension, and he cocked an eyebrow.

"Well, then, I'm afraid you're going to have some trouble here. We don't use credit here, and as for dogs…well, love is a strong word. Let's just say we have an uneasy truce with them," he replied smoothly. "It's the final requirement that intrigues me, though. Human or vampire, have you encountered many suitors who wouldn't want to eat you?"

The words hung in the air between us and I tried to calm the sudden pounding of my heart. What would that mouth feel like on mine? On my neck. My belly.

Lower…

I wanted to reach up and trace his firm lips. Feel the sharp edge of those teeth and—

Some sense of self-preservation deep inside stopped me cold and sent up a word of warning.

Retreat!

I took a step back and thrust out my hand. "I, um, don't think we've been properly introduced yet," I said, my voice shrill. "Sienna."

The intensity of his gaze dimmed as he took my hand and gave it a perfunctory shake. "Dominic Blackthorne."

Of course it was.

"Why the smirk?"

"No reason," I said with a shrug. "I just should've known. Tell me, are there any vampires named, like, Larry Pritchard? Or Bob Klatsky?"

There was that lip-twitch again. He might not want to be here, but he did think I was funny.

Excellent start.

"Now that you've all introduced yourselves, let us begin!" the Duchess's melodic voice boomed, bringing a much-welcome end to the banter that was giving me heart palpitations. "Ladies, come get your weapons. Each will be numbered, and there will be a station in the courtyard with a corresponding number. That is where your training will take place. You'll each have two hours with your partner to learn as much as you can and practice. Remember," she said, holding up one, elegant finger, "the winner will receive an amazing prize that will be the envy of all. So try your very best." She paused for dramatic effect and then threw her arms wide. "Let the games begin!"

Let the games begin, indeed.

Watch out, Dominic Blackthorne, if that is your real name. I'm coming for your secrets and nothing is going to stop me.

Operation "Charm the Enemy" was in full effect.

EIGHT

Dominic

WHAT WERE THE CHANCES?

I stared off into the distance and tried to will this woman's scent from my nostrils as I contemplated my fate.

Of all the kerchiefs on the rack, what were the chances she'd select mine?

One hundred percent, a mocking voice inside my head chimed in.

Because that's how my luck had been running lately. Ever since I'd set eyes on this blasted female. If I'd just walked away... turned my back and let nature take its course, things would've been just fine. But no. The thought of seeing a spirited woman like that offered up as chum had sickened me.

As had the thought of having someone else buy her and use that lush body for their own, that annoying voice in my head interjected.

Now, I was being punished for my weakness as the Gods put her directly under my nose for the entire bloody day.

Not the Gods, I corrected myself mentally, *the Duchess.*

This entire event was foolish. Especially given my concerns about Anthony's recent behavior, but she'd refused to cancel. There was no way I was letting Will come without me. All it would take was one of the aspen arrow's to be switched out for one made with wood from the dragon blood tree. In the hands of a person who wanted to ensure Edmund's claim to the throne forever remained unchallenged, it would be a sure thing.

"Our number is eight. I think it's that way?" she said, pointing a forefinger to the furthest corner of the courtyard.

I nodded and began heading that way when she touched a hand to my forearm for just an instant, stopping me in my tracks.

"Can I ask you something? It's been driving me mad."

"Go on."

"Why did you bid on me?" she asked, shaking her head incredulously. "I behaved like a crazed hellion as opposed to a docile, servant type. And no mirror needed to tell me I looked like something scraped out of the bottom of a frat house toilet. So what made you do it?"

I took a moment to scan the courtyard for Will, making sure he was still in the same general area I'd last seen him, before turning back toward Sienna.

"We had a quota we needed to fill, and I was tired of being there," I replied evenly as I began walking toward our designated practice area again. "As you know, the place is foul. It smells all the bedamned, and my nose is far more sensitive than yours."

She kept pace with me, and I could feel the weight of her dubious stare on my face.

"If you say so."

"I do. In fact, I can tell you exactly what type of soap you used this morning," I said, deliberately misunderstanding her meaning. "Lavender and honey. And I'm willing to bet your breakfast this morning was a croissant with blueberry—" I paused and inhaled before continuing, "No, boysenberry jam."

And even though she'd used some silly, sweet perfume likely provided by her maid, it was her skin's natural smell—like jasmine with a hint of citrus—that had my gums tingling with need. My cock pulsed, a dull ache behind the zipper of my riding pants as I imagined eating her, in more ways than one.

"I should warn you, it's been a while since I've shot a bow and arrow," she said, "and even then it was the foam kind. My dad bought me a Nerf set when I was a kid."

"We'll start from scratch, then," I said as we reached a bale of hay marked with the number eight. A bow and quiver of arrows lay atop it, and Sienna moved toward the weapon.

I held up a staying hand. "Watch me first," I said, selecting out a single arrow and gesturing toward the bright orange pumpkin that'd been placed on another bale of hay in the distance that was clearly meant to serve as our target.

I lifted the bow.

"The most important thing is to keep your grip tender. Hold it more loosely than you think you should," I said, putting arrow to bowstring. I pulled back slowly, taking care not to ruin the flimsy bow, which had clearly been designed for human use. "You'll get the aiming part down with practice," I said, exhaling as I held the bowstring to my cheek and locked in on the target.

I let loose with a twitch of my finger, and tracked the arrow as it hurtled downrange, knowing it would strike true long before it embedded itself in the pumpkin with a fleshy *thunk*.

I held the bow out to her and raised a brow expectantly.

"Your turn, but let's move a little closer for this first one."

Her wide, golden eyes flitted from the target to me. "Okay, but seriously... What a shot. That's really, really far."

"I've had plenty of years to practice," I said, grabbing the quiver and leading the way closer to our now mutilated pumpkin.

"I guess so," she replied, following me about half the distance to the target. When we stopped, she accepted the bow and took a deep breath. She pulled herself up straighter, holding the weapon in a reasonable approximation of the way I'd shown her. Then, she set the arrow I handed her to the string.

She began drawing it back, but I halted her with a hand on her shoulder.

"Wait," I said, glancing down at her legs. "Turn your body a little more, almost sideways. The outside of your left foot should be facing the target."

"Like this?" she asked, turning as instructed.

"Close," I said, a rush of lust coursing through me as I patted her thigh. "Come back a little more, get your legs about shoulder width apart. And straighten your back," I added. Electricity seemed to jump from her body to mine wherever we came into contact, and it took all I had to fight against the primal urge to bend her over, slide my hand into her hair, and—

"Right," I growled, snatching my hand away like it had been burned. "Now go ahead and give it a try."

She fought briefly with the taut bowstring, but managed to get it to her ear. "Heavy," she remarked, staring at the pumpkin with both eyes open.

I blinked in surprise, reminded of just how weak humans were compared to us. No amount of spirit or bravery could close that gap.

I pushed the thought aside and adjusted her elbow just a hair, then nodded.

"Looks good. Now, close one eye and line up the target. Use your knuckle as a guide to aim. It'll take a little trial and error to figure out how high you need to hold it, but let's take the shot."

The arrow whipped from the bow, and I winced as it hurtled upward in a diagonal arc, passing a solid ten feet over the target before whistling past the head of a raven that'd picked the wrong time to leave his perch.

"Oh, geez," she muttered, letting the bow drop to her side. "That was a close one!"

We both watch as the bird flew off, and I had to bite back a grin.

"We'll need to work on the aiming part a bit more unless we want raven for dinner. I'm not a fan of killing an animal I don't plan to eat."

Her cheeks went pink, and my mind instantly went back to our earlier exchange. Would lush, sassy Sienna taste as good as she looked? I could lean in, unbutton that jacket right now. Free those soft, unfettered breasts and suck and lick my way down her belly if I chose to...

And mark her as a potential weakness in the process, you nitwit.

The best thing I could do for this woman was help her win this competition and then get as far away as possible. She would get the attention she needed to make it through the games, as well as a prize of some sort for her troubles. Plus, she would know how to shoot. It might not be much protection against a vampire, especially one of Anthony's ilk, but it would be more than she had now. And for some reason, that mattered to me a lot more than it should.

We spent the better part of the next half hour working on her aim. Her next few attempts went similarly, but her determined expression remained the same throughout, and she grew closer and closer to the pumpkin with each attempt. When her arrow finally struck its mark, she let out a yelp of excitement.

"Well done," I said with a nod of approval.

"How are the others doing, do you think?" she asked, squinting as she glanced to right.

"You're actually ahead of the pack, from what I've seen," I said, following her gaze to see Will's protégé, loosing an arrow. It flew true, striking her target, and he shot her a grin as he clapped her gently on the back.

"The girl who's with my brother seems to be doing well, though. I think you have a shot of winning if you keep it up."

She nodded, "We have more time, so I'll just have to make sure I'm the best shot by then. Do you know what the prize will be?"

I paused, trying to think back to the last time I'd attended this event, then shook my head. "I do not. I attend functions like this only when I'm required to do so, by duty or by command."

"Why do you think the rest do? It seems weird that they'd care about how good we are at shooting a bow. Does that make us more or less attractive?"

I shrugged, "Many of the games aren't about showcasing your skills. They're about entertaining the men whose attention you're vying for. Why do you humans tune in for your reality tv shows? This is no different."

Anger flashed on her face, and her hand tightened into a fist. "No different? Surely, this is far—" she broke off and cleared her throat, her expression softening. "Sorry, I'm only thinking from my own perspective. I guess when you put it like that, it does make sense."

I nodded back at her. "Careful there, Sienna," I said, holding her gaze, "Your mask almost slipped."

"I'm learning," she said, shooting me a smile that almost seemed genuine.

It took a herculean effort to tear my eyes away from it as I gestured back toward the pumpkin. "Let's get some more shots in."

She nodded, settling into her stance. "Tell me, do your soldiers get training in archery?" she asked, pulling back the bowstring.

"They do. A mundane arrow like that won't do much against a werewolf, but there are more destructive versions that are quite successful. That said, we focus most of our training on hand to hand combat."

She let her arrow fly, and cursed softly as it pierced the hay below the target. "And how often do you have to use it?"

"The training? Let's just say that it's come in handy over the past few decades. Preparing for battle is one of those things that seems like a waste until you need it. And then it never seems like enough."

My men and I had saved the king from being murdered more than one time. We'd held off usurpers who would steal our territory if they could. We'd even kept our entire race from being wiped off the planet. Between Vanators, humans, werewolves, and all the other supernaturals, there was no resting on laurels for us.

But this curvy female with the sharp wit and even sharper tongue didn't need to know all that.

"Sounds like a pretty important job. Do they treat you well? I hope they at least give you the best of everything. Your own sleeping quarters, free reign of—" She broke off and shot me a quizzical look. "Wait. Now that I think about it, do vampires even sleep?"

I nodded slowly, slightly taken aback. "We sleep, and the quality of our quarters depends on our rank."

She knocked another arrow, taking aim downrange.

"You mentioned werewolves. Is that what all the training is for? You've got beef with those guys?"

I scratched at the scruff on my jaw and shrugged. "I guess you could call it beef. On the whole, we don't tend to get along with their kind."

"Do they live close by, then?" Sienna pumped her fist in silent celebration as her arrow sank into orange pumpkin-flesh.

I narrowed my eyes at her. "If I didn't think you were too smart to pry, I might be suspicious of all these questions, woman."

Her eyes flickered, and she pulled back almost imperceptibly at the comment, but it was more than enough to confirm my suspicion.

She wasn't making idle conversation. She was digging.

And digging was dangerous.

"Sienna, because I brought you here, I feel it's my duty to warn you." I took firm grip of her chin and forced her to meet my gaze. "Any attempt to flee this place will be met with immediate, brutal consequences. Don't let the thin veneer of elegance fool you. It's as fragile as an egg shell. One false move, the whole thing cracks. And I promise, you don't want to see what's underneath."

Her swan-like throat worked and the pulse in her neck hammered double time.

"Tell me you understand."

"I-I understand," she whispered.

I released her and she instantly turned away to face her target again.

"I'm going to go collect my arrows and try another round," she mumbled before shouldering her bow and scurrying away.

All I could do was give her the information. I couldn't force her to listen.

Well, I could, but I wouldn't. Any woman, especially one that headstrong, would be horrified at the very thought of being mind-controlled. If I forced her into compliance, she would hate me forever.

But she would get out of this whole charade alive.

I tucked the thought away for further examination, later, when I was alone. When the smell of her hair wasn't addling my brain. When the sight of those hips swaying, left to right, wasn't hypnotizing me—

"I think we've got ourselves a real competition brewing here, brother mine."

Will clapped me on the back, his grin wide and full of glee.

"Aubrey is turning out to be a real crack-shot, and your girl looks to be catching on just as quickly. What say we place a little wager on the side?"

I shook my head and let out a grunt. "My wagering days are over for the time being."

The last had saddled me with hellish insomnia and a chronic case of blue-balls.

"You're no fun at all," Will replied, turning his attention to the rest of the field. "I'm sure I'll find someone who is, though. Good luck, brother. You're going to need it."

With that, he loped off to find an easier fish to bait.

A few moments later, Sienna returned with her arrows, renewed determination etched on her face.

"I don't know what the prize is, but I do know I want it. Let's get serious here, shall we? We've got precious little time for you to teach me everything you know about archery."

I didn't want to admire her moxy, but I found it hard not to. So, for the next while, I did my best to get her skills up to snuff.

By the time the Duchess blew the horn to signal the start of the competition, our pumpkin was puree, and me?

Well, I was a seething mass of need.

I'd have chewed my own arm off to free myself from this hell.

One more hour, tops, I reminded myself. A mere blip in my three hundred years on this earth. All I had to do was get through this, and it would be a whole day before I was forced to gaze upon her again.

Plenty of time to get my mind right.

Servants and footmen scurried through the courtyard, clearing away the remnants of the brutalized squash and setting up proper targets with a red bullseye in the center. A crowd of spectators filed in and took their seats, with Edmund in the front row, flanked by his lackeys, An-phony included.

I looked away and took special care not to turn toward Sienna as she spoke.

"I'm so nervous. What if I start shaking and slip and I almost eviscerate another raven?"

"You won't."

"Well, what if I forget everything you taught me and blow it, then?" she demanded, her voice going shrill with panic.

"You won't," I repeated, tonelessly. "Just remember to breathe, exhale, and don't grip too tightly."

She didn't reply and I risked a glance down at her.

"It's going to be all right."

Damn it, stop lying to the woman. It wasn't going to be all right. Today, maybe. But long term? No matter how you turned it, she was still going to end up a prisoner here.

Stuck under the body of another man.

For the rest of her life.

"Gentlemen, the time for instruction is over. Step to the side!" the Duchess called. "Ladies, knock your first arrow!"

I moved away from Sienna, and watched on dispassionately. On the outside, at least. On the inside, I felt like I had always imagined a human felt when watching their favorite sports team. So stupid, all of it. Grown men running around in circles chasing after a ball like a bunch of overgrown children.

But here I was, watching my captive take aim, with baited breath. *That's it. You've got it...*

When the first arrow struck the target, it took everything I had not to howl in triumph. Not a perfect shot, but damn near close, only inches from the bullseye.

I looked around to find there had only been one more accurate shot. As I'd predicted, it had come from Will's protégé, Aubrey. Half dozen others met with varying degrees of success, hitting the target but not close to center. And others still missed altogether.

"Numbers five, eleven, fourteen, and twenty-two, we appreciate your efforts, but you are dismissed. Feel free to enjoy a refreshment and watch the rest of the competition."

There were murmurs of dismay from the females and some ribbing between the men as the non-qualifying teams removed themselves from the range. One girl burst into tears.

And so it went, as each successful team moved back ten paces and fired again. Each time, Sienna managed to hit the target. When only three teams remained, she turned and moved toward me.

"My shoulder is cramping. What do I—"

"Ah, ah, girl. No coaching during the competition," the Duchess called, raising a disapproving brow.

Sienna wet her lips and nodded. "Sorry, Your Grace."

I stood stock still, hands clenched at my side as she strode back toward her mark, face etched with pain.

I couldn't help her, and I had to make it appear as if that didn't bother me in the least, which was easier said than done.

She lifted the bow high and prepared to shoot. I could see the strain and her arm trembling as she waited for the call to fire.

"Loose!"

This one soared low and slow, and I muttered a silent prayer under my breath. It hit, but just barely.

I quickly scanned the other targets and blew out a sigh of relief.

"Number nineteen, you're dismissed. Numbers six and eight, congratulations! You are our final two!" the Duchess declared as the crowd broke into applause. "Each team will move back another ten paces. You will each have one last arrow to make your best shot. One of you will be determined the winner and be the envy of all in the kingdom. The other will...not," she said with a wink and a shrug.

The spectators chuckled at her little joke as the final two competitors, Sienna and Aubrey, prepared to fire.

"Last chance for a wager, brother. What say you?" Will called, his easy grin and clear enjoyment of the games almost enough to settle my nerves for a moment.

But not quite.

"It's still a no from me. That said, I think you'll be glad I didn't oblige you."

"Oooh, big talk from a man who won't put his gold where his mouth is," Will shot back as he rubbed his hands together. "No matter, I've won plenty of coin from the others. Just emerging victorious over the great General Blackthorne will be enough prize for me."

"Indeed," I murmured with an easy smile that belied the turmoil inside me.

Whatever the prize was, I knew it would make Sienna's life here a little more bearable, at least for a time. But more than that, she needed the win. To give her hope. To make her feel strong and capable, and less like a—

Enough.

Sienna lifted her bow, face contorted in pain. I could see the muscle in her shoulder leap and twitch as it visibly spasmed.

Breathe.

Time seemed to slow as she knocked her final arrow.

"Ready...and...loose!"

The noise of the crowd faded away, and I closed my eyes, focusing in on Sienna's breath...the sound of her pounding heart. The snap of the arrow as it leapt from the string.

My gaze never left her face, but I knew it before the tip struck home.

She'd done it.

She'd won.

Cheers erupted from the seats surrounding us and I spared a glance at the targets.

The little minx had scored a bullseye.

She threw her hands up in the air in victory, wincing as her shoulder protested.

"It seems as if we have our winner!" the Duchess proclaimed, face alive with excitement. "Sienna, come join me to claim your prize!"

Sienna set her bow down on a nearby hay bale almost reverently, shooting me a grateful smile before scurrying up to the center of the courtyard to join the Duchess. Her smile put the stars to shame and I couldn't tear my gaze away.

"Congratulations, brother," Will called, a rueful smiling curling his lips. "So close, wasn't it." He moved toward me, hand extended to shake, but an instant later, he was gone from my sight.

"No!"

His shout felt like something out of a dream as I followed the sound of his voice. He stood, arm extended, with the whole of an arrow through his palm. It took a moment to process what was happening, and when I did, I nearly lost my mind.

"Who?" I snarled, wheeling around as I drew my sword and my fangs sprung forth. "Show yourself to me, you bastard."

"It's all right, Dominic," Will muttered, wincing as he yanked the arrow free. "I brought it upon myself. One of the women was attempting to flee. Anthony saw and took action. I reacted instinctively."

The black rage clouding my eyes did not abate as I took in the scene. A young woman with long blonde hair crouched, frozen in place, near a small break in the tree line of the courtyard. She clutched a bow at her side, and her cheeks were ghostly white.

Anthony stood twenty yards away, a bow in his hand as well, head cocked in a challenge.

"The girl nearly escaped with a weapon, and we likely wouldn't have even realized until nightfall. We're obliged not to injure them during the course of the games except in self-defense or if they try to flee. I was well within my rights to take the shot." He sent a glance toward Edmund and shrugged, his face the picture of innocence. "Do we have yet another problem, Dominic? Seems I did you a favor, as security is your purview rather than mine..."

The courtyard was silent, but the blood rushing in my ears was like a torrent.

Think, Dominic. Think.

I turned to Will, who had moved closer to me now, and took stock. He'd been hit, but he was clearly all right. The wound would close in no time. Based on the trajectory of the arrow and the girl's placement, it seemed clear that he was not the intended target.

And still.

It had been way too close of a call.

All because I had been too distracted with some auburn-haired witch to keep watch on my brother. Too distracted to fulfill the singular purpose of an otherwise pointless life.

It would not happen again.

I took the bloodied arrow from my brother and sniffed it. Just an arrow, same as all the rest in courtyard. That settled, I sheathed my sword and turned to face DuMont.

"It is as you say, Earl, your right to fire. In future, when surrounded by countless humans and your brethren, might I suggest stopping her with your hand, or even a command, instead?" I bared my teeth at him in some facsimile of a smile and then turned toward Will. "We'll speak of this more later."

"I, for one, am bored of it already," Edmund called, feigning a yawn. "Can we wrap it up so I can move on to more entertaining pastures?"

"Let's, shall we?" the Duchess replied, pressing a hand to her heart. "Retrieve Marguerite from the bushes and bring her to my chambers to wait until I'm able to join her," she instructed one of the footman before turning to face the crowd again. "Well, that was more excitement than any of us expected, wasn't it?"

Her tone was bright as ever, but I could see the worry in her eyes as she turned to face a now-shaken Sienna.

"Congratulations, my dear! Please accept this medal for your most excellent marksmanship," the Duchess said, slipping a gold medallion around Sienna's neck.

Her cheeks were pale, and a quick glance at some of the other captives nearby revealed that was the case for most of them as well.

Because, in the span of an instant, the truth of their situation had become all too clear.

Good, I thought coldly as I gripped the broken arrow in my hand. The sooner she came to grips with her fate, the sooner she would let go of any silly fantasy she might be harboring about winning her freedom from this place.

"And your prize?" the Duchess said, a mysterious smile spreading across her face. "A boon. A pass. A favor, if you will. You don't need to name it now, but it belongs to you until the end of the games. It could be that you want a larger room, or to skip an event. It could be that you would like to spend alone time with a certain man. Whatever it is, so long as it's within my power to give, it will be yours. The only rules are that it must be used for yourself, and it cannot be exchanged for your freedom." She paused and lowered her voice, holding Sienna's gaze. "Use it wisely, girl."

Sienna curtsied and, when the Duchess dismissed her with a regal nod, she made a beeline in my direction. I stood stock-still as I locked eyes with DuMont, who stood thirty feet behind her, right in my line of sight. The glimmer of a smile that touched his lips left my blood running cold.

"Are you...are you okay?" Sienna asked Will, who stood beside me using his kerchief to staunch the already slowing blood from his wound.

"Nothing but a flesh wound, thank you."

"And you?" she asked, turning that golden gaze on me.

"As am I, now that this day is done. A complete waste of time," I muttered, eyeing her coldly. "Your hair is falling from its braid, and you look like a beggar. Go to your room and get yourself cleaned up, would you?" I turned to my brother and nodded. "My prince."

With that, I strode from the dais like the hounds of hell were at my heels. And, if the crafty look on DuMont's face was any indication, they might as well have been. Damn the Duchess for forcing my hand. If I could've just stayed back and trained with my men instead of joining in this foolishness, none of this would've happened.

"Brother," a low voice called.

I turned to find Will trailing behind me.

"I'm sorry my actions scared you."

I was in no shape to discuss it, so I waved him off. "It's fine. That said, I'd prefer you not do it again. You're far too important to risk yourself for a captive."

"I was never truly at risk."

I glared at him and took a step closer. "You are *always* at risk, Will," I growled. "Never forget that."

He studied me for far too long, like a bug under a microscope, and I took a step back.

"I've got some work to do, so if there's nothing else..."

"Where are you running off to? The others are planning to go on a hunt and then return to the palace for a night of ale and billiards. Join us."

Not happening.

I made a mental note to send my three best men along with my right hand, Scarlett, to follow the men on their hunt and then join them in the study afterwards to keep a close eye on Will. Because what I needed right now was an outlet. To purge myself of this fear and fury. And then? Head to the tavern with the rest of my soldiers, drink my weight in mead laced with Fae honey, and get piss drunk. Maybe I'd actually get some sleep instead of being tortured by dreams of that damnable female that had addled my brain to the point of danger.

"Not tonight, brother. I'll see you tomorrow, though. Enjoy yourself."

"Fine," Will called after me as I walked away. "But all work and no play makes Dom a dull boy. You've got to live a little, otherwise what's the point of being alive for so bloody long?"

His philosophical musings didn't merit a reply, so I continued on. Bypassing the entrance to the castle, I headed straight for the training grounds, unexpressed rage burning a hole in my gut. I almost felt sorry for the challengers who dared to spar with me this day. As I stepped into the arena, though, my pity evaporated. I stripped off my jacket and shirt and yanked my sword from its sheath with a snarl.

"Who wants a piece of me?"

NINE

Sienna

"ARE YOU PROUD OF me?" I demanded, meeting Bee's gaze in the mirror.

She let out a sigh and pulled yet another pin from my admittedly messy hair.

"How many times are you going to make me say it? You were amazing. The belle of the ball, so to speak."

I touched a finger to the medal around my neck and nibbled my lower lip. There was no question, it had been a successful day by any measure. I'd won the contest, my gem had darkened, and I'd also gotten some information from the General, if not as much as I'd hoped.

And still, I felt like I'd been gut-punched, for a lot of reasons. Poor Marguerite. I hardly knew her, but still, her situation was a terrifying one. I pulled the medal over my head and laid it on the vanity.

"But you can't be resting on your laurels now," Bee continued, derailing my thoughts. "It's one thing to be ahead of the pack this early on. It's another to end the games on top. Vigilance is key. You've got to maintain this same energy all the way till the end."

I nodded in agreement, but the fact was, I wouldn't be here till the end. Hopefully, after tonight, I'd have exactly what I needed to find Jordan and make a move. I'd wait another thirty minutes and then I'd slip out. There had been no set rules about wandering the halls at night, so technically I was doing nothing wrong. But even I knew that my plan was a dangerous one.

Especially after seeing what had nearly happened to Marguerite.

"Do you think the Duchess will hurt her. Or worse?"

I'd wanted to ask for hours now, but couldn't stomach hearing the potential answer until now. Between all the adrenaline of the competition, and the drama at the end of it, I'd been a mass of nerves. Not to mention that I was still nursing the wounds the General had inflicted with his ruthless parting remarks.

I was so sure I'd made progress and then—

"I don't think she'll hurt her, no. But she will have to be punished, or what's to stop the rest from trying the same thing?" Bee reasoned.

"Well, I daresay an arrow headed straight at ones throat would be a pretty solid deterrent," I said with a snort, pushing Dominic Blackthorne from my mind for the dozenth time since we'd parted ways. "It was only the young prince's hand that saved her life."

"Will is a true gentleman," Bee said with a nod. "Strong and proud but also kind and warm... I wish he were the one getting the throne. Not to mention, in my humble opinion, he's the most handsome of the three brothers. And he loves it when I make cocoa for him and the Duchess."

"Well, it seems someone has a crush."

"Not a crush," Bee shot back, looking horrified. "He is a prince and I'm a maid. No, just an...admiration, is all."

I wasn't convinced of that at all, but I let her get away with it. A girl should be able to have her secrets if she chose. I wasn't exactly an open book, either.

Again, my thoughts turned to Dominic.

How had things gone from so good to so terrible in an instant?

After the competition had ended, the Duchess had laid out an elaborate feast for us women. I should've been thrilled. No hungry eyes on me, watching my every move. No fear that, at any moment, something horrific might happen in this lair of monsters.

But instead, I could hardly eat. All I could think about was Dominic, General of the vampire army, making me feel things I did not want to feel...

"Your skin is warm and flush, Miss. Are you feeling all right?"

I swatted Bee's hand away and pushed away from the vanity.

"I'm fine. It's just a bit stuffy in here, is all."

She nodded and headed toward the nearest window.

"We'll leave it cracked for you, then, for a bit. Just make sure you close it before you go to sleep."

I narrowed my eyes at her. "And if I forget?"

She let out a weary sigh. "Then you'll probably wake up chilled and with a few mosquito bites. Not everything is life or death here, Sienna."

I rolled my eyes at her as I pulled the last few pins from my hair. "Right, but, like, a lot of stuff is, so maybe cut me some slack until I learn the rules, yeah?"

She had grace to look contrite as she gathered the day's dirty clothing from the floor.

"You're right. I'll do my best. But the faster you learn, the better." She straightened and paused, her blue eyes searching my face. "I like you, Sienna. More than most. Definitely more than I should. That's why I'm so hard on you. I'm invested in seeing you make it through. So when you feel like giving up, or rebelling, or causing trouble, just try to remember that you aren't the only one who will be affected if something bad happens to you. Can you do that for me?"

My throat ached suspiciously and I had to swallow hard to relieve it before replying.

"Sure. I can do that."

She nodded slowly and then backed out of the room.

"Good night, my friend. You did well today."

She closed the door behind her, and I let out a long breath. The guilt was nearly choking me a half hour later as I peeked my head out that same door and looked around.

Not a soul in the hallway, not even a servant. I quickly tugged a robe over my pale green silk sleeping gown, and then padded down the hall, toward the soldier's quarters. Trailing my hands against the stone wall, I stopped when I felt the emblem.

Here we go.

I turned down the long hallway, holding my breath the entire way. According to the Duchess, the men would be occupied until the wee hours, playing billiards and drinking. I had to hope she was right on that front, or else I was going to have a real problem on my hands. Luckily, I had an excuse at the ready, along with my "boon" as an insurance policy. Hopefully, that would be enough to protect me.

A seed of doubt began to take hold and I closed my eyes and pictured Jordan's face.

There was no room for doubt. Knowing the soldiers were gone for the evening made it my best chance to break in unseen. It had to be tonight.

It had to be now.

I continued moving and found that the hallway ended with a large gathering room—chairs spread out, a pool table, a massive fireplace.

Eureka.

I pinned myself to the wall, grimacing. If any vampire was in there, they would have heard my footsteps already.

Bold, time to be bold. Pushing off the wall I stepped out into the main room, eyes wide, and the picture of innocence.

"I apologize, but I appear to have gotten turned around, and—"

Empty.

I let out a sigh of relief and tucked my lost little lamb act away for later as I scanned the room. Heavy leather tomes filled the shelves, but on closer inspection, they seemed to be dedicated to combat strategies and weaponry. No maps or atlases. No desk or cupboards or drawers in sight.

"Damn it to hell," I muttered under my breath.

To my left was another hall and I groaned. No choice but to continue on. Deeper and deeper I crept into the lion's den, knowing that each step took me closer to being caught. Tingles of awareness danced over my skin as I moved swiftly. A thrum of excitement coursed through me that I couldn't deny. A callback from my old days with Jordan when we would have to steal for our supper. Adrenaline pumping, there was again that pull in my gut that told me, as foolhardy as it seemed, I was on the right path.

I stopped when I reached another dead end and settled back on my heels. Doors to either side of me, but which one to choose?

Lie at the ready once again, I moved to the door on my right, and tested the knob.

It swung open without issue and I was stunned to find myself in what appeared to be a bedroom. Strange that it wouldn't be locked.

Not strange at all, I realized with a start. This wing was designated for soldiers...arguably the deadliest of all the vampires. Who in their right mind would be stupid enough to break into their quarters?

Just you, Ceecee.

A panicked giggle threatened, and I clamped my teeth down onto my bottom lip.

Get it together, or you're going to be joining Marguerite in the Almost Decapitated Club, dummy!

Not a sisterhood I was interested in becoming a part of.

I steeled myself and focused on taking stock of what was in front of me. The empty room was masculine and had a smell of leather and musk. By the light of the moon pouring through the windows, I could see a large desk that sat to my left, piled high with books and papers, and a set of simple quills and ink.

My pulse began to pound as I padded forward. Surely, there had to be something of use here. I fanned through the papers, searching for a map or anything of interest. Mail and other useless correspondence about training drills and the like.

"Fecking gobshite, where is the—" My fingers brushed against something a little thicker than the other papers, and I paused. "Please please please please please..."

I pulled it out and, if not for the fact that I was trying desperately to keep quiet, I would have crowed with victory. A perfectly rendered map of the entire territories, sketched out with roads, landmarks, mountains and rivers, even the oceans around were marked where they were safe, and where they were not. I folded the thick paper down and tucked it into the back of my undergarments. There would be time to pore over the map once I was safely back in my room.

As I turned to leave, a sudden chill ran through me, and the hair rose on my arms and neck.

Someone was coming.

The sound of boots on stone echoed down the hall not a moment later, sending a bolt of panic through my chest. I dove beneath the desk, holding every muscle in my body perfectly still as I tried not to breathe.

The door creaked open, the sound a thousand times louder than when I'd opened it just a few short minutes ago.

Boots across the floor, and a low growl from the vampire were all I heard at first, and then a low muttering.

"Gods be damned, where are you when I need you, Scarlett?"

The familiar voice drove straight through me, piercing me to my core.

The General.

I'd have swallowed if the spit in my mouth hadn't dried up like a desert in the summer. My heart was not making this easy as it hammered so loudly that soon it was all I could hear. Surely, Dominic could hear it, too?

And yet, a moment later his boots were kicked off, and the springs of the bed protested as he settled into the mattress.

My mind raced as I tried to think of what he'd told me. Vampires did sleep...but how deeply? Would I be able to slip past him? I had been stealthy enough back when Jordan and I were on the take, but sneak by a vampire stealthy?

Seemed unlikely.

If Marguerite had been spotted trying to escape by Anthony fifty feet away in the courtyard earlier, surely I was as good as busted in a twenty by ten room with the General himself.

"Fucking bastard shoots my brother in the hand," his low voice rasped. "I'll see his head on a pike one of these days, and it won't be soon enough."

A low mumble rolled from him and then a deep sigh. It was then that I smelled it. The astringent scent of alcohol mixed with something sweet. As the roaring in my ears subsided, I realized that, when he'd spoken, his words were slightly slurred.

General Dominic Blackthorne was piss-drunk.

I covered my mouth to hold back my sob of relief. The Duchess had mentioned that the men would be drinking and playing games, but who knew that vampires were susceptible to the effects of alcohol?

I'd lucked out, yet again. But soon enough, my luck was sure to run out and I needed to be long gone before that happened.

Still as a stone, I waited with bated breath for the man who'd paid my way here to go the fuck to sleep.

It seemed like forever when his sporadic mumblings ceased and his breathing went slow and even. Only then did I dare to lift my head and look out across the desk.

His back was to me.

His very broad, very muscled back, sheet pooling across his narrow waist, and low over his hips. The view had my fingers twitching to reach out and touch...

Horror shot through me. This was the man who'd stalked me into my dreams, a hundred times over. The man who had bought me, like some pathetic runt from a puppy mill. The man who had pretended to possess a sliver of humanity today in that courtyard only to turn around and cut me low in front of everyone.

Fuck him, and fuck this.

Taking a slow breath and the only chance I had, I slid quietly out from under the desk, and plotted my path.

Ten feet at best. I was ten feet away from the door. Did I stand? Stay in a crouch? Clutching my nightdress in one hand, I took a tentative step, then another and another. I was halfway there when a low groan rumbled out of the General's mouth.

"Ah, Sienna, you witch. Fuck me."

My feet and legs locked up, my head swiveled toward him of its own accord. In a blink, I was beside him, standing at the edge of the bed.

How in the hell had this happened?

But even as my mind compelled me to run, my hand hovered over the expanse between his shoulders . . .and then I was touching him.

I bit back the gasp at the feel of his warm skin under mine and wondered how he did not wake. Another groan rolled from him and he turned toward me, eyes blessedly closed. My hand splayed across his chest, settling over the left side, where his heart should be, if he had one.

A steady beating told the tale, and I found myself wondering if his heart felt pain, the way us humans did, or if it was nothing more than a biological mechanism.

That pointless musing ended as my gaze traveled lower, over his rippled stomach, to the thick ridge tenting his sheets. He might be out cold, but his body sensed my presence. And mine his, damn me. Parts that I thought had been silenced forever awakened, my core heating and growing slick, demanding that I do exactly what he commanded and fuck him.

No.

He was nothing more than a sadistic bloodsucker who haunted my dreams. A ruthless killer, like all the rest.

I had to get out of here.

Now.

Feeling as though I was moving through mud, I tore my hand from his chest and sprinted for the door, the slap of my bare feet on the floor sounding like gunshots to my ears. A turn of the knob and then I was dashing down the hall. I didn't let myself slow until I'd reached the common room in the center of the palace.

It was only then that the strange pull to return to him, like an unseen fist around my soul, relinquished its hold.

I stood there for a long moment, struggling to catch my breath. Terrifying.

And yet, I could still feel the beat of his heart. Hear the low rasp of his voice, calling my name...

I cocked my head as a strange feeling settled over me. No hands reached out. No one threw me to the ground. I wasn't being followed, and yet I felt eyes on me.

I'd dithered around way too long. Forcing my feet into action, I scurried down the hall toward my bedroom, pausing outside the door to look back one last time. Part of me was certain the General would be right there, breathing down my neck, which only set my pulse beating faster.

The General was not behind me.

But another was, watching me from the other end of the hallway. The one with the evil eyes. Anthony, Earl of DuMont.

He gave a low *tssk*.

"Dangerous, out and about alone at night. Take care, won't you?"

His oily smile pushed me into motion again. I wrenched my door open and slid through, slamming it shut behind me, throwing the simple deadbolt.

Damn it all. I'd been seen. Would I be punished?

Still trembling, I yanked the map from my underwear, and tucked it under my mattress, praying that the Earl didn't attempt to follow me. If discovered, surely the map was worth a beating or two, assuming the Duchess didn't just have me outright killed.

To be fair, as far as he knew, I hadn't done anything against the rules. Still, it took an hour for my heartbeat to return to normal.

And far longer to stop thinking about the way damnable Dominic Blackthorne's skin felt beneath my hands...

TEN

Sienna

I DIDN'T SLEEP THAT night. Not a wink. I told myself that it was because of the map and the creepy Earl. It had nothing to do with touching the naked General while he slept. Nothing at all to do with the fact that he'd given me a command, and I'd been compelled to obey, at least at first...

No, my lack of sleep had nothing to do with the wild sensations rushing through me.

Once the black night sky gave way to the very beginnings of dawn, and I realized no one was going to come for it, I finally gave in to the urge to look at the map.

Tears stung my eyes as I studied this godsend. It was not only a view of the lands surrounding the castle, but it also extended beyond the vampires' realm. The shifter territories were immediately east of the Vampire Kingdom. The two supernaturals shared a border. I stared in stunned disbelief at my luck.

Jordan was closer than I could have ever hoped, but the map had no key to determine true distance. Could I walk there? How much time would I need?

Despite all the unanswered questions, I was filled with hope and a sense of purpose, and, when the sun had crept partway over the horizon, I leapt into action. A quick search of my closet turned up a simple split skirt, dark brown and made of a light material. Much better than some fussy dress if I was going to scout the grounds.

While I was sure that there would be something that I had to do today for the Duchess, I doubted it would be before noon. So long as I got back before then, no one would miss me. My mind tripped back to poor Marguerite, but I pushed the thoughts away.

This wasn't the same thing. The Duchess had been very clear. We were allowed to walk the grounds freely, so long as we stayed on this side of the bridge. And, worst case, if push came to shove, I had my boon to fall back on.

Making my way out of my room for the second time, I hurried down several sets of stairs until I found an exterior door. A guard and a few maids saw me, but none questioned or tried to stop me.

So far, so good.

Once outside, I lifted my face to the sun. It felt . . . not warm the way I expected. Fake sun, fake warmth. I found myself looking at the sky. It was a wonder that the covering that gave them a semblance of human normalcy hadn't been torn apart by an enemy.

A medium sized, white, and black shaggy dog raced over to me, rubbing her side into my leg, her tongue lolling as she looked up at me expectantly.

"I'm sorry," I said as I reached down to pet the top of her head. "I don't have any bickies for you." I bent closer and whispered. "I don't suppose you're a werewolf?"

She barked, jumping about, making me step back.

"She ain't lookin' for treats," an elderly man with a limp said as he carried a woven basket full of carrots on his hip. "She just likes the attention."

"What's her name?"

"Sadie."

"Well hello, Sadie. I'm so happy you came over to say hello." I squatted down to give her a hug and soak in her presence. She went still and then turned to look me in the eyes.

Maybe she *was* a werewolf.

"You've got the touch," the man said.

I kept on rubbing Sadie's head. "The what?"

"The touch. She recognizes something in your soul. Kindred spirits, like."

I laughed. "Oh, you mean she and I both wear collars?" I said, touching the pendant around my neck.

The old man narrowed his eyes at me. "You're one of the new girls. For the Harvest Games."

I hesitated, then nodded. "Who else would be wearing one of these? Not the Duchess, surely."

He didn't wait for confirmation. "Just be sure not to cross the stone bridge into... well, into a part that don't be ours. Stay on this western side and you'll be fine." The old man grabbed a carrot and waved it at me, lecturing on. "But if you get a fool idea to cross, be prepared to die. If the animals in the forest don't get you, the guards will, and one won't be any better than the other. A girl tried it a few years back and the General's men brought her back in pieces to feed the Hunters."

Lovely. Just fecking lovely.

"Warning heeded," I gave him a curtsey and he snorted and tossed me the carrot.

"If you want to see the land"—he eyed up my skirts—"then take a horse at least."

My brows shot up as I tried to keep the excitement off my face. "You encouraging me to run away?"

"Telling you to use the tools at hand you have, to make your life easier," he said as he limped away. "Name's Jep."

"Sienna. Ceecee to my friends."

Jep looked over his shoulder. "That what we are?"

He'd just potentially solved a whole host of problems for me, so it was hard to think of him as anything else.

"Why not, Jep?" I said with a smile and a wink. "I could be dead next week, eaten by Hunters for my bad behavior. At least you know I'll never beg you for money."

His lips twisted into a wry grin. "Lip like that, you'll be dead before the day is out."

My grin widened. "I'll take that wager, sir. Because you're going to see me around here for a while to come."

Maybe as long as fifty-six days, even...

Laughing, he waved me off, and I turned to see a set of stables not far down the lane.

The barn was quiet with the soft sound of hooves shuffling through straw and a few nickers as the horses begged for their breakfast. I walked down the center aisle, checking out the stalls on either side. A few of the horses watched me curiously, but one in particular, a deep black mare at the very end of the row, held my gaze. She kept her dark eyes pinned on me as I headed towards her. When I reached her stall, I pulled to a stop, offering her my hand. She nuzzled my fingers and I rubbed my palm between her eyes.

"You're a love, aren't you?" I murmured as she leaned into my touch. She let out a low blow of air, her eyes half-closing.

I peered over the edge of the stall. She looked to be in good condition...

After one last rub, I went in search of tack, and found a young boy filling buckets with mash.

"I'd like to ride," I said confidently, posing it as a statement rather than a question. "Where are the saddles?"

He scratched his head. "Kinda early, isn't it?"

I shrugged. "I like the morning. Saddles, where are they?"

He peered around me. "These horses are all spoken for. You can't just be riding them and ruining them for the rest of the day."

I grimaced, trying not to let his words deflate me. The potential key to my freedom—to finding Jordan—was only yards away. I wasn't about to just to give up.

"What about the black mare at the end?" I pressed.

The boy's eyes flew wide as if I'd smacked him.

"Havoc?" He shook his head. "You want to stay away from that one, Miss. She's got a helluva bite and she ain't afraid to use it." He turned his arm, showing me a massive bruise across the underside of his bicep.

I shot him a dubious frown. Maybe he was lying because he didn't want me to ride her?

"Are we talking about the same horse? She was just loving on me. Sweet and gentle as a lamb."

He eyed me like I'd lost my mind. "Nope. Not Havoc. She's a right bitch."

I turned and led him down the darkened aisle, stopping in front of the stall. The horse leaned her head over the door and nudged my hand, her tactile lips searching for a treat.

"Hey there, lovely girl," I crooned softly.

"Well, I'll be damned," the stable boy said in awe. "Ain't nobody can touch that horse since she came here."

I wasn't sure what to make of that, especially since she was so friendly. But what I did know was that Jep was right. A horse could cover ground a lot faster than I could on foot.

"Can I ride her or not? You said that every other horse is spoken for..."

"I ain't getting near her, but I guess you're free to do as you want." As if to prove his earlier point, Havoc suddenly snaked her head out, bared her teeth and pinned her ears at him.

Boss mare, indeed.

A moment later, her gaze shifted back to me, and her ears popped forward, friendly as could be.

Weird, but also concerning.

"I'll be fine," I said with some seriously false bravado.

My first job out of the orphanage had been on a horse farm. I'd loved it, but it hadn't paid well enough to take care of me and Jordan, and Jordan hadn't been strong enough for the manual labor. The animals seemed to like me, and I'd never been injured, but there was always a first time. And if Havoc's affections turned out to be fleeting, I could wind up in a world of hurt.

The boy must've come to a similar conclusion and shook his head as he backed away.

"Eh... maybe better if you didn't. Havoc don't like nobody on her back. She's gonna throw you, and I don't wanna get in trouble for the General's property being broken."

I blinked. "This is the General's horse?"

"Supposed to be." The boy shrugged, "But even he can't get near her. She's trained for war."

I had to admit, there was something satisfying about taking Havoc knowing she belonged to the General. I looked deep into the animal's eyes, and she softened further.

"We'll be fine." She nudged the side of my head, her nose wiggling against my hair, mussing it up.

"She's gonna bite your ear off," the boy warned.

"I'll take my chances," I said as I brushed her overzealous nose away.

When he turned away, muttering something under his breath about hardheaded women and broken limbs, I wanted to pump my fist in victory and do a little dance. Instead, I got straight to work.

It took me all of five minutes to tack up and get on Havoc's back. She didn't so much as twitch a muscle wrong.

Once astride, I called to the boy.

"I'm ready!"

He came and flung open the doors, and Havoc didn't hesitate. She burst out of the stable, plunging and dancing. She was strong and chock full of energy, so it took some doing to rein her in on the short path to the gate. The guards opened it for us, and the second we were through, I loosened the reins to give the mare her head. She took full advantage, leaping into a full-tilt gallop, racing over the draw bridge and across the road into the open countryside, and stealing my breath away.

The hair that had hung down my back now flew out behind me, and the winds battered my face. For a moment, it felt like freedom, but I tamped down the sensation. It was just an illusion.

For now.

Once Jordan was riding along with me as we fled this place of nightmares, I would celebrate. As it was, I had work to do in order to get us both to that point.

First up? Find the stone bridge, due east, where the werewolf and vampire territory met.

I counted off the seconds in my mind as I rode.

Ten Mississippi, eleven Mississippi...

Havoc and I galloped through a flower dotted meadow as we ran straight east, past a series of fruit trees on our right, mountain peaks far to the distance on the northern side. Good landmarks, at least.

According to the map, the mountains belonged to one of the other supernatural kingdoms, but I couldn't recall which.

Havoc ran without breaking stride for nearly an hour, and I started to worry she was pushing herself too hard. When she finally began to slow down, I could hear rushing waters nearby. Heart thumping, I led Havoc toward the sound. A moment later, a thirty-foot wide river came into view, weaving its way into a massively dense forest.

And arching over that river?

What had to be the stone bridge everyone had been warning me about.

We'd made it to the eastern edge of the territory. With how fast Havoc was moving, I was betting close to forty miles. It would take me two days if I tried to make that trek on foot. That would never work. Even if I left in the dead of night, I'd have a clutch of bloodsuckers hunting me down by the following morning. When I made my move, it would have to be on horseback.

"Thank you, sweet girl." I stroked Havoc's damp neck, falling just a little more in love with her.

She trotted parallel to the river, her body slick with sweat. As we passed the entrance to the bridge, she gave a sharp whinny and tossed her head.

"Let's get you a drink, girl," I murmured, tugging the reins to urge her down a shallow bank. When we reached the river's edge, she bent her head to the water.

She was still taking her fill when the hair on my arms stood up and a shudder rolled over me. I whipped my head around, searching the tree line. If I'd thought I'd felt eyes on me before, it was nothing compared to the sensation here on the edge of the territory.

Eyes in the forest. I was more sure of it than I was my own name.

"Hello?" I called, cursing myself for a fool even as I did it.

No answer, not that I'd truly expected one. And still, the feeling of being watched—no...studied—only intensified.

"Do you know Jordan?"

I waited, the pulse in my neck pounding so hard, I could've danced to the beat, but again, there was no reply.

With a sigh, I glanced at the position of the fake sun and blew out a sigh. This first day out on my own, I had no interest in pressing my luck any further than I already had. The Duchess had plans for my day, and I wanted to get back with plenty of time to spare. I had to toe the line and stay outwardly obedient, or this excursion would be my last.

But what had me nudging Havoc back up the bank more than anything else?

My sudden fear that the eyes on my back could quickly become hands around my throat.

I was playing a very dangerous game, and making up the rules as I went along.

"I'll be back soon, Jordan. And next time, we leave together," I whispered under my breath as Havoc broke into a canter. "I swear it."

ELEVEN

Dominic

"I REALIZE YOU'RE A misanthrope and a drag, but can you at least make some attempt to hide it? If not for my sake, then for the sake of the fun and enjoyment of others who look to you, foolishly, for a sense of leadership."

Edmund, Crown Prince of the Vampire Kingdom, turned and shot me a withering glance.

I settled more deeply into the seat beside him, and offered a curt nod. "Understood, Your Highness," I said, mockingly.

Edmund scowled at me, a wrinkle marring his smooth brow before it disappeared. "You mistake me if you think I care whether you're enjoying yourself or not, Dominic. I just want to make sure that the ladies here aren't intimidated by your miserable face. Father wants them to be happy, to enjoy this competition. The games are much more delectable if the participants aren't quivering in fear the entire time. At least, until I want them to." He paused to eat a forkful of tender quail. When he was done chewing, he continued, "Speaking of which, Anthony mentioned the other day that you took an interest in one of the girls at the auction. That's new."

Damned Anthony.

I barely resisted the urge to walk over and throttle the bastard where he sat at the table across from us, laughing at something one of his mistresses had said. I tried to keep my expression as bored and uninterested as my tone.

"I think you're somewhat misinformed. There was a scruffy-looking whelp on the block, and she pounded the guard in the face. Raven decided to make things interesting, and unfortunately, I lost the bet. Yesterday, I was saddled with her for the archery competition. Turns out, she's a good shot. Too bad, she's also got a sharp tongue and smells far too human for my liking," I said, lying through my fangs.

I'd thought about that tongue and that body all damned night, despite drinking myself into a stupor, and my mood was even blacker than the day before.

Edmund cocked his head and gazed at me, his blue-grey eyes assessing me carefully. "So you have no interest in this woman, then?" he asked, his voice deceptively low.

I shrugged and shook my head. "None in the least."

"Which one is she, pray tell? I must admit, I didn't pay much attention to the archery contest. Such a bore when we could be doing so much more with our captives..." my brother said, lifting his head to glance around the ballroom, scanning the faces of the women at the tables scattered around the perimeter of the dance floor.

I tamped down the sudden urge to close my fingers over his windpipe, feeling an instant pull to Sienna even though I couldn't see her, almost like I could feel her hands on my skin...

"Was it that one?" he asked with a frown, squinting at a woman in a lemon yellow dress with springy black hair.

Some of the tension in me uncoiled as relief settled in. Sienna was definitely on Anthony's radar, but my older brother had always viewed humans as beneath him. He hadn't even noted her hair color, never mind zeroed in on her, which was good. Dealing with the Earl was one thing. Dealing with the Crown Prince was a whole other kettle of fish. If I could keep him off Sienna's scent, I was confident I could keep her safe.

And what of Will? While you're busy worried about the safety of a stranger, your brother is vulnerable to attack.

I cleared my throat and shrugged. "I haven't seen her tonight."

That much was true. But, I'd seen her last night. Or, at least, I'd dreamt I had. Dreamt of her touch as I commanded her to fuck me. Dreamt of her scent, and sound of her husky gasps ringing in my ears. I'd woken up with a raging hard-on that still hadn't fully abated. It felt so real...

"Are you two bickering again?"

I turned at the familiar voice and looked over my shoulder to see Will standing there with a wide grin.

"Surely not. I do not bicker with those beneath me," Edmund replied, staring at Will with a smile that didn't even come close to reaching his eyes. But our younger brother was oblivious to his disdain.

No. Not disdain.

Hatred.

I often wondered how Will didn't see it. The cruelty that lay within Edmund, with his cold, grey-blue eyes, so like that of a shark. Eyes that saw everything, but felt nothing. How could Will be blind to the fact that Edmund was missing a crucial part of what separated us vampires from true monsters?

A soul.

Edmund gave not a shit about anyone but Edmund.

Oblivious, Will dropped into the chair beside me and picked up a stein full of blood spiked ale and held it aloft.

"Well, cheers, then, brothers. Let this be the best Harvest Games we've ever hosted. I feel it in my bones, it will be one to remember!"

I lifted my cup to his, watching as Edmund followed suit, albeit reluctantly. It never had occurred to Will that he remained in Edmund's graces—I wouldn't say good graces, because Edmund didn't *have* good graces—but graces, because Will possessed the one thing Edmund never would. The love, respect, and adoration of the rest of the kingdom. If Edmund were to openly mistreat Will, there would be instant blowback, of that I was certain. Will might not have the crown but he had something just as valuable.

The hearts of the people.

Mine included. But, despite our bond, I'd never been able to convince him to watch his step around our older brother. If Edmund was a shark, Will was a Labrador, splashing around in the water, looking for the next stick to retrieve, blissfully unaware that an apex predator lurked below the surface, waiting for its chance to strike.

"Cheers," Edmund said softly, then lifted the glass to his lips, taking a long drink. "Tell me, how is your hand?"

"All healed," Will said with a rueful shake of his head. "But Anthony is impetuous. I do believe I'll speak to him about that."

Edmund lifted one shoulder carelessly. "I would say you are the one who behaved impetuously, little brother. There are dozens of other girls. There are only two princes, after all. Me and one spare. Can't be too careful."

He turned a cool eye toward me and I nodded in agreement.

"We are of the same mind, Edmund. It would be best for all involved if you let nature take its course next time, Will."

Will sighed and then nodded. "Yes, well, hopefully such a time won't come to pass. What say we turn the page and enjoy the festivities?

Edmund nodded and set his stein back with a clatter before rising. He held up a hand and, without him saying a word, the chatter around the room began to quiet. Even the human females caught on quickly and, soon enough, the massive ballroom was dead silent.

"On behalf of myself, the Crown Prince, and on behalf of my father, who could not be here tonight, your liege, King Stirling, we welcome you once again to the Harvest Games. It is your honor to be part of them."

I felt a sudden, keen sense that someone was looking at me, and I turned to scan the room. A moment later, I caught sight of a woman tucked in the furthest corner of the hall. Defiant, honey-colored eyes stared back at me.

Blood thrummed in my veins at the very sight of her, and it took everything I had to look away. Even when I did, what I'd seen was etched in my brain as if it'd been carved there by a scalpel. Tumbling auburn curls falling in a riot around creamy rounded shoulders, a pert nose, and a full mouth that made my fangs snap through my gums with the urge to sink them into her lips, to press them to her neck. The riding outfit she'd worn when I'd seen her the day before had been beautiful on her, the color a perfect foil to her creamy skin, but this one outshone even that. A burnished gold that made it seem like she was lit from within, and it offset her hair, giving the impression that she was fire itself.

I could almost taste her vitality from dozens of yards away and the vivid dream from the night before came rushing back.

It had seemed so real, I would've sworn she'd been in the room with me. Her touch on my back had been hot as a brand. And when I'd awakened, bathed in sweat and aching with need.

No bones about it, I was in a very bad way.

Even more reason to keep my distance. If Edmund sensed my interest, he would only cause her grief. And besides, despite her attempts to be charming, she wasn't very good at hiding the truth. The macabre romanticism of the Harvest Games and heady sensuality of being surrounded by vampires that so often entranced the female participants clearly had no effect on her. She didn't want to be here, and the second she had a chance to run, she'd be off like a shot. Who needed an unwilling neck to drink from when there were others available? These Harvest Games were something I was forced to suffer through as the General of the Crown Prince's army, but it was *not* my duty to partake. I'd stay as long as I had to, then slip out as quickly as possible, find another of my kind that wanted to fuck as much as I did, and cure what was ailing me.

That settled, I turned my attention back to my older brother as he closed up his welcome speech.

"Once again, I thank you all for coming, and I wish you the best of luck."

As Edmund took his seat, it took everything I had not to smash the smile on his face right off. Anyone on the outside looking in would think him handsome and easygoing, yet comfortable in his position—a true leader. It was exactly that ability to pretend, along with his good looks and power, that caused the ladies to flutter closer, completely unaware that this particular flame would engulf and reduce them to mere ashes.

It wasn't a question of if. It was only a question of when.

Over the past century, my brother had been married sixteen times, but I had not one living sister-in-law. The countless mistresses he'd taken over the years had each fallen to some bad end or another. To be Edmund's lover meant certain death. To refuse him meant the same. And it was my sworn duty to protect him with my life. If he was a monster, what did that make me?

I shot a glance to Will, who drained the rest of his glass, and then winked. "You ready to mix and mingle, brother? I see you can hardly wait to get out on the dance floor."

I was about to refuse, as always, when a low voice sounded over my shoulder.

"Don't even think about saying no, Nicky."

I blew out a low sigh. "Good evening, Your Grace. Looking lovely, as always."

The Duchess leaned in and tapped me gently on the shoulder with the crimson fan she held. "You'd better say that, child. I spent three hours getting dressed, which is why I'm late. Now, tell me, what did I miss? Anyone pick a girl yet?" she asked as Will scooted down the seat to leave the spot next to me open for our aunt. "Did Eddy already give his speech?"

A flash of annoyance ran over Edmund's face, but he didn't correct her. There were very few people immune to Edmund's wrath, but the Duchess was one of them. Until, or unless, the King passed, she would remain untouchable. It was a good thing, I adored the woman, despite the fact that she was a busybody, always digging at people.

"I did welcome them, yes," Edmund said crisply, "and you would do well to show up on time to hear it in the future." He didn't wait for her response, instead turning to speak with the person on his right and ignoring us entirely, now. Fine by me.

The Duchess rolled her eyes and gave me a conspiratorial smile. "Someone woke up on the wrong side of the coffin this morning," she said with a chuckle.

Will tossed his head back and laughed, then slung his arm around our aunt's shoulders. "See, Your Grace, this is why I can't get married. No one compares to you, in beauty or in wit. You have ruined me. There will never be another like you!"

She patted his hand and shot him an affectionate smile. "Don't waste all that charm on me, boy, get out there and dance, and see if any of these pretty ladies can catch your eye. Finally."

Will didn't need to be asked twice, as he stood and sauntered towards the fray of women, who had all stood up from the table and had begun milling around the edge of the dance floor in search of a partner.

All except one. My jaw tightened, thinking of her phantom touch the night before. I'd woken and been sure I could smell her even.

I was losing my fucking mind.

"I know you don't want to hear it, Nicky, but it's a long life for our kind, and it'd do you well to find some joy in it." She leaned her head closer. "Besides, you getting out there can only help the girls in the long run. Help them be seen as desirable by a General and the other men will take note. They look up to you."

I knew it was true. The less terrified and more engaged the females were, the better their chances of survival. But I held no delusions about most of their futures, regardless. The deck was stacked against them. We were predators and they were prey. Those weren't my rules, but the law of nature. Even for me, it was a struggle to maintain self-discipline when it came to the weaker species—and no one knew it better than I. Human blood, and the promise of it, did things to a vampire that a human couldn't possibly understand. Biological things...psychological things. Things that could derail even the most careful planning.

Once I'd matured enough to manage the power of the blood lust, I made sure I was never in the presence of humans when I was in need. Instead, I drank from a cup, or took from the vein of a more than willing vampire woman weekly, rather than waiting a month between feedings. It wasn't the same, of course. Akin to eating stale bread while a feast of crispy-skinned duck a L'orange, parsnip puree and caramelized onions sat an arm's length away. But it worked. I had drunk as little as possible directly from humans for the last fifty years and hadn't drained one dry in a decade more than that. Given that most of my brethren viewed humans as an entertaining distraction, at best, or as a crop for their consumption in every sense of the word, at worst, I supposed it was something.

Some still believed that the more human blood they drank, the more powerful they'd be. Another myth, thank the gods.

Still, as I watched the young women peering nervously around the room, trying to keep their smiles from quivering when the men moved in, I was keenly aware that my 'stale bread' wasn't enough on days like this.

"Go on, then," my aunt murmured, rousing me from my macabre thoughts. "And if you promise you'll dance with at least three of them, I'll make your excuses to Edmund myself, and you can retire to your quarters."

"That's a bargain I will gladly accept," I replied, pushing myself to my feet. The sooner I could get the hell out of this place and this ridiculous waistcoat, the better.

Of their own accord, my eyes flicked around the massive room, again searching out auburn hair. Sienna was tucked in the opposite corner, now, alone, head bowed. I hadn't been watching her more than a moment or two, when she looked up. This time, I held her gaze. She wet her lips reflexively and my gums throbbed as my fangs tried to break free for a second time.

I gritted my teeth and did a quick bout of mental math. It had been four days since my last blood meal. Normally, I'd have another few days before the desire would be this sharp. Then again, these weren't normal circumstances. We were surrounded by human girls, and the scent of it was overpowering everything. Not even the smell of succulent, roasted meats, exotic hothouse flowers, or expensive perfumes could compete.

Lifeblood had a scent that obliterated all others.

And the urge to taste *hers* was like a clawing, needful thing in my belly; needful in other places too. The constant barrage, day and night, in my dreams and while I was awake…It was too much.

Three twirls around the floor, and done.

"Sir…w-would you like to dance?"

I turned to find a pretty young woman with golden hair and a tentative smile gazing up at me. She was a slight little thing…long, lean muscles and sharp collar bones with visible hollows and valleys that most vampires prized. As attractive as she was, I found myself blessedly unmoved by her, and the pressure in my gums receded as I took her arm.

"I would," I said with a nod.

SHANNON MAYER

Human waitstaff bustled by, clearing the dishes and leftover food, as the ten-piece orchestra in the corner of the room grew louder.

I led her to the dance floor and swept her into my arms. To her credit, she didn't seem all that nervous. In fact, as I steered her around the floor in a lively reel, she started to giggle.

"You're a fabulous dancer," she called over the music. Her cheeks turned a pretty shade of pink as she tightened her grip on my shoulder.

"Thank you," I replied, trying not to let my irritation with the small talk show. "My mother was a dance instructor when I was growing up. I had little choice in the matter."

She pressed her body closer to mine, until our hips were flush.

"Well, she did a great job teaching you. My name is Martha, by the way. And yours?"

I started to say General, and then faded off. "Dominic will do."

She was still mooning up at me when the song ended and I pulled away with a tight smile.

"I won't monopolize your time. There are many men here who, I'm sure, would love a dance."

The gem nestled between her modest breasts was glowing pink, giving credence to my words.

"Oh!" she exclaimed, following my gaze. "That's good, right?" she asked, searching my face anxiously.

"It is," I confirmed with a clipped nod. She moved to lean into me and I took a step back. "If I were you, I'd make a beeline for the gentleman by the fountain in the blue jacket, staring at you."

138

Peter Vasilli wasn't of royal blood, but he was well connected, respected, and as good a man as any in the palace. If Martha could win him over now, and hold his attention for the next seven weeks, she had a good chance of seeing this thing through to the end, and landing herself a spot in the ladies' court. If she was lucky, Peter might even fall in love and take her as a permanent mistress or even his wife.

Martha followed my gaze and bit her lip.

"And if I'd rather stay here with you?" she asked softly.

"I'm afraid that's not an option. I am not looking for . . .what you would need from me."

Her cheeks flushed again, but this time with embarrassment. "I see. Well, thank you for the dance. And the advice."

With that, she hurried off, in the direction of the fountain, leaving me to breathe a sigh of relief.

One down, two to go.

I could almost taste my freedom. Maybe I would go to the courtyard and convince one of my men to spar with me. This excess energy had been building for days, and needed an outlet.

"I can't stop thinking about it. Why did you help me?"

I looked up, irritated at having let my guard down twice in less than ten minutes, and found myself looking into a pair of liquid honey eyes.

Very pissed off, liquid honey eyes.

"Beg your pardon?" I drawled.

She moved closer and glared up at me.

"No more bullshit about needing to fill your quota so you could leave. You bought me. *Me*, specifically. Then, you helped me with the archery competition. Only now, you're acting like you don't know me and can't wait to get away from me. So why did you do it?"

I resisted the urge to step back as I tried not to breathe through my nose.

Shit. Too late.

Her essence hit me like a sucker punch. Jasmine and vitality and the sweet heat of her sex coiled around me, sending a hot wave of blood rushing through me, lighting me up, even as my fangs broke free of my gums with a snap.

I called on every ounce of self-discipline to retract them before replying.

"I made a bet with an old friend." My words were clipped. Hard. "And I lost, which meant I had no choice but to purchase you. And as General, my protégé losing an archery competition would hardly reflect well on me. Now, if you'll excuse me." I made a move to turn away. To escape her.

The Duchess passed my field of vision and skewered me with an icy stare and an arched brow. At this point, it would cause more of a scene if I walked away than if I played the part of a gentleman.

"Shall we dance, then?" I snapped, unable to keep my tone anything but fierce. Sienna frowned for a moment and looked like she was about to refuse, but then nodded.

"Can I ask you something else?" she said as I led her around the floor.

I clenched my jaw. "Given that I doubt I can stop you, go right ahead."

"How would you feel if you were in my shoes?"

My concentration that had been wholly focused on blocking out her scent and the feeling of her ripe body brushing against mine slipped, and I winced.

"How would you feel if you were kidnapped, and forced to parade around like a show poodle in hopes to get the attention of a creature who would just as soon drain your blood as fuck you?"

Her cut-to-the-heart-of-it words were just grim enough to soften the edges of my need, but I refused to apologize to her for my kin and their ways. She was just a pet, at best. A meal at worst.

"I would realize escape is futile and I would accept my lot."

She studied me through narrowed eyes. "Somehow, I doubt that, Dominic. Have you no advice for me then?"

Hearing my name from her lips sent another rush of blood south and I swallowed a growl even as I answered her.

"You want advice? Fine. The Crown Prince has all the power here." I knew I should bite my tongue, but I couldn't fight the compulsion. "You'd do well to stay out of his way and under his radar for your own safety."

And I'd do well to mind my own fucking business, but here we were. Chatting.

She nodded slowly. "All right. Given that I have no one here I can trust, and you helped me once, I will take that under consideration. Which brings me back to my original question...why me?" Her question had an intensity to it that made me think she believed there was some other reason.

"I told you. A bet gone wrong. With the fist fight, I knew you'd end up as chum. Filthy, and miserable, and pathetic. I felt sorry for you," I said, only lying through my still slightly distended fangs. I sure as shit didn't want to tell her that she made my heart race.

Her throat worked as she swallowed hard, before lifting her chin proudly. "And I feel sorry for you that you have to kidnap women and force them into some crazy-ass Hunger Games type nonsense in order to convince them to fuck you."

Touche, little kitten.

I probably should've been irritated at her impertinence, but damned if that didn't make me want her more.

I drew her closer, until she was a breath away, her eyes widening and a tremor rolling through her.

"I can assure you that if I wanted to fuck you—or any of the women here—there would be no coercion required."

Godsdamn it, man, shut your trap.

I spun her in a circle and then pulled her back sharply, a move that caused her heel to catch and sent her stumbling. I tightened my arms around her to steady her, and wound up with her soft breasts mashed against my chest.

For a second, I couldn't move. All attempts to dance ceased as a wave of lust rolled through me, so strong, my biceps started to quake.

She stared up at me, eyes wide, lips parted, her stone sliding from dark pink into a steady purple. It took all my strength not to crush my mouth against hers. Grab those full hips in both hands and grind her against my aching cock. Close my teeth over that smooth swell of breast and sink my fangs into—

"I'll take my leave now," I rasped, steadying her on her feet before stepping back. "I've grown weary of this party. And of you."

I turned on my heel and headed straight for the exit.

Duchess be damned. I'd danced with two, and she'd better be glad for it. I'd wasted more than enough time on this stupidity. I was the General of the Crown Prince's army and Protector of the Empire. I had important things to do.

Things that didn't involve an auburn-haired, golden-eyed witch seemingly intent on bringing me low.

TWELVE

Sienna

I STARED AFTER THE General as he strode out of the ballroom, a knot of disappointment low in my belly competing with the desire to call after him with one final insult. I'd only agreed to dance with him in order to get some intel on the werewolves. It had nothing to do with the way his skin had felt the night before, or how the ridged scars across his shoulders intrigued me. The back and forth with him on the dance floor, the feel of his large hands on my waist and engulfing my own fingers was . . .interesting. Yes, that was the word I was going to use.

Interesting.

I sure as bloody hell wasn't going to say sexy.

Or hot enough to light my clothes on fire and leave me naked in his arms...especially after his round dismissal of me. Especially knowing that he'd kill me in an instant if I displeased him.

Even as I tried to deny all the feelings, a flush of heat rolled through me and I found myself fanning my face with one hand in a vain attempt to cool myself. He could say what he wanted. If he was bored by me, I'd eat my golden hairpin.

A touch on my elbow turned me away from the rather lovely view of the General just before he made a full exit from the room.

"Well, hello, *precious*," a smooth voice I recognized purred.

I blinked and met the gaze of the greasy man from the auction. The one with the cruel eyes and sinister face.

The one who'd seen me outside my room the night before.

Fecker could drop dead and I'd be happier for it.

A wave of disgust rolled over me. I twisted my arm to unhook his fingers from me, but his grip was tight and he bore down on the bones in my arm. His smile grew.

"A fighter, then? You think you can out-muscle me like you did that pen warden? Please, you're a weak little human. You should be grateful for my attention."

I should have been afraid, terrified. I should have just nodded and smiled—the Duchess had drilled the etiquette into us. Except that he looked like a wet noodle that could be pushed over with a simple shove, and I despised wet noodles. I snapped my hand straight down and while his fingers raked through layers of my skin, his hold slid off me.

"I think that a child could out-muscle you." I tipped my chin up, a shiver of fear finally catching me as the burn of his scratches shot up my arm.

Idiot, what are you doing? I scolded myself. *Play nice!*

But I couldn't help it. He wasn't wrong, I'd been a fighter my whole life. I wasn't about to give up now, not to a slimy prick like this one. "You fight like a schoolgirl, scratching at me," I said.

Just keep digging, Sienna. Just keep digging.

145

His eyes narrowed and he stepped closer, but I stepped back, bumping into another body.

"Anthony," a rich velvet voice drawled. "Are you scaring the girls again?"

Anthony cleared his throat and gave a slight bow. "Young prince, of course not. This one and I were about to take a turn around the dance floor."

"Then you won't mind if I take her for the next dance? That is, unless you wanted to shoot her in the neck with an arrow, first?"

My lips twitched but I managed to hold back a smile as I turned to see who my rescuer was. Green eyes that sparked with humor, and dark brown hair that was far too long and unkempt. William, the younger of the two princes, who had risked his limb to stop Marguerite from being shot.

I had only spoken a few words to him after his injury at the archery competition, but Bee had told me all about him. No, not told—gushed. She'd gone on and on about the many qualities of the lovely William and how exquisite and kind he was. While I doubted any vampire could be all those things, I had witnessed proof that he at least had some compassion, which made him a far better dance partner than Anthony.

"Your Majesty," I curtsied to the prince, my arm on fire, but I grit my teeth against it.

He took me out onto the dance floor, turning my arm so he could see the finger scratches that were cut into my skin, his eyes tracking the trails of blood, but he didn't seem all that interested.

At least, not what I would have thought for a vampire seeing fresh blood.

"Hmm. Seems he's damaging the girls again. The Duchess is going to be pissed." He gave what had to be a mock shiver.

I blinked up at him. "You almost sound afraid."

"Of her? She beat me with a wooden spoon once, and when it broke, threatened to stake me with what remained."

My jaw dropped. "What?"

His grin was infectious. "I was twelve and I'd put itching powder in her panty drawer." His grin widened and I couldn't help the laugh that tripped out of me.

"You didn't. You're lying to me."

"Couldn't sit for a week and didn't sleep most of that time for fear she'd make good on her threat." He watched me like he was trying to see inside my head.

"What?"

"Curious. That's all. Very curious."

He spun me around, then pulled me carefully back into his space. But not too close. "About what? My horoscope? I'm a Pisces."

His smile was bright and a tad too wide. The smile of someone who used laughter to cover pain. And a little part of me hurt for him, which was stupid. He was not my friend. He was just another one of my captors. Albeit a charming one.

"I'm wondering what interest my brother has in you," he said, still smiling.

I blinked. "Wait. I thought your brothers were Dominic and Edmund? That troll back there was your brother as well?"

Probably not the best thing to say to a prince.

"Gods no!" He burst out laughing. "An-phony is just an Earl of the realm and a real—"

"Prick?" I offered.

William winked. "Amongst other things. No, I mean my brother Dominic."

"Oh, he's definitely not interested in me," I corrected with a harsh laugh. "In fact, I'm quite certain he hates me now."

William shook his head slowly. "Nope. Unless I was seeing things, he certainly does not hate you, Sienna."

"Can I ask...why is he a General and the two of you are princes?"

"He's a bastard," William said with a shrug.

"Well, yes, I know that, but why isn't he a prince?"

William's eyes flew open wide and his mouth hung open, showing the very tips of his fangs. Miracle of miracles, he threw his head back and laughed so hard he had to stop dancing, which drew everyone's gaze.

"Stake me now, I'm dead. Yes, he *is* a bastard from time to time, but he's also an actual bastard." He shook his head. "Let me explain . . .no, there is too much. Let me sum up. The King is his father, but it was an oops that produced Dominic."

William pulled me back into a hold, even though the song had changed and he should have changed partners. More gazes followed us. I did not like this. I glanced down at my pendant to see it glowing the same soft pink it had before. So William wasn't lusting after me, at least.

"And that means he can't be heir to the throne?"

"It does," he conceded with a nod. "Not fair, in my view, but there you have it."

Once more around the dance floor we went, and if we'd had eyes on us when William had been laughing, it was nothing compared to now.

Anthony the Earl of whatever stared hard at us, a veritable weight to his gaze, and the wounds on my arm ached as if he'd scratched me again.

The Duchess was tapping her fingers against her chin, her eyes following us closely.

And the Crown Prince even had a gander at us. His gaze was . . .cold with a chill that I could feel wherever my skin was bared to his eyes.

William never pulled me closer than what any good school marm would say was appropriate, at least. There was easily a bible's width of space between our bodies. My pendant continued to fade from the pink, to a not quite clear stone, once more. Just as the Duchess had said it would. Whatever desire An-phony was throwing at me was gone now. At least the stone wasn't completely devoid of color.

"Very, very interesting. You aren't terribly afraid of us, are you? You don't smell afraid at all," William said as he spun me out, holding me by one hand.

Correction. I wasn't afraid of *him*. But I was afraid. Afraid of being stuck here for eternity, living as a prisoner. Afraid of making one false move and being pierced by an arrow for my troubles. Afraid of failing Jordan, and cursing him to the same potential fates. William was wrong. I was afraid. I was just very, very good at hiding it.

"As lovely as this is, I should let you go," I said, loosening my hold. Dominic's words about staying off the Crown Prince's radar ringing in my ears, I took a step back. Edmund was clearly very interested in watching William and whoever he spent his time with. For that reason alone, it was best to take my leave. "I do believe there are others that would like to dance with you. And I should tend to my scratches."

I curtsied and he gave me an odd tilt to his head, dismissing me.

"Till we meet on the battlefield, Sienna of the spit fire."

His words gave me pause, but I hurried off the dance floor to the room that we'd all been brought into, at first.

I hurried to get inside and away from all those eyes. I finally let myself truly feel the scratches in my arm, the four of them digging deeper than I would have thought from simple fingernails. I hissed as I touched one of them. They stung something fierce and were still bleeding steadily, droplets landing on my skirt and ruining the bright gold material.

Strange. There had been moments where I'd not felt them while I danced with the young prince.

"Sienna!" Bee's voice cut through the chatter of the other maids waiting for their charges. She was at my side in a flash, her eyes horrified as she took in the scratches. "What happened, Miss?"

"What indeed?" The hard voice of the Duchess snapped through my spine, straightening me as if she'd whacked me with a stick right on the ass. She appeared as if from nowhere.

Damn vampire speed.

The maids scattered and, while Bee stood her ground, the Duchess snapped her fingers. "Out, I wish to speak with this one." Her pause was weighted. "Alone."

Once the maids were all gone, the Duchess scooped my uninjured arm in hers and guided me toward the sinks. Like the young prince, her eyes tracked the blood, but she didn't seem overly affected by the sight or smell of it. Was that because she'd already fed? Or maybe there was something wrong with my blood? "You seem to have caught the eye of the Earl. It was his desire that filled your pendant for a time."

As I'd thought.

The gilded mirrors over the sink reflected back to me my face, still flushed from the dancing, and the stark red of my blood dripping off my arm. I held it over the sink. "I am sorry about the stains."

"Posh, it is not the material of the skirt that bothers me." She took a cloth and ran it under cold water before pressing it to my arm. "It is that you did not seem to feel the wounds while you danced with the prince."

I looked at her in the mirror, part of me wondering how I was seeing her.

"Don't even think of asking that stupid question. You humans and your foolish entertainment. Bram Stoker met one vampire who was a known provocateur, and he took everything that idiot Dracula said at face value. A vampire who was kicked out of our Kingdom for his sheer stupidity. Both of them are morons. Then again, I find most men rather oblivious when it comes to important things." Her hands were surprisingly gentle on my arm. "Better?"

"A little. It...stings."

"Yes, a vampire who means you harm can make their wounds incredibly painful. And if you're not careful, you'll have scars by morning." She rinsed the cloth, and reapplied it.

Silence fell between us. Not as uncomfortable as I would have thought. Of course, it was me who broke it.

"Why are you helping me? Being kind to me?"

Her eyes slid to mine. "Would you rather I were cruel? That I tortured you and beat you and then asked you to dance with the men who will drain you of every drop of your blood, given the chance?"

I couldn't swallow, fear stealing my voice. Well, not entirely. "A rather vivid picture."

Her lips twitched. "You are . . . interesting, Sienna."

Interesting. The same word I'd used for the General. "I don't want to be interesting, I want to be free."

Bollocks, I did not mean to let that slip out. My mind was flushed with heat and the pain in my arm. I would blame my mouth on that alone.

The Duchess picked up a clean towel and pressed it against my arm, drying it before she directed me to sit at one of the small prepping stations. Again, she moved as comfortably in the space of servants, as Duchess.

"If freedom is what you want, then you would do well to fight your way into Gold Status. Five girls are given that status, five only. They will be fought over, desired, and they will be auctioned off to only the richest men in our world. Men who have many possessions. Men who are easily distracted. Men who will bid on another woman next year, and the year after, and the year after." She moved so quickly I couldn't follow her movement, and I was suddenly looking at a well-wrapped arm.

"Why is that important?" Because her words felt like she was trying to tell me something that I wasn't quite catching hold of.

She did not sigh and smack my face. She explained herself patiently, like one would to a child.

"Men of power, who have many possessions, are less likely to notice you. A man with few possessions, one who spends his entire life savings to bid on you, that one will notice if you scratch your backside in your sleep." Her eyes drifted over me. "The question is, which do you want to be, Sienna? Owned by a man who will eventually forget you, or owned by a man who will keep you on a leash so tight that it will strangle you long before you ever die?"

Horror squeezed my throat as if I could feel that leash even in that moment, and I struggled to speak. But this felt like a time I would not get with her again. I would need to be able to slip away. I needed to have that fecking gold status, just in case I couldn't get free of this place and find Jordan before the games were over.

Before I could say more, she helped me to my feet and the world swayed. "I feel ill."

"That is the scratches. They are meant to incapacitate you, making you easy prey for the one who injured you. I suppose it was not my sweet William?" Her hold tightened on me, and was about the only thing keeping me upright.

"No, he was kind to me."

"My nephew *is* kind. It is a weakness he gets from my side of the family." She snapped her fingers and, a moment later, Bee was there at my side.

"Oh, Miss, what happened?"

The Duchess answered for me. "She's taken ill. Get her to her room, and lock the door. Do not let anyone but myself in. Understood?"

Bee's face paled, but her voice had an edge to it. "Yes, I understand. I won't let anyone past me."

"Good girl." The Duchess patted her on the cheek. "And in the morning, I want my cocoa out on the balcony. William will be there, so bring two cups."

Bee steered me around and I wobbled, even in my slippers. I turned back to the Duchess.

"Marguerite...Can you tell me, is she all right?"

The Duchess paused for a long moment before inclining her head.

"She is. And she will stay that way, if I have anything to say about it. We told you girls you had free reign of the grounds, but she clearly overstepped by attempting to sneak off and take the bow with her. I just need to keep her out of Edmund and Anthony's sight for a time, until they forget about her. Let her actions be a warning to you, child. There will be opportunities for you to get what you want, but you need to be patient. Much more patient than Marguerite."

"Why are you really helping me?" I whispered.

She leaned in close and pressed her mouth to my ear. "Because I believe I know who, and more importantly . . . *what* you really are."

THIRTEEN

Dominic

AFTER I LEFT THAT godsdamned ball, I sparred with one of my guards for two hours, yet again trying fruitlessly to work off some of my frustration. I'd left the sand pit drenched in sweat, but as soon as I wasn't fighting, thoughts of an auburn-haired woman filled my head.

Sienna.

What the hell kind of name was Sienna?

I stomped off and found Scarlett, the captain of my guard. We had an arrangement that served us both well. She was in a common room with several other guards, but I stopped in the shadow of the doorway until she saw me. Her smile faded as she got up from her seat and headed in my direction. A bloom of guilt spread across my chest, but I reminded myself that our relationship worked both ways. She'd come to me on countless occasions to work out her own . . . frustrations.

I turned and walked down a narrow hall toward my room, leaving her to follow me, but thoughts of the auburn human filled my head. The slight pulsing of the vein in her neck, the way the silk of her dress clung to her breasts, and I couldn't wait. I needed release.

Now.

I spun around to face Scarlett, the irony of her name hitting me full force as I pinned her to the stone wall.

She could have fought me off. She was well trained. But her eyes widened, filled with lust, and she waited.

Raw hunger filled my head and my groin, and I reached for my pants, needing to purge this ache in my chest, the near constant throbbing of my cock that hadn't let up since I'd seen the girl in the auction.

Still, Scarlett waited. She knew this game. She knew me well, but it was usually behind closed doors, not in a public hallway. Not that it mattered. Vampires weren't prudes. We saw no shame in fucking, and monogamy was a rare trait.

Children were too rare to be overly fussed with who you were producing them with.

Holding my forearm over her upper chest, I reached for Scarlett's pants and ripped them open at the waist, wishing she was wearing a dress, a gold one that looked like it had been spun by fairies, so I could be inside her in mere seconds instead of fumbling in frustration.

I growled, a low sound that rumbled through my chest, and she reached down to shove her pants over her thighs and down to her boots.

My annoyance rose and I roared, not wanting to wait, needing to purge this demon inside me *now*.

Wrapping an arm around her waist, I carried her to a doorway leading to a store room several feet away and kicked it open. Then, I dropped her and turned her to lean over a table by the door, her bare ass waiting for me.

An ass that was lean with muscle, nowhere near the rounded curves I ached for.

I paused, hand on her low back.

Scarlett looked over her shoulder, lips parted, fangs gleaming, and pupils dilated. "Dominic?"

Her voice cut through the fog. Fucking her would do nothing to slake my thirst.

A step back, and then another, and I laced up the front of my breeches. "Fuck. I'm sorry, Scarlett."

She rolled and stood, pulling her own clothes back into place. "Sorry for what? This is not that kind of . . .arrangement, General. No apologies between us."

"No, I know, I just..." I shook my head, not sure what to say to her.

"Look, you don't have to tell me anything, that's not how this," she motioned her hand between us, "works. We both know that. So tell me who she is? Who has you all riled up?"

I looked past her, unable to meet her gaze. "It doesn't matter."

"I think it does. Am I out of a job?" And then she laughed at me. "Let me know so I can fill your position. I have a man in the wings." She winked as she strode past me and patted me on the ass for good measure. "Pity, I did like where this was headed. I enjoy being *royally* fucked." Her laughter followed and I couldn't help but smile after her.

"It's nothing, Scarlett. Don't fill my position."

Yet.

She called back over her shoulder, eyes sparkling, "I very much look forward to meeting this 'nothing', General."

Attempting to sleep that night was fucking futile. At best, it was fitful, and I couldn't help wondering if Sienna was really human and not some magical creature sent to haunt me. No one else had the same reaction to her that I'd had, either at the auction or here at the castle.

Those who noticed her at all saw her for the problem she was—for the woman who didn't fit with the other girls.

I gave up on sleep as the 'sun' rose. I needed to clear my head, so I dressed, then headed to the stable. I needed distance and space to breathe and fresh air.

When I reached the stable, I went straight to my horse. Men like Anthony had the stable boy prep their horses, but I saddled my stallion myself. I grabbed the gear from the wall and headed for Ares' stall. As I set to work, I heard murmurs down at the other end of the stable that didn't sound like Timmy or the other stable hands.

Just as I was about to lead Ares out of the stall, I heard a horse release a frustrated snort.

Timmy spoke in a near whisper, "I really don't think you should be taking her out, Miss. She seems even more agitated than usual today."

The miss murmured something even I couldn't hear, but I felt the same pull I'd felt last night, and at the auction. I moved to stand in the aisle.

A woman wearing a full gray skirt and a loose white blouse exited the stall, her long auburn hair hanging down her back in gentle waves. I couldn't see her face, but I didn't need to. I could *feel* the draw to her. She had a pull to her that I felt in every fiber of my being.

Godsdamn it. The one person I wanted to escape all fucking night, and now she was ruining my morning too.

But then I really looked at her, and the scene in front of me. She sat astride Havoc, the most untamed horse in the barn. The horse that I'd been prepping to fill Ares' boots as he aged. The mare had been purchased a year ago, and no one had been able to get close to her since. The horse was wild and dangerous, so much so, just a week ago, I'd suggested she be moved out of the royal stable and out to the countryside to be used for breeding stock only.

But now Sienna was sitting on her back, barely keeping her under control as the mare plunged and danced, grabbing at the bit.

What in the hell was she thinking?

She ignored Timmy, leaning over the horse's neck as it bolted for the already open doors, blowing past me. Not even seeing me.

"Why did you let her take that horse?" I shouted.

Timmy turned to me with a look of terror. "I tried to stop her, General."

"Havoc's going to throw her and break her fucking neck!" I didn't stop to think. I'd barely gotten into the saddle before my heels were hard against Ares' sides, surprised by the unexpected fear that sank into my marrow.

I disliked the woman intensely for the disruptions she caused to my life.

The idea of her being hurt though, did something strange to my body.

I raced for the open castle gates, not surprised that the girl and Havoc were nowhere in sight. That black mare was built for speed and stamina—the whole reason she'd been purchased.

The guards jumped out of the way as I galloped after her, starting down the road, toward the docks, then catching a glimpse of black already far out in the fields.

Motherfucker.

My first thought was her horse had gotten away from her and her life was in danger. That she was inexperienced and had chosen to take Havoc out for a ride and was now at the horse's mercy. But then, I realized she was riding low over the horse's neck and her posture suggested she was experienced with horses. She was totally in control. But how?

That realization led to another—this wasn't for a stroll in the pasture. Sienna was trying to escape, and she was headed straight for Werewolf Territory and the eastern bridge.

Dread filled my gut. That was one of the first things they were supposed to learn when they got off the ship. I'd repeated the threat to her myself.

Stay away from the eastern border.

The tension between the werewolves and the vampires was at an all-time high right now, more so than with any other Alpha Territory, and they wouldn't stop from killing anyone who crossed into their border, no matter their species.

Bloody hell.

I dug my heels into Ares' flank, urging him to go faster. If I could reach her side, I could grab her reins and pull her horse to a halt.

Only, Sienna and Havoc had no intentions of being caught, and we couldn't draw close to the pair. By the time we reached the eastern forest, she glanced back for the first time, saw us, and urged her horse to go faster. Unbelievably, Havoc got a new spurt of energy and put even more distance between us, Sienna's hair flying behind her like a curtain, rippling in the wind.

How was she controlling that horse when no one else in the kingdom had been able to even get close to her?

We were approaching the bridge to Werewolf Territory and she showed no sign of slowing down. I urged Ares, pushing him to dig deep. I had to stop her.

I had to cut her off.

We were finally gaining on them, Ares' training and stamina coming through. Thirty feet turned to twenty, ten, five, then I passed her just in time for Ares to block her from crossing the bridge. She turned her horse in a wide arc away from me, and her horse slowed. Before Havoc came to a full halt, Sienna leapt off, holding a wooden stake she'd pulled from her boot. Her chest heaved as she pointed it toward me in a defensive stance, her pale cheeks flushed from the wind. Her eyes were bright and wide. What I'd taken for a skirt were full-legged pants some of the women wore to ride astride instead of side-saddle.

"Stay away from me, you ass! I'm not going to go down without a fight!"

I jerked Ares to a halt and jumped off, standing about ten feet from her.

"Have you lost your mind?" I shouted. "You can't cross into Werewolf Territory!"

"Who said I was crossing into Werewolf Territory?" she shouted back.

"You were headed straight for it! If I hadn't cut you off, you'd have crossed the bridge!" I stalked toward her, my body vibrating with adrenaline and other things. Darker things.

Like the idea of turning her over my knee and spanking her ass until it was bright red and begging for my teeth and lips. Spanking her until she was wet with desire, and she begged for me to take her right there in the field.

"Stay back!" she growled, her eyes fierce, her brows furrowed.

My gaze dipped slightly to her full hips, then swept up and over her breasts to the determined expression on her face. Fuck me. Indeed, that was exactly what I wanted from her. The predator in me demanded to take her and mark her as my own.

"You think you can stake me?" I asked in disbelief, and my fangs ached as they descended.

"I won't just let you kill me, I won't!" she said, her breath coming in rapid pants. The rise and fall of her breasts was a distraction to say the least.

I paused, deciding to play with my prey. Why not? We were alone.

"And how will you explain staking the General when you go back? What if you don't kill me? What if you just injure me? Then you will be in deep, Kitten."

Her eyes widened in confusion. "Don't you turn to dust? They'll think you just took off."

"We don't turn to dust," I said, with a predatory grin, partially amused and fully turned on by her brassiness.

"Then, I'll toss your body into the river."

I tilted my head. "How will you explain the fact I took my horse out after yours? Are you planning to murder Timmy, as well?"

Her eyes widened even farther. "I'm not murdering anyone. I'm protecting myself. You chased me down. I'll tell the Duchess you tried to kill me."

"Protecting yourself against the General of the Crown Prince's army?" I asked. "I have hundreds of years fighting much more dangerous opponents than you." I grinned. "You're merely a slip of a girl. I could easily crush you. No one would believe you." I paused and laughed at her. "Perhaps that was your plan? That no one would believe you could possibly kill me?"

"Don't be so sure," she said, her breath becoming more controlled, but the vein in her neck pulsed, calling to my fangs. "No one believed that I could ride Havoc."

"Touché. So then you would wish to be known as a vampire hunter? A Vanator?" I couldn't help poking at her. Or drawing closer to her. Fuck. I needed to walk away, but then, I'd be neglecting my duties. She'd tried to escape, and I needed to do my job.

Her chin tipped up. "I will do what I must, to survive, General. Even if it is surviving you."

We were so close now I could see the individual shades of gold in her eyes. "Why are you truly out here?"

"I was riding Havoc."

"At breakneck speed?"

"When was the last time she was ridden?" she asked, her voice full of accusation. "I let her run as she wished, both yesterday and today and she galloped straight out here, but I had no intention of crossing the bridge. Even if I'd wanted to cross, Havoc steered clear of the bridge yesterday. And today, *someone* raced ahead of us to block us."

"You rode her yesterday?" I demanded. "How did she let you on her back?"

"I don't know why you all think there's something wrong with her," Sienna said. Then, as though the horse understood, she shook her head tossing her mane, sides heaving as she sucked for air. The mare walked over and nuzzled her shoulder.

What the hell? That horse had been mean since the day it had arrived in the kingdom. Perhaps Sienna *was* some kind of witch, a siren full of magic, or even a sorceress? I nearly laughed at my own wild imagination. There was no such thing as a sorceress. At least, not anymore, but there was no denying my strange reaction to her, or the horse's connection.

Perhaps Edmund had sent her out to torture me? More likely it would be Anthony though.

"I'm supposed to believe you rode out here like a bat out of hell on a joy ride? When I was trying to stop you? Why didn't you stop?"

"Because you were *chasing* me!" she protested. "I had no idea who was behind me or what you wanted. But if you want the honest truth, I would have been riding like that anyway. Havoc needed the run and I liked riding with her. We were out for exercise. I was told I had the run of the land as long as I didn't leave the territory or go over the bridge. You yourself told me that! Are you changing your mind?"

"You're telling me you weren't trying to escape?"

"I'm not stupid. As you so eloquently intimated, escape is impossible," she said. "We're surrounded by mountains on one side, an ocean full of sharks and other supernatural creatures on two others, and the Werewolf Territory on the fourth. Not to mention, the guard towers that are always staffed with at least two guards, as well as the guards at the docks and the castle gates. The only escape is to win this competition."

She sounded convincing except for two things. One, she'd paid far too much attention to the borders and the guard staffing. And two, she had too much fire in her eyes for a woman who planned to play the game.

She was on a recon mission.

It made me want her even more.

My eyes drifted down her body, and that's when I noticed the long gashes on her arm, undeniably fingernail scrapes. Gashes that hadn't been there the night before when we'd danced.

My vision darkened, and I asked in a deep voice, "Who touched you?"

She looked confused, then she followed my gaze to her bare forearm. "No one."

"Do not lie to me," my voice rumbled with power. "Tell me his name. *Now.*"

She flinched and took a step back, even while her own eyes darkened. She was fighting the power in my voice. She shook her head, not unlike the mare before she spit out the words. "Earl Anthony, but the Duchess dressed my wounds. They aren't anything big."

I saw instant red, and I wanted to jump on Ares' back and sprint to the castle so I could rip Anthony's head off with my bare hands, as I'd promised him on more than one occasion. But I couldn't. Edmund would demand an explanation and I didn't dare give the truthful one.

The pendant on her neck glowed a deep shade of burgundy.

Fuck me. She couldn't know how much I wanted her. For her sake, as well as mine.

"Go back to the castle. Now." I ground the words out.

Her chin lifted as defiance filled her eyes even as I saw her tremor. "No."

Gods be damned! I flexed my hands, and her eyes dipped to them. She took a step back.

"The Duchess will not allow you to hurt me." She threw the words at me like a gauntlet.

I crossed the short distance between us, faster than she could blink.

"The Duchess has no say over me, Kitten. If I wanted to strangle you here, and leave you for dead, none would deny me that right."

The tremors ran through her harder. "You admit to wanting to kill me? Even as you get a hard on?"

She dared to brush the back of her hand against my cock.

I took another step and she was against her horse, staring up at me.

Defiant to the end.

My already warm blood ignited, and my dick made its own push to get closer to her. Fucking traitor.

I wanted her, and if one of us didn't leave soon, I wasn't sure I wouldn't pin her to a tree and fuck her senseless.

The thin cotton of her blouse clung to her breasts and I could see her hard nipples through the fabric—the desire was not one sided.

I salivated with the need to touch them, suck them.

I wanted her, and I fucking hated myself for it.

It took all I had to step away from her.

"Don't cross the fucking bridge," I barked, then spun, and mounted my horse. I pointed a finger at her and glowered. "If you do it and survive, mark me, woman. I'll kill you myself."

With that, I sped off, damning the day I ever met her. Sienna was a problem and I needed to stay far, far away.

Even though it would mean another man would have her.

FOURTEEN

Sienna

"WELL, I, FOR ONE, think the Crown Prince is devilishly handsome," a low voice murmured to my left as I stared down at my reflection in the empty silver plate before me.

"I'm kind of hoping Will might notice me," another said with a giggle that rang out over the clang of silverware and chatter.

All two dozen or so of us were seated in the Great Hall for lunch, and, for now, it was just us. No men sniffing around and staring at us like we were animals in a zoo. That alone should've been cause for celebration. What with the exquisite-looking butter-poached lobster and miniature teacakes, along with the fact that none of us had gotten murdered yet, it should've been a banner day.

Instead, I was a bundle of nerves and stress and anger.

The fear still hadn't left me after being busted by the General. He could have killed me. He'd even closed the distance between us, pinning me to Havoc. Instead . . .instead he'd just stared at me and, for once, I'd been at a loss for words.

"What about you, Sienna? Which of the men would you like to get the attention of?"

I looked up to find the handful of women seated closest to me waiting expectantly for my answer.

I blinked as I addressed Holly who had posed the question.

"You mean of the bloodsucking creatures who had a hand in having us kidnapped from our homes, thrown in pens, and then auctioned off like cuts of beef, which one would I give a rose to?" I asked with a fake smile. "Let me think." I paused and cocked my head like I was considering it deeply, and then frowned. "You know what? I'm going to take a hard pass on any of them this time, but thanks for asking."

Holly turned a ruddy shade of red as the other girls stared at me in stunned silence.

Part of me knew I was out of line for being snarky with them. They were in the same horrible spot I was, with little in the way of hope, and even less in the way of choices. But I'd had a rough night and even a rougher morning. My arm throbbed, I'd barely slept, and I'd walked into this luncheon already drained from my encounter with the General.

I'd wanted to see if I could find another way into Werewolf Territory, a path that was not used like the bridge.

And what had I gotten?

Too much testosterone and a deep desire to touch his stupid face.

As much as I wanted to treat the other girls with kindness no matter how silly their chatter got, diplomacy was beyond me at the moment.

"You realize that if you don't get selected by someone, you'll die."

These stark words were spoken by a raven-haired beauty directly across from me and I regarded her silently for a long moment. I dredged through my sleep deprived brain for her name. Anya.

I locked eyes with her. "I guess that's the problem. A part of me still feels certain there are things far worse than death."

The words surprised even me, and I closed my mouth with a snap. I hadn't meant to be quite that honest. With them or with myself. I was here, with a job to do—get to Jordan, and get us on the damn boat.

Until then, I needed to play the part better, I knew I did. But it was not easy for me to be false.

I lifted an absent hand to my hair and traced the golden butterfly nestled there with my fingertip.

I'd made a vow to myself to honor Hannah. To be brave enough for the both of us.

Living in terror minute to minute wasn't sustainable—a body ran out of adrenaline and could adapt to almost anything, even constant fear.

Now I was stupidly finding myself attracted to the one man I was sure would kill me given the chance and opportunity.

My heart wanted to fight, but today...at this moment? My mind and body felt spent. The altercation with the Earl, my shameful and confounding reactions to Dominic, and trying to figure out how to use what little I'd learned to help me, combined with the lack of sleep, had truly taken the stuffing out of me.

Add to that another dream of Dominic, hunting me in a forest, bellowing my name.

Chasing me.

Part of me had wanted to turn to him, to go back.

The other part . . .the other part that had kept me alive all these years knew I had to keep running.

And then to literally have him chase me in the open field? Fecking bollocks, it was too much.

As I scanned the faces around the table, I realized everyone was looking at me now, and the last of the chatter even further down the table had ceased.

Anya cocked her head, eyes narrowed. "I'm glad you feel that way." She turned and skimmed her eyes over the other girls before continuing. "If any of the rest of you don't want to live, feel free to bow out now. I, for one, am going to win this whole fucking thing. And, at the end, I'm going to have half a dozen wealthy men vying for my attention. If you'd rather throw in the towel, get drained of blood and then fed to the Hunters, be my guest. Less competition as far as I am concerned."

"Well," a loud, female voice rang out from the entrance to the Great Hall. "I do applaud your determination, Anya, but I must say, your lack of empathy for your fellow competitors isn't the most attractive look."

The Duchess swept into the room dressed to the nines, as always, her signature, red-bottomed stilettos clicking against the marble floor.

"Those of you who do make it to the end will become part of our society here. And whatever you might think of us, in this society, like any other, friends are good to have."

Funny, how she said that and yet I'd seen no human women around other than maids. Which made me doubt her words.

Still, her admonishment had an effect on the girl. Anya squirmed uncomfortably in her seat.

"Yes, Your Grace."

As I stared up at the Duchess, her strange words the night before played again in my mind.

"I know who, and more importantly, what you really are."

I'd tried to press her then, before she'd left, but she had clearly not even meant to say that much as she strode from the room without another word.

I'd considered asking Bee this morning, but I had the sense that whatever the Duchess was keeping from me was important enough that she wouldn't be sharing it with the maid, or anyone else, for that matter.

It was a mystery. Like my fate, and everything else in this gods-awful place.

"Shall we begin our etiquette lessons for the day, now?"

It took everything I had not to laugh out loud at the absurdity of it all.

Yes, Your Grace. By all means. Let us practice drinking a cup of tea, pinky extended, and without slurping, in hopes that it will aid us in our efforts to avoid being disemboweled in a most grisly fashion by something called a "Hunter".

I was officially in Crazy Town, and like Hotel California, there was no way out.

Unless, of course, I pulled a Hannah and just ended it right then and there.

I closed my eyes and conjured up a memory of my mom. What would she do if she was in my shoes? Moreover, what would she council *me* to do?

How to save both me and Jordan?

The words she'd spoken to me when I'd gotten my lunchbox stomped on the first day of primary school—and my stomach stomped on the second day—ran through my mind.

"Suck it up, stop your crying and give as good as you get. They've already shown their colors, so believe them. Next time, don't wait for them to strike first."

Roger that, Mama Bear.

It wasn't much, but the memory was the little boost I needed to get through this luncheon without slicing my carotid with a hairpin, at least.

Huzzah.

For the next few hours—not lying, it felt like a hundred—we listened as the Duchess taught us how to behave in court. And, by the time it was over, the most important thing I'd learned was that there were way too many forks with very specific jobs. One for shrimp, one for salad, one for meats, one for dessert, and even one just for oysters. I'd only been trying to be helpful when I'd pointed out that I'd managed fine with just the one my whole life up to now, but the Duchess didn't seem to hear me as she continued on without missing a beat.

Now that we'd gotten through the whole meal, most of which had been eaten cold while she spent countless minutes teaching us how to eat each component, I was praying we would be done for the day. The ache in my arm was getting worse with each passing moment, and I now had a headache to go along with it.

"I'm very pleased with your efforts today, ladies. Before you're dismissed, let me remind you that we have the Secondary Ball tonight, outside in the courtyard. I urge you to look your very best as always. The first couple gatherings tend to be tame as you acclimate to your surroundings. Typically, the Secondary Ball marks the true beginning of the games in earnest. You will see things that you haven't before and those things may shock you. Rest assured that your best path remains unchanged. Garner as much attention as you can. The brighter and longer your gem glows, the more likely your story will have a happy ending. Are we clear?"

"Yes, Your Grace," we all murmured in unison, like that happy little cult family we were.

"Sienna, please remain behind for a moment. I need to speak with you."

I slumped in my chair as I swallowed a groan. This couldn't be good. Judging by the smug look Anya shot me, she was pretty sure I wasn't being asked to stay after class to receive my commendation and gold star sticker for excellence, either.

I resisted the urge to flip her the bird as she and the others scattered from the table and headed toward the wide double doors.

The moment they were closed, the Duchess turned to me, smooth brow knitted in concern.

"How is your arm, child?"

She moved closer and gestured for me to show her.

I lifted my hand and rolled the cotton sleeve of my day-dress to the elbow, revealing four, angry-looking lines.

"Well, at least they aren't getting worse," she observed with a satisfied nod. "He will have been spoken to by the Crown Prince for touching you in that way at this stage of the game. You don't belong to him. Yet, at least. It's unacceptable."

"I agree with that last part...it's unacceptable. You can keep the rest of it, though. I don't now, nor will I ever, belong to anyone but myself," I shot back sharply.

The Duchess's silver eyes flashed for a moment before she shook her head slowly. "Sweet, summer child. You need to stop this."

A knot wedged in my throat and I coughed to loosen it. Even though I knew I had to play the part of the proper woman...even though I knew if I didn't, I would surely end up dead, I was struggling. The constant emotional rollercoaster of terror and fury and despair and lust—

"Stop what?"

"Fighting the inevitable. It's sapping your strength to fight the things you actually have no control over." She pulled the chair beside me away from the table and took a seat, facing me. When she reached for my hand, I didn't pull away. "We are very different, my kind and yours, but men are the same no matter their species. They deal in perception. Within the confines of these games, to their minds, the power lies with them. They get to watch and wait and choose and bid. At the end, they walk away with their prize like preening cocks. But do not discount your role in this. It is you...your actions, your body, your face, and yes, that sharp tongue of yours, that will dictate where you'll end up and how you'll be treated when you get there. The man is the horse. The woman is the rider. Use that understanding, Sienna. Use what the gods have given you to enthrall a man of worth, and once you have him enthralled, don't let go. On paper, he will own you. But in truth?" She stared at me long and hard. "He will be yours."

An image of dark eyes and a broad naked chest filled my mind, and I could not stop the way my heart picked up speed even as I shoved it away.

She reached out and gently rolled my sleeve back down.

"So what's it going to be, Sienna? Are you going to do your best to win this, or are you going to let your stubbornness be the death of you?"

She was too smart for her own good, this woman. And, whether I was being conned by the best of them or her words were sincere, there was no question that they spoke to the deepest part of me. The part that Hannah had seen in the pens and that had set me on this path to find Jordan.

The part that refused to be a pawn in this twisted fucking game.

I was being forced to play, that much was true, but that didn't mean I couldn't still win and play by my own set of rules. I needed the time to hammer out my path to Jordan, and getting killed for my smart mouth was not it.

For my remaining time here, I would learn to play like a Grand Master. If things panned out the way I hoped, I'd be gone, a ghost in the wind, before the games wrapped up.

"I will heed your words." I dipped my head in her direction. "Thank you."

"There she is," the Duchess whispered. "Go on, then, child. Prepare for tonight. I'll be watching as you show us just how . . .interesting . . . you are."

FIFTEEN

Dominic

"GENERAL, WILL YOU BE sparring with us this afternoon?" The voice pulled me out of my thoughts of a certain human that I could not seem to escape.

I turned a slow look toward the captain of my guard, and one of my best fighters. And my occasional fuck buddy prior to a certain human arriving.

"Captain Scarlett. What division will you be training with today?"

"Staffs." She gave me a quick smile that crinkled the skin around the edges of her light brown eyes. Her hair was a similar color and pulled back in a braid that she was never without. "I do know how you and the other boys like to play with sticks."

If my mind had not been so distracted, not only would I have laughed at her poke at me and the men, I would have said yes to sparring. "Perhaps another—"

"William will be there," Scarlett added. "If that makes a difference."

My jaw tightened and I nodded as I changed direction. "You know it does."

Scarlett fell into step beside me and after a dozen steps spoke. "How long will you protect him?"

"Which him?" I murmured.

"The one that holds us all at his beck and call, the one that is going to be the death of us." She kept her voice low. As one of the few who truly understood my dilemma, she was as flummoxed as I on how to keep this charade up. On how to bring it to an end that would leave Will on the throne and not on a fiery pyre, myself along with him.

We walked, stepping in time through the stone halls that curled down through the castle to the first level basement and the armory before I answered her.

"As long as I must." I shucked off my tunic and undershirt and let my hands drift over the ironwood staffs until I found a good one. Black and nearly as strong as iron—hence the name—they had an eerie quality to them that not everyone appreciated. There were harmonics within the wood that hummed and even sang when you fought with them. They were one of my favorite weapons, and rather untraditional when it came to being a General's personal choice.

A good sword was fine, but rather ordinary, in my mind. It took years of training to be good with a staff, but once you conquered it, it would help you beat a swordsman any day.

I took the weapon with me up the short flight of stairs that led into the training courtyard, the bright sun making me squint.

SHANNON MAYER

While the magically created sunlight would not kill me, it irritated my eyes when it was this bright and when I'd not been drinking enough human blood.

"You need a drink, first?" Scarlett asked. "We have some on the side for those who've been neglecting themselves." She motioned to a handful of men and women off to one side of the courtyard—Feeders.

I shook my head and waved her off, ignoring the needy ache in my belly at the thought. "I'm fine."

Loose sand had been laid out in the circular court that was two hundred feet in diameter, leaving plenty of room for multiple training quads. Four men to a group, who took turns sparring and mentoring one another. I'd always found that teaching was as good a tool to learning as only being taught.

The clatter of staffs slamming into one another, the shuffle of hundreds of feet, the grunts of the men slithered through my ears, along with the smell of sweat and blood.

As I stepped onto the sand, silence fell, as the men training stopped, faced my direction, lowered their weapons and saluted me.

I saluted them back as I continued across the sand, straight toward my younger brother. "Carry on, men."

Will saw me coming and he winked as if . . .as if this was just another game. Like me, he'd stripped to the waist. Unlike me, he was showing some bruises already across his ribs and a good sheen of sweat. Sure, they'd heal up within a few hours, but not quite as fast as lore would have humans believe. If he took some blood, he'd

182

heal faster yet. "General, so glad to have you here. You have been avoiding me and we never did get to have our conversation I'd asked you about." He waved his partners away, fist bumping the three of them and promising them a drink at the ball.

I motioned for him to continue on as I began to slide through a warm-up. Working the staff in a circle with one hand, I moved it across my back to the other hand, around and around my body. Faster and faster until the ironwood hummed lightly, the staff warming against my skin.

"Show off," Will grumped.

"What do you wish to discuss?" I kept moving through the katas I'd been taught as a boy, letting the movements ease my mind. Perhaps this was what I should have been doing to forget the human. Training had always been a respite for me. I made a note to come back daily if I could until the Harvest Games was over.

The staff was an extension of my body and arms as I let the steps take me into a zone that allowed me a measure of calm I never had found anywhere else.

"You do remember I wanted it to be a private conversation, do you not? Not in the middle of a courtyard with many eyes and ears on us?" Will said as he leaned on his staff to watch me. "Seriously, do you even know that you aren't supposed to be that good?"

A smile slid over my lips as I slid the staff between my legs, stepping over it and swirling it up and around my neck. "Don't flatter me. And if it was all that private or important, you would have hunted me down by now."

He shot forward with his own staff, lightning fast, and I caught it with my own, turning it away just before it drove into my neck. I pointed my weapon at him. "Be careful what you start, young prince."

He swung a second time but telegraphed it so far ahead that I leaned on my own staff, waiting for him.

"Asshole," he barked as he missed me.

"Wannabe," I threw back and he burst into laughter as we sparred back and forth, both of us grinning now.

Defense and offense, we trained as we always had—teasing the shit out of each other.

"Terrible, who taught you, Auntie?" Will tossed at me.

"Please, I saw her with that wooden spoon. You ran for your life. Chicken shit."

He ducked a blow and popped up like a damn gopher. "I was not nearly as afraid as you at the dance the other night. I saw you running away."

From anyone else, I would have been right pissed off. With Will . . . "I did not run," I paused and held my staff out horizontally before spinning it again. "I strode gracefully. At a rapid speed." Another burst of laughter from him and that sound only made me more determined to keep him safe.

He was a bright spot in our world that would not be put out—not if I continued to have any say.

Spinning around one another as we continued to ramp up our speed and the power of our hits until the ironwood began to reverberate in my hands like a tuning fork.

The sounds of the two weapons hummed in the air and I knew that everyone else had stopped to watch, and could feel their eyes on us.

"Edmund is sending me into the Werewolf Territory for negotiations, I leave as soon as the Harvest Games are complete," Will said suddenly, and I jerked to a halt, his words snapping me out of the rhythm of the fight. His final strike slammed against my upper thigh, and sent me across the ground, a spray of sand slicing through the air.

I rolled to my feet despite the intense pain that shot from my leg straight through me. "What did you say?"

We both knew I'd heard him.

Worse and worse.

"I'm sending him to do the negotiations for us," Edmund's voice rang out clearly across the training ground. Will and I turned to face our older brother as he strode toward us, stripped to the waist and an ironwood staff in his hands. "Perhaps a little more sparring?"

The glint in his eyes said it all. He was up to something. "Another time—"

"Oh, I did not mean you, General. I meant *my brother*."

Will startled. "Well, sure, I guess. I mean, of course, Your Highness." He gave a short bow from the waist, just short of mocking Edmund.

This was a terrible idea, and with this many witnesses, I had no way to stop it. But I could only hope that, *also*, with this many witnesses, Edmund would restrain himself. Flicking my staff up out of the sand with a toe, I caught it in mid-air. "I'll take the winner, then," I said.

"Oh, a family tournament. Excellent!" Will spun his staff and faced off against Edmund. "I do look forward to beating you again, General!"

My heart squeezed at the sight because, again, to Will this was just a game.

To Edmund, though . . . this was an opportunity to hurt us both. To make us pay for being born.

I clenched my hands around the ironwood as I locked eyes on Edmund, reading his body as if I were facing him myself. The best I could do was hope I could find a moment to distract Edmund and slow him down. Not that I didn't want to face him. But facing him would mean that Will had lost.

And if Will lost, it would be because Edmund wasn't sparring, but trying to hurt or even kill our younger brother, all the while making it look like an accident. Just like he'd done with all his wives and mistresses.

The two men circled, eyes intent on one another. Will took the first swing and Edmund blocked it easily. "Do not humor me, Will. Let us see what you're made of. For once, let's see if there is anything of worth in you."

Will's normally jovial face hardened and, for a split second, I saw a piece of myself in him. Of a rage so deep that it burned the blue of his eyes into shards of glass. His hands shifted, as did his stance, and suddenly he was moving far faster than he had with me, his response to Edmund's cajoling immediate.

And it caught the Crown Prince off guard. A hush fell through the onlookers.

The hum of the ironwood reverberated through the air and Edmund was forced back step by step, barely able to keep Will at bay. I didn't dare cheer. I didn't dare grin.

I kept my mouth shut and my eyes on them as Will struck a glancing blow against Edmund's ribs. In the past, that would have been enough to end the fight. A moment where Will would claim he'd won and back off.

Will pressed on. "Perhaps you should be careful what you ask for, brother."

I wasn't sure my heart could take it and, though I knew it couldn't happen, a part of me couldn't help the words ringing through my mind.

Kill him, Will, fucking kill him and be done with it!

I couldn't kill Edmund, but Will could and be within his rights to do so, and take the position of Crown Prince.

As if hearing my thoughts, Edmund suddenly dropped, avoiding a wicked blow to the head, grabbed a handful of sand and flung it up into Will's face. Will tried to keep his eyes open. Tears flowed down his cheeks as he strained, squinting to see through the grit.

Taking that moment, Edmund snapped his staff straight up in a perfect undercut to Will's jaw, the crack of ironwood and snapping bone blasting through the too silent air.

Will fell backward, eyes rolling, blood dripping from his jaw where the skin had split and the jaw bone was visible.

Edmund turned and smiled at me, his fangs showing. "Oh dear. I do believe I don't know how strong I am some days."

A careful bit of applause came from the men around us. Edmund waved and bowed to them. They did what they did because I'd coached them for years how to behave around their Crown Prince.

"Captain," I snapped to Scarlett as I struggled to contain my growing rage. "Get the young prince to the medics. That jaw is going to need attention so it heals straight and to make sure his fangs aren't shattered." I glared at Edmund, not bothering to hide the anger. He knew exactly how I felt about him.

He smiled. "And? General, are you feeling up to meeting me on the field of battle?"

This was . . .interesting. He'd rarely offered to spar with me because he knew I could hand him his ass in a burlap sack with both my fangs knocked out and missing an eye.

He was no fighter. He was more like the spider spinning his web, waiting for his prey to make a mistake. Which meant he was up to something.

"As you wish," I drawled as I pulled the staff across in front of me, stretched it out and tapped it to the middle of his.

The two ironwood staffs rang, a greeting, if you will. And then I slid to the side and stepped back as he swung hard toward me.

I let him come at me so that he was overpitched to the front, all but chasing me around the ring. Will had pushed him and I let him come at me, always staying just out of reach. Holding the end of my staff, I drove it toward his foot, and took him out at the ankle, making him stumble. Nothing serious. No bad injuries.

Over and over again, I made him look . . .stupid. A dangerous game, but I was so fucking pissed at him for hurting Will. Shattered fangs couldn't be fixed. It was the one thing we couldn't regenerate.

Edmund swiped a hand through the sand and tossed it at my face as if that move would work again, but I wasn't there, I shot to his side, pulled his feet out from under him and sent him flat onto his belly. "One day, Edmund." I pressed my staff to the back of his neck. He flicked his hand upward. A signal?

A tingle crept along my spine and I felt eyes on my bare skin like a caress, freezing me to the spot, taking me mentally right out of the fight.

Hot and cold, I turned as the girls from the Harvest Games slid through a doorway and lined up on the side.

And the one in the front?

Sienna and her damn golden eyes, wide, dilated and very much locked on me. My fangs popped through my gums and—

A blow to the back of my knees sent me to the ground, to all fours, and then the ironwood staff was pressed to the back of my neck.

"One day soon, Dominic," Edmund whispered in my ear, "I will find the one that has you so very, very distracted."

Sixteen

Sienna

I STARED ACROSS THE training courtyard as the scene played out in front of me. The General's body moved like . . . like he was more panther than man, his steps smooth and his skin slick with sweat.

The other girls around me whispered and giggled and all I could do was stare.

Jesus H Christ, the man was hard in all the right places. He swung a black staff, connecting it to his opponent's and then he just stopped, turned and stared at us.

At me.

His eyes locked on mine and there was a moment where I heard that whisper that had pulled me across the continent, that whisper that said I was still looking for home.

The world disappeared in that moment, everyone around us nothing but static and white noise, a hum of what had to be magic filling me. He had to be putting a spell on me because I didn't like him, not one bit. Yet, right then, I would have given everything to just . . .touch him.

I blinked and he was on his knees, his opponent behind him and I recognized him finally. The Crown Prince. I looked at my feet as the Crown Prince's eyes swept across the group of us women.

And suddenly, our having to wait in the small room off the courtyard, then being shoved out quickly into the training area made sense. We were being used as a distraction so he could win his bout with Dominic.

No, not Dominic. The General.

I curled my fingers around my dark blue silk skirt, focusing on the feel of it instead of the indignation that flared on Dominic's behalf.

"What I wouldn't give to lick him like a lollipop," Anya purred. "All of him."

I looked over at her. "Which one?"

She smirked. "Why, does one interest you more than the other?"

I knew a trap when I saw one, and I smiled back. "Does it matter? Either would be a catch."

Mind you, I'd rather dig my own eye out with a spoon than get close to the Crown Prince, but perhaps Anya preferred power over safety. And I had a feeling that if she knew that there was anything even remotely interesting about the General to me, she'd deliberately try to get his attention.

There was a shuffle at the back of our group and then the Duchess was there, in all her glory.

"Eddy, what have you done?" She snapped the words out like a whip and both men in the center of the courtyard stood, dusting themselves off.

"Eddy?" I mouthed. Had she really just called the Crown Prince by a nickname?

"Your Grace." Edmund bowed at the waist. "Sparring is an integral part—"

Her dark gray skirts swirled across the sand as she strode over. "I do not mean the sparring, you boys do as you wish with your sticks and play swords."

A low chuckle rumbled out of Dominic and I had to press my legs tightly together as a thrum of heat started there and tried to get my attention, as I tried not to stare at him with my tongue hanging out. Anya wasn't wrong—I wouldn't mind licking him like a lollipop.

Truly, what in the world had gotten a hold of me? Was this a vampire's power on full display? Or was it reality coalescing with the dreams that had plagued me since I was old enough to feel need that caused me to feel this way about him?

"Then, what is the issue, Duchess?" the Crown Prince asked, and even I could hear the threat in his voice.

"You clearly are not in a place to behave like a gentleman, and after seeing what you did, I'm of the mind that you need some time to reflect. You'll not be attending the ball tonight." She flicked her hand out, a folded fan in it, and whacked him on the arm. "Consider yourself punished. Get your apparent bloodlust under control tonight so that you may rejoin us tomorrow."

His preternatural eyes snapped with cold fury. "This is *my* kingdom. I'll do what I damned well like."

My breath was suspended in my chest as the Duchess took a step closer and glared up at him.

"And these are *my* girls. Your father agreed to those terms decades ago. It's my duty to protect them until the games have commenced. You're a danger to them in your current state, so you shall sit this one out until you've mastered the art of self-discipline once again. Is that understood?"

There was a hard silence, and I noticed Dominic's body language. He was almost quaking with tension, nostrils flaring and on high alert.

The pressure was broken an instant later as the Crown Prince smirked, mirroring Anya in a way I didn't like. He bowed from the waist again. "As you see fit, Duchess. I will retire to my room and leave you all to the festivities."

Turning her back on them, the Duchess snapped her fan open and waved it at us. "To your rooms, all of you, for there is a ball to attend and very little time to prepare."

I was still contemplating all I'd seen, an hour later, as I bathed. What had I missed that had caused the Duchess to come down on the Crown Prince like that?

Whatever it was, it must have been pretty bad. But the scarier part was the look in his eyes when she'd challenged him. His words had indicated he would obey, but those eyes?

They spoke of vengeance.

My thoughts shifted to Dominic. He and the Crown Prince clearly had an adversarial relationship, and I couldn't help but wonder where that had originated.

Maids always had the best gossip...

"Bee, what do you know about the General and Prince Edmund?"

"Not much, Miss. They don't see eye-to-eye very often, but I don't know the reason. Maybe due to the General's illegitimacy? Oh! Speaking of him, did you hear what happened to Prince William today, though?" Bee sat beside me while I soaked in the scented water of the deep copper tub. I picked up a bar of soap that smelled like fresh rain and scrubbed it over my arm.

"No, what happened?"

"His brother snapped his jaw in half!" Her words were whispered, but shrill on behalf of the young prince.

"Why would Dom—the General hurt his brother like that?" I stared at the soap in my hands, not liking the thought of Dominic hurting Will. Not liking that I was bothered at all by the thought of either of them being hurt.

She whapped me on the shoulder with a towel. "No, you ninny! Edmund did it."

A weird sense of relief flowed through me. "That makes more sense." And it also explained the Duchess's fury. But why had he done it? During the sparring, he could've passed it off as an accident. Somehow, I doubted that was the case, though. And apparently, the Duchess agreed.

"Wait . . .do you . . .has the General caught your eye?" Bee grinned down at me and I ducked under the water to rinse.

When I came up for a breath, she hauled me out of the tub still blinking past the water that streamed down my head.

"He's going to be hard for you to catch, Miss, real hard, but oh what a prize! And just think, you'd be sister-in-law to Will! I mean, if he married you!"

"That's not the goal," I said, "the goal is to be safe and . . .yes. He is my mark." Mark, like he was a job I needed to do.

An image of a different kind of job I'd like to do for him fluttered through my head. On my knees, the bare skin of his belly shivering as I slid my fingers down to the laces of his breeches.

"Oh, look, your skin all goosied up! Let's get you warm." She toweled me down rapidly and in a matter of seconds had laid out my clothing options.

"You all will be required to show your ability to be graceful tonight, taking turns in groups of four to dance for everyone," Bee said, repeating what I already knew. "So something that flows."

I needed to stand out. I needed to start gaining juice in the damn gem around my neck. "What do you think everyone else will be wearing?"

"Oh, bold colors, for sure. Deep reds, blues, blacks, nothing pale and light. Edmund's preference." She paused and looked me over. "What are you thinking?"

"Maybe a pale yellow or ivory, something . . .innocent," I said. Not that I was anything of the sort, but an image could be helpful.

She clapped her hands and ran to the closet, pulling out a stunning butter yellow two-piece dress that was fitted through the body and covered with subtle daisy appliques, but then the skirt flowed out in a gauzy cloud that spilled to my feet with slits here and there to allow for free movement.

The front clasped with tiny pearl buttons rather than the back, adding to the ensemble. "I love it." This is something I would have dreamed of dancing in, all those years ago when ballet was my one true love.

"What about your hair?" Bee held it up. "Everyone else will be doing updos, trying to look graceful."

I thought about Dominic out for a ride with his horse, about the way his eyes had gone to my hair. Will was right.

I was on a battlefield and I had to use every weapon at hand.

"Leave it down, let's put a few flowers in it."

Bee clapped her hands and went to work. In no time, she was weaving flowers in and I was seeing a very different Sienna looking back at me in the mirror. This one looked closer to the real me than I'd been since I'd arrived. A little bit wild and a little bit defiant to the constructs. But when it came to Dominic, I had a feeling it was exactly what I needed to do.

If no one had caught his eye in all these years, maybe it was time to give him a different look.

My thoughts were rudely interrupted by a bellowing roar that echoed through the castle. I clutched the edge of the table and jerked forward, which meant Bee ended up pulling my hair. "What the hell was that?"

She didn't even pause in her movements, carefully untangling the knot I'd created. "The Hunters. Their mating season is starting, and the males get snarly."

"Snarly." My eyes widened. "Wait, they're *real*?"

"Of course, they're real, and they're horny, which makes them snarly. Just like every other man who gets horny without any relief." She leaned over my head and pulled up a few more pale yellow flowers for my hair.

Another bellow, deep and threatening, lifted my skin as if it would dance right off my body.

"Do they ever get…loose?" I'd not seen the beasts, but I'd been partly hoping that the mention of them had been like the boogeyman. Meant to scare, but not a real threat.

Apparently, this boogeyman was very much alive and well.

"No, never. They're allowed to fly freely in their lair during the day. But there aren't many left, and those that are, are kept well contained far from the castle. You only hear them during mating season."

I stared out the window, eyes straining as if I could see the creatures, but nothing stirred in the forest beyond the castle. Not even a flutter of birds, and the bellows receded.

Interesting that no one had warned us to stay away from the southern side of the realm. Where the bellows had come from.

"There, you're all done."

Bee helped me stand. The skirt flared out around my legs and a few glimpses of bare skin here and there were peeking out. A tease.

"Shoes?"

"No, if we're going to dance, I want to be barefoot." I moved to follow her out of the room and then paused. "Wait."

"What? You don't want to be late."

I frowned. "The General is often late to these things."

Bee nodded. "He is."

"Then let him see me make my entrance."

Bee clapped her hands together. "Oh, I love it. But not too late or we'll both be in for it."

I didn't think she was right, but I wasn't going to stop her when she told me to hurry. My feet sunk into the plush carpet of the upper halls, then cooled as we reached the patterned tiles that led to the main ballroom.

Bee paused for a moment outside the door and then I pushed it open and swept inside, just late enough to make an entrance.

The other girls were across the room with the Duchess, who was watching me with an arched brow. They wore the darkest of hues, each of them opting for rich colors that were stunning in their own right.

But I was the only one that had dared something different. I hiked up the front of my skirt as delicately as I could and hurried across the room, flashing bare legs and bare feet.

As I passed the main tables, a weight settled on my body of a gaze so intense it might as well have burned my clothes right off. I didn't pause but I did look over my shoulder and straight to him.

And just as he went to look away...

I winked.

Eyes forward once more, I reached the Duchess.

"You're late."

"But on purpose." I smiled and curtsied to her.

"You are in the last grouping, and we will be eliminating a girl from the competition tonight." She snapped her fan out and caught me on the wrist with it, a sharp slap but really minor in the context of things.

Eliminate.

Bee had not warned me, which meant that something had changed.

"But why? I don't recall hearing about an elimination when you explained the rules…"

"This is a monarchy. Rules change, child. And often without warning." She turned her molten silver gaze on me, and I realized with a start that she was afraid. For the first time, she was afraid, and that chilled me to the bone.

It took a moment for her words to sink in, but when they did, I physically shivered. "Edmund. He did this to get back at you for…"

"This is my kingdom."

"These are my girls."

But apparently, the games fell under Edmund's purview, a fact that he'd taken full advantage of. She was wrong about one thing, though. The rule change hadn't been without warning. Edmund's expression had promised retribution, and he was hitting the Duchess where it hurt.

She lifted her chin and straightened her shoulders. "Never mind that, child. Suffice it to say, if you hope to make it to the end of this, the time to press is now."

"But what will happen to the eliminated girl? Will she become a maid or something else?"

"That's the million-dollar question, isn't it? The prince has not seen fit to share that information with me at this time. I will do my best to speak to the King and intervene, but as of now, we work off the assumption that whatever the outcome, it isn't one to be desired. Get out there and win their hearts...and their interest. Am I understood?"

I nodded and wet my suddenly dry lips.

"Yes, Your Grace."

"Now, sit and watch your competitors. Moreover, watch the reactions of the men observing. See what works. What doesn't. Adjust accordingly."

I settled in behind the Duchess to watch the other girls dance. Four at a time they did a poor imitation of a Maypole Dance around the circus performers' standing pole.

In most groups, at least one girl stumbled. One barely held her tears in check.

I did my best to remain calm despite all I'd learned. Of all the things I could do, dance was in my blood and I was ready to show what I had.

"Sienna, you will be with Anya, Jade, and Holly," the Duchess said, directing us out onto the floor.

Anya stepped out in front and I let her lead, let the others go ahead of me. As we took our practiced positions around the pole, Anya turned when she shouldn't have and walked into me, rather than gliding forward.

She tucked a foot between mine and sent me off balance into the center of the circle. I grasped a hold of the pole for balance to keep from falling on my face. The other girls tightened their circle so that there was no way for me to push my way back into the dance without looking like I was pushing my way in.

So be it.

I stood quietly, a hand on the pole, waiting, my heart pounding. Someone was going to be eliminated. I was already an underdog despite my win at the archery contest—I did not want it to be my boon that would save me should I fail here. As the other three danced and wove their way around me, their gems glowed to a deep pink, bordering on red.

The music stopped and they curtsied to the high table and I stood there, fear slicing through me.

I lifted a hand and summoned every bit of courage I had in me. "Music, please, I didn't have a chance to dance."

I caught the Duchess's eye and she may have smiled, but it was quick.

The music started, a slow beat, and I snapped my fingers. "Faster."

The tempo picked up immediately and I kept a hand on the pole as I stepped around it, stepping high and flashing my legs as the skirt flared out behind me. Gripping tight, I pulled myself up, used the momentum of my steps and let it carry me around like a carousel, my legs crossed over one another.

I kept my steps steady as I pirouetted, once, twice, three times, skirt billowing as the music ticked up again.

It had been some time since I'd danced like this. But desperate times called for desperate measures.

I pressed a bare arm against the pole and pulled upward, reaching hand over hand as I pushed off with my legs. Pretty, it was all about the image, and as I climbed to the top of the pole, I let the music flow through me, the moves I'd been taught sliding through my body.

As the music finally began to slow, I let myself feel the ache in my hands, the bruising in my inner legs and thighs that would show up in the morning.

But as I stretched out in a plank position, belly up, with the pole gripped tight between my thighs, bending backward to stare down at the table far below, I knew I had him.

His eyes were locked on me, a glint of fangs peeking out from his lips.

And that's when I let go of my grip on the pole.

SEVENTEEN

Dominic

I STRODE INTO THE banquet hall, pissed that the Duchess had strong-armed me into attending.

"You must go," she'd said. "With Edmund banned and Will indisposed, there needs to be some royal presence."

"I'm the bastard," I'd told her dryly.

"But you still have royal blood flowing through your veins," she'd said, having the audacity to pinch my cheek. "And while everyone pretends to ignore that, the fact still remains. Besides, you're the *General*." Then, she'd turned on her heels and left me furious enough to smash something.

I had no time for balls and banquets. Edmund's jealousy of Will was growing, which meant my younger brother wasn't safe. Today was proof enough of that.

But if Edmund was losing control, maintaining the status quo was important, for now. Or at least until I could figure out how to handle him.

What was Edmund thinking, sending him to the Werewolf Territory? I needed to find a way to broach it with Edmund the first chance I got. Strike that, I knew exactly why he was doing it. That assignment was quite possibly the most dangerous negotiations to be made and there was a good chance Will would be killed.

And yet here I was stuck in the banquet hall, surrounded by vampires decked to the nines, an orchestra playing, while rich food was being served. The Harvest candidates were grouped together, waiting for their cue to dance around the idiotic pole, a tradition going back to when our father sat in the Games. He loved to watch them weave ribbons in and out of one another, but it had changed over the past century.

The vampires were evolving, yet not.

We were the apex predators, but Edmund must be worried if he was sending our brother on a peace mission. The wolves had embraced technology while we were still living in a mishmash of centuries past. The dropping of the Veil had changed many things, and we had been slow to respond.

My gaze kept drifting to the women, stuffed into their richly colored ball gowns, and I grew anxious. One, in particular, was missing. Had she gone riding again and failed to return to the stable? Surely, the Duchess would have come to me if she hadn't, if for no other reason than to send out a search party in fear that she had gotten lost.

Anthony was to my right, babbling about something, when the doors opened, and Sienna walked in. She was wearing a pale yellow dress embroidered with tiny white flowers. Her long auburn hair hung down her back and flowers were woven through it at the top of her head like a crown. She padded across the room, her back straight, her toes pointed. She moved with the grace of a dancer.

The Duchess frowned as Sienna approached and, after a short exchange, the Duchess rapped her wrist with a fan and sent her to the back of the group. But for a split second, Sienna had turned to me, her eyes boring into mine. And then she had the audacity to wink.

Wink!

Heat spread through my chest and down to my groin, my cock instantly growing hard. What was it with this woman? Why did I react to her so? I felt like a young boy, unable to control his own body.

"You seem more interested in the girls this season, Dominic," Anthony murmured as he cut a piece of meat on his plate.

I turned to him and lifted a brow. "Perhaps it's because I've been part of the process since the beginning."

"Perhaps," he conceded, but looked far too smug for my liking. "Are you thinking of bidding this year?"

I snorted, as I lifted my glass of spiced wine. "I never have in the past. Why would I start this year?"

The reason came to me in the form of a single memory. Sienna on Havoc's back, racing across the countryside. Her look of defiance as she faced me with a pitiful stake, as though she thought she could fight me and win. As a man who thrived on control, my fascination was unsettling.

The girls began to dance in groups, and the men watched with lust-filled eyes. The Duchess had been smart to make touching the girls off limits until the auction. It made the men much more interested. Perhaps that was the appeal to this archaic ritual. For creatures who were used to getting practically anything they wanted, for once, they had to wait. It only made the prize that much sweeter.

Several groups of women had danced, but none held my attention. I began to wonder if I could leave without risking the ire of the Duchess. Doubtful. She'd expect me to stay, at least until all the girls had danced. As the highest ranking official in the court, at the moment, my departure might signal that the women who hadn't entertained the crowd yet weren't worthy of attention.

That, and a certain auburn-headed woman hadn't performed.

Finally, the last group headed toward the pole, Sienna with them. Three of them took their position, then the music started. They began to move, and since they were the last group, the men seemed restless, their attention wandering.

So much so, I don't think many of them saw the raven-haired girl in the burgundy dress make a wrong turn and bump into Sienna, sending her sprawling into the pole.

Sienna grabbed it for balance, but made no move to return to her position. Not that she could. The three other women tightened their circle.

"Oh, dear," Anthony mused. "That's a shame."

For some reason, I found myself turning toward him.

A wicked gleam filled his eyes. "Our prince has decided to up the ante tonight, you know. The woman with the lightest stone will be eliminated from the games."

It was only centuries of facing deadly opponents that allowed me to hide my surprise.

He tilted his head. "Odd he didn't see fit to mention it to you."

Not odd at all. The bastard knew I'd take issue with changing the rules mid-game. Not that I would put anything past him. My concern now was, what would be done with the eliminated girl?

Nothing good, that was for certain.

I made a concentrated effort not to glance Sienna's way as I replied. This was a tricky line to walk. Sienna needed to be desired in order to make it through, but I couldn't allow Anthony to see any more than he'd already seen of my attraction to her.

Think, Dominic.

"Not odd at all. He does what he wants, and I have no vested interest in all this silliness. He knows that. As do you, Anthony." I returned my attention to my half-empty plate, and said in a surly tone, "I'd rather trade places with Timmy and be mucking stalls right now."

"And yet, you've been to practically every single event this season."

"Not by my choice. Take it up with the Duchess."

My molars ground together, both in irritation of Anthony's barbs, but also the fact that the song was ending, and Sienna was still standing next to the pole.

Her stone was paler than the others. Enough that if something didn't happen, she would be eliminated. Was I saving her from one potentially perilous ending, only to face one that was far worse?

But then she called out for music, and after a sharp nod from the Duchess, the orchestra began to play.

"Faster," Sienna said in a clear voice, full of assurance as she snapped her fingers. A change had taken over her. Sienna had brought her game face, and I couldn't look away.

The orchestra kicked it up a notch and instead of the pretty prance the other women had executed, Sienna grabbed the pole, and then with a fire in her eyes, she made magic, spinning her body around in a series of intricate moves that were a combination of lover and warrior.

I was mesmerized, as was every other man in the room. Her dress and her hair flew around her as she spun and climbed higher, defying gravity.

And then, she was perpendicular to the floor. Her dress was hiked up, exposing her bare thighs, and it was apparent the only thing keeping her from hitting the floor was the strength of her thighs, and her hands, one below and the other above. Then, she released her top hand, and arched her back, her gaze locking on mine.

Something hit me like a blast, filling me with an overwhelming urge to take her. Right there. Right now. To pin her back to that pole and lift the hem of her dress and fill her.

I fisted my hands to control myself.

And then, she fell.

A gasp spread throughout the room, but she didn't hit the floor, instead, her body twisted, curling around the pole and she stopped herself just inches above it.

The room filled with pressure and I heard a sound of bursting glass or crystal.

Sienna dropped her feet to the floor, then, pushing out her belly and arching her back, she rose, using the pole to guide her until she was standing.

Her stone was gone, the pieces scattered across the floor, only, one must have scraped the delicate skin of the hollow of her throat. A single line of blood began to flow down her chest and into her cleavage.

The room erupted with applause, but her gaze was firmly on me.

I never wanted anyone or anything so much in all my life. I could smell her blood from here.

The alpha in me rose, the predator demanding to claim his prey, and I didn't trust myself not to act. Pushing my chair away from the table, I got to my feet.

"Leaving so soon?" Anthony asked with a lustful grin. "The Crown Prince decreed that you're to pick the loser in his absence."

Of course he did, the bastard.

"The task is yours," I ground out, thanking the gods that my coat hid my cock, straining against the confines of my pants.

"And the last girl?" he asked. "Sienna? Is she not the loser? She no longer has a stone."

The room had hushed, and the women all watched in fear and confusion.

"The last woman is spared," I said, "her stone was practically black before it broke."

"How can you be sure?" Anthony asked, arching a brow. "She was twirling, so everything was a daze."

The image of Sienna on the pole, leaning back and locking eyes with me. The dark red, nearly ebony stone was burned into my head.

Speaking for her now would only confirm Anthony's suspicions, but I had no choice. At least it would buy her another day, and me time to figure out how to rectify this mess.

"She is spared. I leave it to you and the Duchess to decide the fate of another." Then, I strode from the room and into a dimmed antechamber that led to the hall.

"General," a woman called after me, her voice soft and delicate. For a moment, I prayed she was Sienna, just as I equally prayed she was not.

I turned slightly to see the dancer that had been in Sienna's group. The one that had tripped her.

I stopped and lifted a brow, giving her my most derisive glare.

As I'd intended, she came to a halt, fear filling her eyes. Her heartbeat picked up.

"Shouldn't you be with the others?" I asked in a growl. "Discovering your fate?"

Her chin lifted defiantly. "My stone was dark purple. I already know my fate."

"I wouldn't be so certain of it." My anger boiled, not only because I didn't want to be speaking to this woman who tried to have Sienna eliminated, but because my cock was so hard, if I didn't find release within the next minute or two, I would lose all sense of reason. "Go with the others before I drain you dry."

Her eyes flew wide. "B- but that's against the rules."

"I'm the godsdamned General of the bloody Vampire Territories!" I bellowed. "I make my own fucking rules!"

She scampered off, properly terrified, and I contemplated the long walk to my chambers.

Fuck it all. I didn't think I'd last that long. Instead, I ducked into an alcove, cut off from the room by a curtain, then fumbled with my breeches to free my cock. Grasping it in my hand, I released a groan, images of Sienna filling my head. Sienna on the dance pole, wild and free. Sienna on Havoc, her hair flying. I imagined her on a bed, her hair spilled around her, glaring up at me in defiance.

My blood surged and my cock ached as I stroked harder. I didn't want my hand, I wanted to be buried deep inside her.

In my mind, she was on my bed, her legs around my waist as I pinned her arms to the bed over her head, but she wasn't fighting me. Her ankles were locked around my back as I rode her, capturing her nipple in my mouth and sucking.

Oh, how I hated her for making me want her so badly. Hated that she made me weak.

She gasped, arching up to me so I could go deeper, only, I realized the gasp had come from my side, not in my head.

Sienna, behind a small gap in the curtain, watching me, her face flushed as her gaze drifted to my cock.

A host of options filled my head. I needed to stop. I needed to send her away.

I needed to grab her and fuck her right here and now and get her out of my system.

But despite what I'd told that little dark-haired bitch, I wasn't a rule breaker. My life was bound by them.

So instead, I squeezed my eyes shut, made my strokes more deliberate, letting my imagination take control. She may have been standing there, watching, but in my mind, I was forcing her to her knees and letting her wrap her lips around me.

That wouldn't be breaking the rules, would it? But I damn well knew it would.

My eyes opened, and my gaze drifted to her chest, the trickle of blood. I imagined my tongue on her chest, lapping it up and, in the end, that was what pushed me over the edge—imagining my fangs in her neck, drinking her blood as I exploded inside her.

I came hard, bending over and grunting. I rested my free arm on the stone wall as I soiled my shirt. I gave myself a few seconds to recover, then stood upright, surprised to see her still standing there. Her eyes were wide with fear, but also hunger.

Fucking hell.

That did not bode well for either of us. She was supposed to hate me. Her life very well depended on it.

I refastened my pants and then slowly stalked toward her, backing her up so her back was to the wide doorframe.

Her breath came in shallow pants and I cursed when I felt myself already hardening again.

I considered trying to scare her away from me, but my gaze dropped to her blood, and suddenly, I was desperate for it.

Dropping my head below her chin, I flicked my tongue against the hollow of her throat.

She moaned, but I hardly registered the sound, instead, growing light-headed from the power in her blood.

Sienna was supposed to be a human. What was this?

She sucked in a breath and her chest rose and fell, sending me closer to the edge of reason again.

Needing to taste more of her. I swept my tongue down the trail, stopping at the edge of her cleavage. And then, I lifted my head, practically high from the essence of her blood.

What the hell was this awful magic?

"Get out," I growled, trying not to lose myself in her golden-green eyes. "Get the fuck out of here and don't come back."

Her lips parted, but she didn't respond, staring up at me in a daze.

"Fine. If you won't go, I will," I snarled, clenching my fists to keep myself from touching her.

But as I walked away, I couldn't shake the terrible sense that no matter how far I went, this woman would be the end of me.

Eighteen

Sienna

Dominic stalked off, but I was frozen, my back against the doorframe. My mind was racing. What had just happened? Why had I stood there and watched? Why had I let him lick the blood from my skin?

Because there was no doubt that I had let him.

What the hell are you doing?

Everything felt too much. The room was too hot. Too cold. Too confining. My chest tightened and I struggled to take a breath.

An image of Holly filled my head as the Earl announced she was to be eliminated, and her terrified face as two guards led her away. But it was the horror in the Duchess's eyes that made me realize Holly was in real trouble. I'd begged her to let me use my boon, but she reminded me that it couldn't be used on anyone but myself.

I had to get out of here. I had to find a way to escape. I had to find out where they took Holly and see if I could find a way to save her. Sure, she hadn't exactly been nice to me when she helped the others cut me out of the circle, but she was a human being and in this nest of vipers, we had to stick together.

"There you are," Bee whisper-hissed next to me, and I flinched. "I've been looking for you everywhere! I heard your pendant exploded and you were cut." Her gaze drifted to my chest.

"That's not important," I said. "What's happening to Holly? Why didn't you tell me they were eliminating someone?"

"I didn't know they were," she shot back with a frown. "I think this was Prince Edmund's way of taking revenge on the Duchess for how she treated him."

"So you don't know where they took her?"

She shook her head. "No, Miss." She paused, then added, "But who can say? There's a chance they'll make her part of the staff. That's what happened to me."

I gave her a hard stare. "Wait. Are you saying you did this stupid Harvest contest?"

"I did." Her cheeks turned a splotchy red and her gaze lowered. "Five years ago."

I was aching to ask her more details, but I needed to focus on finding Holly before it was too late. After witnessing Edmund's fury at the Duchess this afternoon, and then the terror in her eyes a short while ago, I had a terrible feeling of foreboding. If all a girl had to do was fail to garner enough interest, I would bet at least three quarters of us would choose it rather than become a vampire's sex toy/meal plan. Surely, Edmund knew that making her a servant now would cause a chain reaction and he'd lose half his participants inside a week.

Holly wasn't going to be relegated to servitude.

Edmund was going to have her killed.

I said as much to Bee and she nodded slowly.

"Yes, but they could also send her to another castle or noble family in the kingdom to work. Then none of us would be the wiser."

Still didn't feel on brand for Edmund, but I couldn't kick that possibility out of bed without at least checking into it. "Assuming that was the plan, once they removed her from the competition, where would they have taken her?"

Bee's brow furrowed. "They could've just moved her into the servant's quarters. Or, they might decide to keep her locked up until daybreak when she can be delivered to her new home. But it doesn't matter where she is, Sienna. You have to let it go."

"If you won't tell me where they might be keeping her, I'll just find someone else who will."

She grimaced, a war brewing in her eyes, but then her shoulders slumped. "Since it just happened, it's possible she is still in Ms. McConnell's office. She's in charge of the staff. She'd be the one looking for a family in need of a servant."

"And where's her office?"

"Off the kitchen." But then she hastily added, "But you can't just show up there demanding what happened to Holly!"

"I won't. I'll just do a little spying." Then, I headed for the door to the hall.

"Sienna!" Bee whispered loudly as she followed. "This is a really bad idea. The Duchess told all the girls to go straight to their rooms. That was one of the reasons I was so desperate to find you."

I stopped and turned to face her. "What were the other reasons?"

She glared at me. "I was worried about you. I heard you were bleeding. Probably should've just let you bleed out for as much trouble as you're determined to cause," she added with a sniff.

I pulled her into a quick, impulsive hug. "Thank you for caring, my friend." I released her and stepped back. "But there is no reason to stick around. Why don't you go back to the room and cover for me if they decide to do a room check?"

She gave me another hard stare. "No. You don't even know where you're going."

"Bee, I don't want to get you in trouble."

"Seems like it's the other way around," she muttered, grabbing me by the arm and yanking. "This way. We'll take the servants' hallway."

"The what?"

"You don't see the butlers and maids traipsing around the main hallways with plates of food, do you?"

"Now that you mention it..."

I didn't see a lot of things around here that I'd have expected. Like kids, or bats. I'd definitely been expecting more bats.

I let her lead me down a long, dim hallway with occasional doors with signs that read Banquet Room West Door, and Music Room 1. The hall turned and in the corner was a doorway leading to a set of stairs. Bee led me down a floor, into the bowels of the castle, and I briefly had to wonder if she was a plant for Anthony and was leading me to a dungeon to be tortured and murdered. But soon, she turned into a large room with multiple fireplaces and even more clotheslines filled with all sorts of linens and simple clothing.

"Let's make sure you blend in," she said, already rifling through the clothes. Seconds later, she was tugging a simple brown dress off the line. "This will work. Come stand over by the fire and I'll get you out of that."

She made quick work of the lacings, and I let the yellow and white dress fall to my feet, standing in front of her in only my lacey underwear. Lifting the new dress up, she tugged it over my head, letting me slip my arms through the sleeves.

"Your hair's still a problem," she said as I made quick work of the buttons in the front. She snatched the flowers out and tossed them in the fire, then gathered my hair into a low ponytail before making a bun and using the hairpin buried in my hair to hold it in place.

Frowning, she took a look at me and said, "You're still too pretty with your makeup, so keep your face down if we pass anyone."

"Okay."

"Also, you're not wearing any shoes--"

"There's no time for that," I said, slicing my hand through the air.

"Try to stick to the shadows and maybe no one will notice."

I nodded, more determined than ever to find out what happened to Holly, and if she was in danger, find a way to help her.

Bee picked up my discarded gown and held it to her chest, then took my hand and pulled me out into the hallway. The room next door looked to be the washing part of the laundry, so she dumped the dress into a large cart then tugged me back into the hall, going deeper and deeper into the darkness until we came up another set of stairs. When we reached the top, we came to a closed door. Bee peeked through a crack. Apparently satisfied, she pushed it open more, to let herself through the opening, then beckoned me to join her.

I was surprised to see we were in the kitchen, which was empty except for two women, one kneading dough and the other sitting in a rocking chair by one of the many fireplaces, knitting. Neither looked over as we emerged. Bee led me toward the back door I'd taken to get to the stables, but then she turned left into a narrow hallway that ran along the outside wall. She reached a closed door and glanced back at me.

"There's no one here. Ms. McConnell's office is locked up tight. She'd still be reading her the rules if they had brought Holly here."

"So where next?"

She seemed to give it a moment's thought, but then a loud scream pierced the night, somewhere outside. It wasn't human, and it sent a chill down my back. Another soon followed, and I met Bee's gaze.

"Was that what I think it was?" I demanded, icy fingers of fear closing around my throat.

Bee still looked horrified as she whispered, "The Hunters. They must have taken her there."

I started to run to the back door.

Bee grabbed my forearm, the one with the scratches, and held tight, despite my gasp of pain. "You can't go out there. They'll kill you too."

I jerked my arm free and kept moving. Deep in my head, I knew that if those sounds had something to do with Holly, it was probably too late, but I still had to know. I had to see my eventual fate if I failed.

Bee slowed to a halt as we reached a wooden door.

"That would take us out of the castle," she said. "But it will lock behind us."

"You don't have to do this," I said. "Stay here and let me in when I come back."

She shook her head, then started looking around on the ground. She picked up a rock the size of a grapefruit and turned back to me. "I'm going."

I thought she planned to use it as a weapon, only, when we exited through the wooden door, she turned and put the rock between the door and the doorframe.

"Not many people use this door, so no one will disturb it."

"And if they do?" I asked.

"Then, we'll likely be spending the night in the forest, because I don't know how we'll explain being out here after sunset." Then, she gave me a pleading look. "We shouldn't be doing this."

She had a point. The sounds, which were coming from a grove of trees to the south of the castle, were settling down.

But what of Holly?

I couldn't bear not knowing what had become of her. Not just for the girl herself, but for me...for all of us.

I had to keep going.

"You stay here."

Turning my back to her, I kept close to the castle wall to escape detection from the guards above us. I sprinted, my bare feet helping me move quietly. When I reached the corner of the wall, I saw several soldiers walking out of the trees, heading toward a castle gate. Instead of a moat, the castle was surrounded by about fifty feet of flat, unobstructed land on all sides. All the better to see an approaching enemy, I suspected, but also made us potentially discovered.

"How do you plan to slip past the guards?" Bee whispered behind me.

I winced at the sound of her voice, wishing she wasn't here. Wishing I didn't need her. But the fact was, I had no earthly idea how to get past the guards.

"The Duchess said we were allowed to walk the grounds freely..."

Bee snorted. "Not past dark, and you know it. Besides, all these rules, they don't apply to everyone equally. The Crown Prince and his lackeys can get away with almost anything."

Including murder. She didn't say it, she didn't have to.

"I know the guard who mans this tower," she continued reluctantly. "He's likely sleeping on the job."

I shot her a grim smile, grateful for the help, but terrified I might be leading her to her death.

"So you're saying we could make a break for the trees and no one would spot us?"

"After the soldiers are all inside and they close the gate."

"And if he spots us?" I asked, my stomach in knots.

"Then, I'll tell him I'm taking my new apprentice out to search for nocturnal blooming herbs for my demanding mistress, and to take it up with the Duchess if he decides not to let me go."

"And if he goes to her and asks?"

She snorted. "He won't. Most of the men are terrified of her." She peered around the corner. "They closed the gate. Let's go now."

Stepping away from the corner, she headed straight for the woods, leaving me to follow. We'd gotten about fifteen feet when a man overhead called out, "Who goes there?"

Bee turned around and glanced up. "Nathan? Is that you?"

"Bethany?" the man called out in surprise. "What are you doing out here this late?"

She gave him her excuse, embellishing it with a tale about how demanding her mistress was ailing and needed something to sooth her stomach."

Nathan looked at her hard and long but then nodded. "Alright, then. Go on with you, but stay out of the south clearing. It sounds like the Hunters are riled up tonight."

"Thanks for the warning," Bee said, before turning and leading us to the trees.

For the next few minutes, we snaked our way through the eerily quiet forest. The insects, frogs and owls had all given up their songs, likely in deference to the blood-curdling sounds of the Hunters in the distance. As Bee led us deeper and deeper, the snarls of the creatures grew louder.

Above the tree-line, a massive, stone structure came into view, backlit by the glow of the moon.

"The Aviary," Bee whispered, her voice filled with dread. "That's where they keep them."

The throng of trees gave way to a clearing, and we both stopped dead in our tracks. Three tall, steel poles were staked to the ground. Spread out around them were three creatures, each about twenty feet long, all with thick chains attached to leather collars around their necks, the end of the chains attached to the poles. They were all black, lean yet muscular, and covered in leather-like skin. They looked like a cross between a lizard and dragon from a Tolkien novel, from large heads and beady eyes to the tucked wings on their backs and long tails.

My palms went clammy as I stared at them in shock and awe.

"Hunters," Bee said, trembling in fear.

They might have been riled up before, but they seemed fairly quiet now. Even though the one closest to us had lifted its head slightly and seemed to be sniffing the air.

"What do the vampires do with them?" I croaked.

"King Stirling made them over a thousand years ago for protection and combat. The blood of all the supernatural creatures runs through their veins. Their power is unmatched."

"Those...*things* are a thousand years old?" I asked in disbelief.

"No, not them. The species," she said. "They aren't immortal, and only a dozen or so live at any given time. I've heard whispers that the population is controlled by others challenging the alpha for dominance, resulting in battles to the death. They lay eggs, but since the Veil fell, I hear they are laying fewer and most don't hatch."

I turned back to look at her. "And the vampires think it has to do with the Veil coming down?"

"That's the presumption. There have been other strange happenings since then," she said. "King Stirling isn't well. It's been a slow decline, but I overheard Prince Will say he thinks he's dying."

My mouth parted in shock. "Can vampires die without being killed?"

"No," she said. "That's just it. Yet he keeps getting sicker and sicker. The Duchess is beside herself..." Her voice trailed off. "In any case, years ago, or so they say, there used to be hundreds of them and soldiers used to ride them into battle. But now, they're far too temperamental to approach, let alone ride."

"So why are these three here now?"

"To alert the guards to invaders, from the south, I suspect."

"They're expecting invaders?" I asked in shock.

"There's always that chance." She shrugged. "Things aren't good between the vamps and the wolves."

I frowned. If they were glorified guard dogs, why hadn't the soldiers come out in force when they started to screech and howl?

Only one answer floated to my mind, and it filled me with horror.

Bee released a soft cry, covering her mouth with one hand and pointing toward a Hunter with the other. There, off to the side, was a single shoe. Nausea rolled through me as I took another step closer, recognizing the nude-colored pump with crystals shaped into a holly leaf.

I'd seen it on Holly's foot when she was dancing around the Maypole. Only now, it was partly chewed up and covered in blood.

"That's Holly's," Bee said in a strangled voice as she moved next to me. "Oh my gods. That's her shoe."

We had the attention of the Hunters now, the one farthest away, lumbering to its feet and lifting its head to sniff the air.

"They fed her to these monsters?" I asked, my anger rising above my horror.

The other two creatures got up, too, all three watching us closely through narrowed eyes.

"They must have," she said through her tears. A wail slipped out of her and I slapped my hand over her mouth. It was too late, though, and now all three Hunters were on the move, their wings tucked tightly to their back. Their tails dragged the ground behind them as they took a step toward us in unison. One of them let out a low growl, revealing a top row of vicious-looking jagged teeth.

The better to tear you into tiny pieces, my dear, a voice said in the back of my head.

The chains on their necks looked strong enough to hold them, but I didn't want to push my luck

"Bee, take a step backward—slowly—so we don't rile them any more than we already have."

She did as I instructed, but she tripped on something and fell sideways, sprawled out on the ground beside me.

The Hunter closest to us didn't waste time. Its wings spread wide, twenty feet on either side of its body, as it roared and pounced toward Bee.

And that's when I realized we'd underestimated the length of the chain.

Bee was definitely within snacking distance.

I reached for the hairpin, not stopping to acknowledge that a six-inch, thin, metal pin was no match for a monster this size. Instead, I leapt in front of Bee and let out a war cry, hoping it was enough to startle the monster and give us a chance to escape.

To my amazement, it froze, then lowered itself slowly until its nose was a foot from my face. The slight slack chain hanging from its neck made it clear I wasn't at a safe distance.

It raised its head to the sky and roared, the power shaking the ground beneath my feet. Then, it lowered its head again, face to face with me as its wings spread impossibly wider.

"Get back!" I shouted.

It growled, then pushed out a large puff of air that stank of rotten meat. The force nearly knocked me over, but I held my ground, knowing instinctively if I turned my back to the creature, I'd be Hunter chow.

The beast snapped its teeth at me three times, then tipped its head back and roared again as I scrambled away, dragging Bee with me out of distance of the Hunter's reach.

The Hunter snorted and strained to get closer, but its tether stopped him just short, as it gnashed its teeth and snarled.

"What just happened?" Bee asked in a quivering voice.

"I don't know." I was freaked out, myself, but I wasn't about to question it.

We were alive, that was all that mattered.

We continued our quick march back toward the palace until we reached the trees, and then, by tacit agreement, we both broke into a sprint. We didn't stop for a hundred yards, and even then, only because Bee grabbed my arm and yanked hard.

She gasped in shuddering breaths, her cheeks pale as she gaped at me. "Seriously, Sienna. What the bloody hell just happened back there?"

I tried to calm the beating of my heart as I stared back at her helplessly.

"How are we still alive right now?"

"I don't know," I managed, wetting my bone-dry lips. "Maybe it wasn't hungry?"

They'd just had a meal, after all...

"We need to get out of this place, Bee," I pressed, still shaking. "I don't think we should go back. We can take our chances and try to make a run, try to get to the next territory. There's a ship—"

"No!" She shook her head furiously, face covered in dirt and streaked with tears. "That was our once in a lifetime miracle right there. We won't be granted another, Sienna. You have to do this the right way. Give yourself time to formulate an actual plan that has a chance of succeeding, or you might as well just go back and let that monster tear you to bits right now. Buy yourself that time." Her face was earnest, and her tone pleading.

In my heart of hearts, I knew she was right. But how could I go on pretending everything was okay? Flirting, dancing, laughing? Was I that good of an actress?

Jordan needed me to be, if I was to get us out of here.

Just the thought of having to face Anthony or The Crown Prince made my stomach heave in revulsion.

And having to look Dominic in the face after watching him? Wanting him, in spite of all of this?

Bee grabbed my upper arms and shook me from my tortured thoughts. "Promise me you'll put more effort into this contest. Promise me or I'll never help you with anything again!"

"I am!" I snapped back, my mind churning. "Bee, I am."

Dominic still obviously had an interest in me. It might be mixed in with a healthy dose of irritation, but there was no denying that something powerful arced between us when we were together.

Maybe my dreams of him were not because he would be my destruction, but because he would be my path out of here somehow?

If I wanted to survive long enough to escape this nightmare and find Jordan, I needed protection.

And who better to give it than the General of the Crown Prince's Army? I reminded myself grimly.

I gave Bee a dark look as a renewed sense of resolve settled over me.

There was no going back, no matter how much I wished I could.

Now that the games had taken an even darker turn, I knew that if I could, my plans had to be moved up. Whether I liked it or not.

NINETEEN

Dominic

I PINCHED THE BRIDGE of my nose between my thumb and forefinger as my head began to throb. It had been a long, sleepless night. Between erotic thoughts of a dancing witch who tasted like the nectar of the gods, and the stress of wondering what my evil brother would do next, I hadn't gotten a single wink. Our kind didn't need much, but aside from the night I'd fallen into a drunken stupor, I hadn't strung together more than thirty minutes of sleep since the Games had begun.

"He cannot be allowed to run roughshod, unchecked, over this process," the Duchess continued. "Gods, brother, this is already a barbaric enough process without allowing a petulant man-child to make it even more horrific."

Her words echoed through the King's royal study and then hung there for a long, silent moment.

I had to admit, I was impressed with her. When she'd called this meeting between the three of us, I'd wondered exactly how much she would tell him. Edmund was a delicate subject to broach with the King, and one she and I had a tacit agreement to handle with a light, deft touch.

Apparently, his unprovoked attack on Will, and his actions and the elimination of one of her girls from the Games, had been the final straw. Gone was diplomacy, leaving nothing but fury in its wake.

There was a reason all the men were afraid of her.

"The Games are tradition, Evangeline," King Stirling rasped, shifting awkwardly in his seat and not making eye contact with his sister.

I squashed the twinge of pity that tried to rear its head as I regarded him. He'd aged ten years since I'd seen him last, just a month before. He was a thousand years old if he was a day, the oldest of our kind by centuries and one of the only originals remaining, but he still had the countenance of a fifty-year-old man. Only now, it was that of a rather sickly, fifty-year-old man. His decline had started when the Veil had lifted fifteen years before and, thus far, no one had been able to determine why or how to stop it. But it was almost like the ancient magic that slowed the aging process in our kind had begun to break down. I had no doubt he would live for years to come, but the deterioration was very rapid by our standards, and made me wonder if it would catch up with us all if we weren't able to put the Veil back in place.

And, despite having put our best minds to that task and reaching out across bridges and overseas to other supernaturals—even our enemies—we were no closer to an answer than we'd been on the day it had happened. Other creatures were seeing changes, as well.

The fae had seen children born twisted and ugly that were from the purest of bloodlines, the werewolves had begun to see a madness echo through their packs as they lost themselves to their animalistic sides, and that was only problems we'd been able to suss out. No race had remained unaffected. Even our Hunters, born of my father's ingenuity and desire to protect our kind from those who would seek to destroy us, were suffering.

The eggs were lain but refused to hatch.

The Veil may have dropped and given us more freedoms, but whatever powers it protected our world with now had turned on all of us.

"It's a tradition that needs to die, brother," the Duchess declared passionately, regaining my attention as she shot to her feet and began pacing, her sweeping skirts swishing against the wooden floor as she moved. "This was something conceived as a punishment...just desserts for those barbarians who feared and hunted anything they didn't understand. With our evolution, and the evolution of human thought and tolerance, surely we can cease and desist with this?"

Stirling's gray brows caved into a frown as he leaned forward on the mahogany desk before him. "With all the strife going on in our world right now, we need this break for both morale and unity. And you know without it, we run the risk of the men heading off to the mainland, themselves, and wreaking havoc on humans there. The Games are a necessary evil to keep some of our mens' most base urges at bay. But moreover, if we cease with the Games, what comes next for us, Evangeline? We stop taking human blood altogether? We cower in the shadows, feeding on rats and vermin the way we were forced to centuries ago?"

The Duchess let her eyes drift closed as she slowed to a halt. "I don't know, brother. Gods' truth, I don't have all the answers. I just know that bringing these girls here and forcing them to do this isn't right. It's never been right. And your son's actions—"

"Your *prince's* actions," Stirling shot back, his voice stronger, now, as he straightened in his seat. "He is the first-born son of mine, and don't ever forget it."

I silently willed the Duchess to stand down, hoping she realized how close she was to the edge...

My father didn't possess Edmund's inherent cruelty, but he also wasn't a man to be trifled with. He was both proud and stubborn, and secretly furious at feeling weak and ineffectual as his body failed him. It was a dangerous combination.

"Yes, Your Majesty. Of course he is," she said, clearly reading his mood. "And he is my nephew, as well. His word is law unless you say otherwise. But I implore you to consider taking control of the Games for the remainder of the month. Or allowing Will to do so. He's a prince, too, and equally capable. And Edmund is clearly distracted with his duties and the noble task of trying to reinstate the Veil. Surely, he can't be expected to bother himself with games during this time of impending crisis."

Stirling leaned back with a heavy sigh and ran a hand through his long, graying locks.

"William is not the first heir to the throne. Edmund is, and he wouldn't take kindly to me inserting myself in this trivial matter.

Nor should he. It's inconsequential, in the scheme of things, and if I don't trust him to handle such a thing, then what does that say of my trust in him on the whole?" He shook his head grimly. "I'm sorry we cannot agree, sister, but I won't create tensions between my sons over human women. I know you allow yourself to become attached to some of them, at points, but the risk of such a move, politically, is not one I'm willing to take."

I hated to admit, I agreed with him, on some level. After what Edmund had done to Will the day before in the sparring arena, it was clear the leash he'd kept himself on in regards to our younger brother was fraying. Hastening that process could have disastrous consequences.

"So what do you suggest we do, then, Your Highness?" the Duchess asked, spreading her hands wide, tone almost pleading. "The girls are going to start to panic if they learn that the eliminated girl was fed to the Hunters."

I pinched my eyes closed at that. Part of me had known that would be the girl's fate. Edmund was so furious that the Duchess had embarrassed him, it would've been out of character for him to choose a less horrible punishment. But a little piece of me had held out some hope that he would choose diplomacy over pride and settle for a less grisly form of retaliation.

He hadn't. And now the battle lines were drawn. I could see it in the Duchess's face. Edmund had gone too far this time. Things would only get worse from here between them. Soon enough, I would be forced to choose a side.

I loved my aunt. She was controlling and could be manipulative, but at the core, she was a good soul. But the safety of my younger brother and my mother relied on me protecting Edmund to the bitter end.

Maybe the time had come to end this charade. Until now, I'd been resigned to my fate, so long as it meant those I cared for most were somewhat shielded from Edmund's cruelty.

Things had changed.

It would be a risk. I would have to place full trust in my allies to help me unroot and unmask Edmund's secret loyalists. Then, I would need to eliminate them. If I was caught, I'd be convicted of treason and killed. But if I wasn't?

Freedom. Freedom to stage a coup and seat Will on the throne, where he belonged. If our father was a casualty in the process, so be it.

I realized it was the thought that had been there, sitting in the back of my mind for months now, waiting for me to be ready.

And I knew that a part of that readiness had to do with a pair of golden eyes. Even if I only ever admitted that to myself.

My path now clear, I tuned back to the conversation to hear the very end.

"I'll speak with Edmund and see what I can do to calm the waters some, but you'll stand down, for now, Evangeline. That's not a suggestion. It's an order," Stirling said, his eyes on the papers in front of him.

The Duchess's mouth collapsed into a thin line, but she bent into a full curtsy. "Yes, Your Majesty."

She turned and stalked from the room, making no effort to disguise her displeasure. I stood to follow but Stirling's voice stopped me.

"There are times that I wish things were different, you know."

I turned to face him, keeping my expression blank despite the sudden rush of blood to my ears.

"In what way, Your Majesty?"

"Your brother Edmund's heart is too hard to ever be a truly great leader. And, truth be told, Will's is too soft. It's a shame, is all...that it couldn't have been you."

It took everything I had not to leap across the massive desk and wrap my hands around his throat. He was to blame for all of this. He kept the status quo by continuing to support a monster.

"Well, it couldn't have been. I'm a bastard, after all."

With that, I turned and strode from the room.

"Interesting little confab with our father, brother mine?"

I turned to see Edmund lounging against the wall in the corridor, sharp gaze studying my face.

"Not really. Just guard business," I replied easily. But I had to wonder what he'd heard of our discussion, if anything. Had he been close enough?

"Indeed," he drawled, never taking his eyes off me. "Well, enjoy the rest of your day and I'll see you tonight at the festivities."

I didn't bother with a reply, stalking down the hall, desperate for some air to clear my head.

Last night had been a clusterfuck of epic proportions. Not only had things gone too far with Sienna, now both Anthony and

Edmund were suspicious and on the lookout for the girl who had piqued my interest.

I had to maintain my distance more than ever.

But now that I'd tasted her? I bit back a snarl as I kicked open the door to the courtyard. I could think of nothing else.

The best thing I could do going forward would be to ignore her completely. If they never knew I wanted her, they couldn't use her to control or punish me. After her dance last night, there was no question she'd garner enough male attention to keep her safe from elimination...

The very thought made my fists clench. The idea of another man looking at her made me want to break things. Another man touching her?

I let out a low hiss as my fangs broke free of my gums.

She was damned if I did, and I was damned if I didn't. Given the choice...well, there really was no choice, was there?

No matter how badly I wanted her. No matter how she'd tasted, or smelled. No matter how her pulse had leapt under my tongue.

Sienna was off limits.

TWENTY

Sienna

"THAT'S ALL FOR TODAY, ladies. The rest of the afternoon is yours. Then, tonight, we have an amazing meet and greet where you'll get a chance to have a few minutes of one-on-one time with every eligible man in the palace. Sharpen your wit," our hostess advised with a knowing flash of fangs that I assumed was supposed to pass for a smile, "a beautiful mind can be as attractive as one's physical appearance. Dismissed!"

I let out a low hiss of relief and stood, making a beeline for the door. It had been an interminable two hours of listening to some female vampire named Hecula, of all things, as she droned on and on about the history of the monarchy. That, followed by a test on the titles of various vampire nobility who I could give two shits about. The only interesting parts? Apparently, King Stirling had been the first and only king of their kind. He'd had several wives over the course of that time, but not as many as one would think, given he was literally thousands of years old. His sister, Duchess Evangeline, however, only had one husband.

Maxim the Bold.

Hecula's violet-colored eyes had lit with excitement as she wove stories of his bravery in battle against those who would eradicate their kind. He'd met an untimely end after a group of pitchfork-wielding villagers ambushed him on a visit to the mainland for human blood. He killed forty-six of them before they were able to finally take him down.

Upon his death, the Duchess had sworn that she would never marry again, as no man could possibly compare. It was a vow she'd held true to for the past two centuries.

I shoved aside the twinge of pity and practically sprinted for the doors to the courtyard, suddenly feeling like I was suffocating.

It had been a hell of a day, after an even worse night.

An image of that bloody shoe with the cheery little holly leaf on it ran through my mind, and I sucked in a breath of crisp, fresh air as the door slammed behind me.

"Damn you, Edmund, you bastard," I whispered, blinking back a hot rush of tears. Yanking my skirts to my knees, I dashed toward the lush gardens in the distance. I'd only seen them from the window in my bedroom, but surely they were as good a place as any to get lost for a while.

In all my days, I couldn't recall being so confused, angry, and afraid all at once. Even in the auction pens, there had been some comfort in the pure hatred and disdain I felt for my enemies. Here, in the palace, there was a whole new element of...something else.

From Will, with his charming grin and warm laugh, to Evangeline, who clearly struggled with the moral implications of the Harvest Games and cared for us girls in her own way.

My brain instantly supplied a visual of Dominic, and my stomach flopped. Thick cock in hand, stroking up and down as he stared at me, cowering in my hiding place.

Wet.

Wanting.

Coming to terms with the fact that I needed him to survive was bad enough. Feeling this ungodly pull... like a magnet to a blade, was fucking unconscionable.

"Get out of my head, Dominic," I muttered as I picked my way through row upon row of rose bushes. Their scent was almost intoxicating, mixing with that of impending rain, and I picked up the pace.

Just breathe, I reminded myself. I would work myself into a full-blown panic attack if I didn't get a grip.

So something terrible had happened last night. At least I had a plan now. I would continue to explore the grounds until I found a way out while I worked on enthralling Dominic. After last night, there was no question that he wanted me. All I had to do was harness that want and I'd have him exactly where I needed him. He would protect me until I could escape, and I'd be able to get to Jordan. Surely, I could withstand his attentions long enough to—

A semi-hysterical bubble of laughter escaped my lips at that thought, and I slapped a hand over my mouth.

Withstand his attentions? Last night, as I lay in my soft, warm bed, it was all I could do not to reach between my thighs and rid myself of the ache that had built there. A girl had been killed, and still, my dreams were of a gorgeous man, with dark eyes, watching me, jaw clenched as he came on his stomach.

"Oh, Sienna, you are a piece of work," I whispered as I continued to the other side of the gardens. Here, vegetables grew aplenty, and the earthy scent was like a balm to my soul. A familiar smell tickled my nose and I frowned.

Garlic?

I searched the crops, looking for the source, and initially couldn't find it. It was only when I looked to the massive, stone wall circling the gardens that I saw it. The long, slender bunches of reeds. Wild garlic.

I picked my way through the plants and leaned down to pull up a handful of tiny bulbs. On a whim, I plucked them free of their fronds and stuffed a few down the front of my dress. Despite the history lesson, they'd kept us in the dark about what vampire lore was true and what wasn't, thus far. Given the fact that I hadn't seen anyone turn into a bat yet, the garlic wasn't likely to help. Then again, having it sure couldn't hurt, I reasoned. If there was even a slim chance it would get me out of a situation like the one I'd found myself in with Anthony, it was worth it.

A flash of lightning lit the sky and thunder rolled a moment later.

I hated the thought of being cooped up indoors all day, but with the chill in the air, the thought of getting hypothermia was even worse. I clutched my skirts high and began to pick my way back through the gardens.

I was just entering the throng of rose bushes when a low voice called my name.

"Sienna?"

I froze as every nerve-ending in my body fired to life. Dominic.

I turned to see him standing near a bush of massive, crimson blooms.

"What are you doing out here?" he demanded, his voice low and raspy.

"I'm allowed to go where I please, so long as I stay on this side of the bridge," I shot back with more bravado than I felt. Fact was, I could barely keep my eyes from drifting lower...away from his gaze, past those broad, strong shoulders, down, down—

"That's all well and good, but only an idiot stays outside when it's about to downpour, not to mention when there is lightning."

Anger coursed through me, but I bit back a sharp retort about him being out here, too, as I remembered my goal.

It was fight or flight and I'd already made my choice.

I would fight.

Dominic and I had a rare moment alone, and I needed to use times like this to press my advantage.

I swallowed a rush of nerves and forced a smile to my lips.

"You're right, of course, General. Silly of me to be out here. I just love the smell of coming rain, don't you?"

I tipped my face to the sky and sucked in a breath until I could feel my breasts straining against the sweetheart neckline of my dress. Take that, big boy.

I didn't need to look to know he was staring. I could feel the heat of his gaze.

"No, actually," he said sharply. "I prefer to stay dry. And, in an effort to do so, I'll leave you to whatever foolishness you're up to out here."

He turned on his heel and started walking away before I could even process what was happening.

"W-where are you going?" I called after him.

"Inside. But feel free to remain. In fact, I prefer it."

My mind raced as I tried to make sense of his words. What was it with this infernal man? One second he was hot, the next cold. Last night, he'd seemed like he wanted nothing more than to get closer to me. He'd even licked me—

A thought popped into my brain and dug its hooks in.

Was my blood not to his liking?

Moreover, why did the possibility sting like a physical slap?

As I stood having some Stockholm syndrome-fueled existential crisis, Dominic was still walking away. Panic coursed through me and I shambled after him.

"Wait, please!"

He slowed to a stop but didn't turn to face me. "What is it, Sienna?"

I latched on to the first thing that came to mind. "I have a...splinter. In my finger. I was admiring the roses and one of the thorns got me. I can't see it, but I can feel it. Would you take a look?"

He blew out an impatient sigh and turned. "Come on, then," he ground out, waving me over.

I rushed toward him and held out my hand. "As I said, I can't see it, but—"

His big, warm hand encircled my wrist, making me gasp. What was it about him that made me feel this way? Like I'd been living in grayscale my entire life, and now, in his presence, the world was in full color? The sound of the thunder like a sensual growl, the scent of the roses sweeter, the feel of his thumb on my pulse enough to make my knees weak.

I blinked and stared up at him in shock.

"You're doing this to me," I declared, yanking my hand away, completely forgetting my mission as I poked him sharply in the chest. "You're making me feel this way with your vampire mind control. I bet that's what you were doing in my dreams last night, too. I won't have it. Get the fuck out of my head!"

For a second, he just looked puzzled. And then, he started to laugh.

It was a strange, rusty sound, at first. Like he didn't do it much. But once he started, it began to come more naturally, which only irritated me more.

"What's so funny?" I demanded.

"You," he said when he could finally speak again. "Is that what you honestly thought? That I was making you dream about me with my spooky powers, then?" He wiggled his fingers at me, and I barely resisted the urge to bite one of them clean off.

"Why is that so funny?" I shot back. "You drink blood, don't you? And you are preternaturally strong, and hardly seem to age."

"Yes, well, all that is true, but a lot of what you humans believe about us is just nonsense. For example," he continued, mirth still filling his eyes, "we can be seen in mirrors. We can come inside your house uninvited."

"But that garlic you have stuffed down your dress?" He reached out and plucked it free with a move so fast, I barely even felt it. "Tastes delicious with our latest crop of tomatoes that we imported from San Marzano."

My cheeks went hot as he tossed the garlic over his shoulder.

"Well, none of you have exactly been forthcoming about much since we got here," I shot back, "so forgive me for trying to take a few precautions. I would have been raped the other night, if not for the Duchess intervening. I'd like to avoid that particular scenario where possible."

All trace of humor vanished, and Dominic leaned into me, his expression fierce.

"That will never happen," he declared, his tone so icy, it chilled me to the bone. "Not while I'm alive."

My throat went dry as I stared up at him.

"Don't make promises you can't keep, Dominic. We have no idea how the Games will end, or if I will even make it the whole way through."

"My word is my bond, and whatever should happen here, I will not allow that."

I inched forward until our bodies were an inch from touching.

"And how will you manage that? Unless you take me for yourself..."

A tiny pulse in his jaw beat as he studied my mouth with something like longing.

"I cannot. I will not. In fact, the safest place for you is as far from me as possible."

I wasn't sure why he thought that, but I knew I had to press my advantage before it disappeared. He wanted me still. It was written all over his face.

"What if I'd prefer to be close..." I whispered.

My bold declaration had its desired effect, and need swirled in his eyes.

"You don't know what you're asking for, Sienna. There are others who could treat you with kindness, as well. Men with more friends here at the palace than me...and far fewer enemies."

"And if I don't want them?" I pressed my breasts against his chest and rolled up onto my tiptoes, sliding my arms around his neck. "If I want you?"

His low groan brought a rush of heat to my core and he pinched his eyes shut. "Stop. Stop this, right now."

Plan forgotten and driven by nothing but pure need, I tipped my hips forward, grinding against him.

"I couldn't stop thinking about it," I whispered, just as the first raindrops splattered against my overheated cheeks. "You touching yourself. That was for me, wasn't it? You liked watching me dance?"

One arm crept around me, pinning me close as his free hand cupped my nape, sending a shiver rolling through me.

"You are a witch," he rasped.

My hips began to pulse of their own accord, and he pressed back.

On a growl, he slanted his mouth over mine in a tangle of tongues and teeth. Some part of me knew I should fear his fangs, but the other part? The bigger part? Wanted to feel them sink into my bottom lip as he drank from me.

I clenched my legs together as I ground helplessly against his rock hard length, every inch of my flesh alive with need.

A blinding flash of lightning painted my closed eyelids with a red haze, and the following crack of thunder shook the ground. An instant later, the skies opened up and a deluge of icy rain came down in buckets.

Dominic pulled away with a grunt, releasing me and taking a giant step back.

Rain sluiced down his painfully beautiful face, but even through that veil, I could see the anguish there, right beneath the unslaked need.

"Stay away from me, Sienna," he managed through gritted teeth. "I don't have the strength to say no to you, so I need you to do it for me. For your own safety, stay the fuck away."

With those ominous words, he turned and stalked off, leaving me in the rain.

Alone.

TWENTY-ONE

Dominic

Two days had passed since the incident in the gardens.

The incident.

I snorted to myself. As if I could reduce that moment into a single word. The taste of Sienna's blood, the feel of her body, the desire that I could not purge from my system no matter what I did.

And that was far from my largest problem.

I swept the room with my gaze, taking in the curls of smoke, the male laughter, the anticipation that fueled the head-to-head matches within the room.

"You look as though you expect an attack, even now," Will drawled across from me.

I looked back to him, to the jaw that had been so clearly shattered and put back together by our most skilled healers.

"Rather," I said as I leaned over the playing board. Blitzkrieg was a game of strategy, with armies arrayed across the table, and I clearly had my younger brother on the run. Just as Edmund did in our current situation.

The dark red of my army covered three quarters of the board. He leaned back in his chair and his eyes narrowed ever so slightly. "You think it was not an accident."

I glanced around. Though the other men were obviously deep in their games, that did not mean they were not listening.

"I think that you are a fool if you believe it, and from what I saw in the training grounds, you are holding your cards far closer to your chest than even I realized." I motioned for him to make his move on the board.

There was nowhere for him to go in this game.

Or in the game we were both living.

"Whatever do you mean?"

"I mean," I kept my words even, "that I've never seen you fight like that in all your sessions with me. Not once have I seen a fire in you that I thought worthy of a battle-hardened warrior. And yet, there it was."

Will didn't meet my gaze. "I find it best, in our world, not to tip one's hand when it comes to true strength, to true abilities. Don't you, General?"

Holy shit. I'd been right, then—Will had it in him to be the leader we needed, but he'd been hiding. That moment in the courtyard had shown me what I needed to know. What I knew was worth fighting for—a prince that would be strong enough to stop Edmund.

His smile said otherwise, though, and he adjusted his seat so that he pressed his forearms to the table, as though giving the game a steady look. "You think that I am cornered."

I looked over the pieces of the board. "I am sure of it."

Will spread his hands above the pieces. "It is not the size of the army, General, but the heart of the soldiers that determines if they win the war."

I mimicked him, leaning on my elbows to stare at the board. This moment had been a long time coming, and I wondered if he was ready to understand the depth of what was being played out in this kingdom. If he was truly ready to take on Edmund, as I was. I had to believe he was ready, for that fight had shown me something in him that I thought was missing.

Clever, clever boy, he'd been hiding in plain sight.

"This war that is being waged is no small thing, and no matter the hearts of the soldiers, they can be overrun should the enemy be insidious in their tactics. Like snakes let loose within the sleeping soldier's barracks." I touched one of my pieces as if to move it and then withdrew my hand. Pulling from the stash of other colors off the side of the table, I took a number of black pieces and slipped them into various positions on the map. Both within my own color, and within Will's. "If you do not know who is who, how can you trust any move made? How can you know that the moves you make will keep you safe?"

Will's eyes slowly lifted to mine, a slow horror filtering through them as the understanding dawned. "I was right to keep my hand hidden."

"Very much so," I said.

"Then, I would say our auntie loves me best, for it was on her advice," Will said. "When I was twelve."

Twelve. He'd been hiding for over two hundred years. Godsdamn. Talk about a long con. I couldn't help but be impressed, by both him and my devious aunt.

His hand hovered over the board. "So, now what is the best move, General?"

Slowly, I knocked each of the black pieces down. "To eradicate a nest of vipers, kill the little ones, first, while the mother is out hunting. For if the mother is struck first, surely all the little ones would attack."

He picked up his drink and tipped it to his mouth before answering. "That is a damn pickle. But I agree with your thoughts."

Even then, he made me want to laugh. "Yes, a pickle, indeed."

A bell rang through the room, and I grimaced. "I do believe you are about to be joined by the Harvest Candidates." I stood, and Will motioned at me to sit back down.

"I have no interest in them, either, let us continue our game," he said.

"Not even the redhead?"

Damn it, if my cock did not get me into trouble, my mouth surely would. Will shot a look at me as the women filtered in one at a time from the hidden paneled door behind me. I could not see them, and I kept my back that way. Will looked them over.

"She is lovely, and I found her highly amusing, but in a rather friendly way. Nothing more, General. I prefer a beauty whose hair shines like the sun." His eyes swung my way. "Not you, though."

Fuck. I was going to get myself hung up by my own jealousy.

"Blonde, brunette, redhead. It matters to me not." I shrugged and picked up my glass. "Curious, is all. I heard from my gossiping squire the castle is abuzz. They're saying she made you laugh during your dance the other night and that she might be your choice."

"We laughed together, it is true. All at your expense." Will smiled and then grimaced as he rubbed at his jaw. "Ah, the lady in question seems to be joining us."

It took all my effort not to react to the heady smell of the confounding woman as she approached our table. Dressed in a silver gown studded with black sparkling jewels, the cut of it gave no illusions as to the curving shape underneath, the dip of her waist and the gentle swell of hips and breasts.

A shape I could still feel filling my palms as I crushed her lips to my own, tasting her desire as I drank her down, licking my way across her skin. . . I shifted in my seat, fighting all the urges that rushed through me. Godsdamn it all, I had to get out of here before my body gave me away completely.

Sienna managed a perfect curtsey as she held out a golden tray laden with chocolates, which allowed me a perfect view of the tops of her breasts, all but begging for my fangs as they pressed up and outward from the corseted top.

I struggled to breathe, though she did not, the gentle rise and fall of her flesh damn mesmerizing.

"Apparently, we are to pretend we made these ourselves," she said, holding herself in that lowered position, eyes downcast for but a moment before they lifted, practically twinkling with laughter. "But I did not. I tasted one and I suggest you avoid them, as they are quite foul. I would not even feed them to the dogs."

Will laughed. "You may stand, Sienna." He paused and cocked his head. "An unusual name, Sienna. Is it a given name or a nickname?"

She stood and lowered the tray. "Funny you should ask. A nickname, yes."

"Your hair?" I asked.

Shut up, shut up. Do not encourage her to meet your gaze!

Too late.

Those golden eyes turned to me. "Yes, indeed, though not likely for the reason you think. I was in an . . .an accident, I suppose you would call it, as a child. Prior to that, I was fair, quite blonde. After, the roots began growing in this color."

Will shook his head. "You jest. If you'd come here blonde, I would have swept you off your feet by now."

She laughed up at him and I had to grip the table from reaching across and snatching her away from his gaze. "No, it is true, the doctors said it can happen when a great shock occurs, especially to a young child." Her smile hadn't slipped but there was a sheen of sweat on her skin that looked . . .delectable as she spoke about her past. The need to pin her down and lick my way across her body had me shifting in my seat once more.

"And your real name—"

She leaned over the board. "Let me guess, you are winning, General?" she said, deftly changing the subject. Interesting. She didn't want me to know her real name?

Will spread his hands wide. "He always wins, Sienna. That is why he is the General."

She bestowed on him a wide smile that made me want to smash something, flip the table, anything to draw her eyes back to me. To keep her looking at me as though I'd set the moon in the sky and named every star for her.

What in the actual fuck was wrong with me?

Her gaze slid over the table. "Truly, he always wins? Well then, let me help you, Your Majesty. Perhaps you only need someone who understands strategy as well or better than he."

Moving one of Will's pieces to a small island in the center of the board, she finally turned to me.

"Sometimes, it is the one piece everyone would claim as...useless ...that can become the most important piece of all."

With that, she made her way from the room, hips swaying.

And within fifteen minutes, Will had swept the board with me, all but cackling with laughter. "How did she know what piece would cause the cascade effect? I do not think I've ever beaten you before, brother." He clapped me on the back and left me there, still laughing to himself.

More than that, how could she have possibly become more desirable by beating me at my own game? I didn't think it would be possible to want her more, and yet here I was, all but on fire for her.

The room slowly emptied and I sat there alone, staring at the pieces. The red army of mine. The blue of William's. And the black pieces I'd set up for Edmund. I picked them up and rolled them in my hand.

They were cool, as if they'd been in an icebox, and the reality of Edmund's threat leached the desire out of me. I needed help to root out the traitors. To root out Edmund's people he'd placed near to those I loved the best in this world.

I needed someone's eyes and ears within this place. Someone I could trust. Someone no one would suspect.

I stood, still holding the pieces in my hand for a long moment, before tucking them into my pocket. Decision made, I knew that I would have to move quickly. Whatever plans Edmund had, he was setting them in play, and I could feel the undercurrents pulling at me. The same way I knew when a battle was about to turn. It was a sensation I felt deep in my gut, and one I'd learned never to ignore.

That thought fresh in my mind, to the stables I went, pausing at Havoc's stall. The black bitch of a mare gave me a serious side eye and then lunged at me, teeth bared.

"Yet she rides you as if you were the finest of pets," I muttered. Whatever spell Sienna was weaving around the mare, she seemed to be weaving around me, too. That gave me pause, and then I shook it off. I would not fall to the same weakness as others of our kingdom when it came to superstitions.

I pulled Ares out of his stall and quickly tacked him up. He gave me a snort, as if to ask why such a late night ride, and I gave him a quick scratch on the poll. "We are going to find an old friend."

Sienna was infecting me with her ridiculousness. Now, *I* was speaking to my horse as if he understood.

In the saddle, I gave him my heels, urging him forward into a steady, ground-covering canter. Down across open fields, I headed toward the Hunters, first, passing by close enough that I could hear their unsettled snarls, then angling further east. The forest reared up in front of me and I guided Ares to the narrow path, slowing him to a walk and then finally stopping him.

"From here on, I go alone." I patted his neck and tied him loosely to a tree.

Quickening my own stride, I found my way to the line between territories in no time.

Tipping my head back, cupping my hands around my mouth, I let out a howl, pitching it just as I'd been shown all those years ago. Near on seventy years, and in those seventy years, I'd only used it once before.

The sound died slowly in the air, and I knew I would have to wait. But not as long as I'd thought.

A crack of a branch snapping was my only warning, a short while later. I turned to see a massive beast of a man standing on his side of the territory.

"Dom," he growled my name in his familiar, Scottish brogue. "I am rather in the middle of something."

I shrugged. "Trouble rarely shows itself when we have all the time in the world for it."

He grinned, the scar that bisected his face from the corner of his mouth to his right ear pulling tight, making it more of a grimace. "You are admitting, finally, that you are trouble."

I held a hand out, and his massive hand engulfed mine as we shook. "It has been too long, Lochlin."

"That is because we cannot be friends." He shrugged. "I watched 'The Fox and the Hound' with my niece, just last week. I do believe that is you and I."

I laughed. "You would relate our childhood friendship with a *Disney* movie?"

Lochlin shrugged his wide shoulders and leaned against the sturdy trunk of a nearby oak tree. "I would. You were, and still are, the one friend that I know is true."

His words sunk into me. "You show too much of your heart, wolf."

"Better than my beastly nature," he said. "What is happening that you need me?"

I found myself pacing in front of him. "The Crown Prince . . .he has people in league with him, set up in various . . .placements." I shot him a look and he nodded for me to continue. "Should anything happen to him, they will strike those that they are positioned near."

He blew out a slow breath, his deep brown eyes thoughtful. "And?"

"I cannot suss them out without being caught, and having the repercussions be the same. I need someone to help find them, someone that no one will suspect."

He laughed as he spread his hands wide. "You don't think they would notice me?"

"In perhaps a different form, you would go unnoticed."

Lochlin lowered his hands and wrinkled up his nose. "As a dog."

"Is that not one of your shapes?"

He rolled his eyes. "I prefer for others not to know that I carry more than one form within my belly. You know that my father's . . .gifts . . .dinna be something I like on display, 'specially not for my pack to see."

He had a point, and I understood. Being part fae and part shifter had given Lochlin a unique set of skills that no other shifter had. His magic allowed him multiple shapes within the canine family.

"A wolf would be rather . . . obvious. But a sweet mutt? One that I could gift to my aunt?" It was my turn to spread my hands wide. "No one would be amiss."

"Do you often gift your auntie small dogs to eat?" He tipped his head to the side. "I do not wish to be feasted on."

My pacing slowed. "It is my aunt's birthday in a few weeks, I will tell her it—you—are an early gift. As a pet, of course. You wouldn't be the first."

Lochlin gave a slow sigh. "I almost regret letting you save my life."

"Twice," I reminded him.

He grimaced. "Twice. Fine. I will do it, but I need a little time to get some of my affairs in order for an extended absence. I will meet you back here tomorrow night."

He held out his hand and I took it, shocked when he pulled me into a bear hug. "You are in deep, brother. But I've got your back." He let me go and I stepped back.

"You have my thanks, wolf."

He barked a laugh. "Tomorrow night."

Lochlin melted back into the trees and I turned back toward my own kingdom.

And the treachery I was determined to dig out.

TWENTY-TWO

Sienna

I STIFLED A YAWN as I sat in a stiff parlor chair while listening to the six-piece orchestra playing what I was sure to be a very complicated piece from some dead composer—one whom some of the vampires around me might have actually known personally. The musicians and the piece were impressive, but I was growing more anxious by the minute. It had been three days since my encounter with Dominic in the garden—four since I'd watched him pleasure himself while thinking of me—and he'd been avoiding me like I was a contagious disease.

But in his absence, I had new potential bidders. Since my pole dance, I'd caught the attention of several vampires, two of whom were flanking me now, both pawing at me, even if it was against the rules. But there were subtle ways to cop a feel...like George to my right, who dropped his program and fondled my ankle when he bent to retrieve it. Or Michael to my left, who *accidentally* slid his fingers down the side of my breast. But neither of them affected me the way Dominic had, and other than the board game the night before, I hadn't seen him.

Did he really plan to stay away from me? Why did he think it was dangerous to be with him? He was strong, incredibly so, but he'd also vowed to protect me, so why did he think he would hurt me?

Finally—mercifully—the concert ended, and the Duchess announced that we were to adjourn to the next room for refreshments and conversation. I was restless. I told myself that it was from sitting so long—not that I was bothered that the General hadn't attended. The Harvest clock was ticking, but the thought of enduring the attention of any more of these lechers was more than I could bear, even if they might be my back up plan for survival.

But I wanted Dominic, not because I was attracted to him. No, that was actually a detriment. I wanted him because...

"Would you like a cup of punch?" George asked with a polite smile.

"That would be lovely," I said demurely.

This was all a game, just like the one Dominic and Prince Will were playing the night before, only this game had real consequences. It was a matter of life and death, and I needed to get myself together. Dominic wasn't here, he chose to purposely stay away from me, so I needed to focus on the men who were interested.

At least long enough to make my escape. I had forty-eight beads left on my bracelet.

George returned with my punch, then began to tell me he'd met the composer from our concert in Paris during a night of debauchery, all while his gaze kept dropping to my breasts popping out of my low neckline. I'd had Bee cinch my corset tighter for that very reason, but it hadn't been George's eyes I'd hoped to capture.

My companion's story segued into another involving George and F. Scott Fitzgerald, and I zoned out, glancing around the room. The men were hovering around the women like vultures, waiting for approval to claim their meals. It didn't seem to be a good analogy, considering vultures typically devoured dead flesh, but after finding Holly's shoe, I wasn't sure I was that far off the mark.

But suddenly, I realized that someone else was missing from the evening—Earl Anthony DuMont. I was certain I'd seen him sitting in the front row during the performance, but he was absent now. I wasn't sad to see him gone—quite the opposite—but he'd attended every other function, so it seemed strange he was gone now. It felt rather like that time I'd spotted a massive spider on the bedroom wall, only to have it disappear before I returned with my shoe in hand to get rid of it. Unsettling.

After forcing myself to endure ten minutes of George's bragging, it felt like the walls were closing in. I wasn't sure how much more of George I could take, and there wasn't anyone else in the room I was interested in even talking to, let alone wanted touching me.

The thought of my encounter with Dominic in the garden filled my head, making my cheeks flush. I thought of George capturing me in an embrace as Dominic had, covering his mouth with mine, and it left me nauseous.

I only wanted Dominic. Why didn't he want *me*?

Scratch that, I amended, recalling the hard length of him wedged against me in the garden. Why didn't he *want* to want me?

"Excuse me, George," I said as I winced. "A sudden headache has hit me. I'm so sorry, but I need to go back to my room and lay down."

Concern filled his eyes. "Would you like me to escort you?" George wasn't much of an actor, because his concern was obviously manufactured, and it was equally obvious that he hoped to get me alone.

I was starting to think the rules of this game were merely suggestions...

I forced a smile. "While that is very kind of you, my maid will be more than happy to escort me. I've felt this coming on all day, so she's waiting in the wings to help me back."

Bee wasn't due back for likely another hour, but he didn't need to know that.

I didn't wait for his reply, instead, I hurried out of the room and down the hall, not stopping until I turned a corner and found myself in a long hallway of windows overlooking part of the castle grounds, including the stable. I pressed my back against the wall, taking in the view as my mind raced.

What was I doing? This charade was stupid and pointless. If Dominic wasn't going to be a viable solution anymore, then I needed to step up my game at finding a way to escape before things got ugly. The thin veneer of civility and fake concern couldn't disguise the bloodlust in George's eyes, or the salacious way he licked his chops when he looked at me. He'd as soon bleed me dry as fuck me, and I was wholeheartedly opposed to both. Stepping away from the wall, I rested my hand on the window sill, studying the castle walls and the land surrounding it. I'd explored the flat land to the east, up to the edge of the Werewolf Territory border, but I still had no idea if there was another, less obvious entry point. One that didn't involve me getting instantly murdered the second I crossed over the line.

I'd start investigating with Havoc tomorrow.

Feeling bolstered by my plan, I started to turn away, but then stopped when I saw a horse and rider emerge from the gate that Bee and I had used the night we'd found the Hunters. Narrowing my eyes, I stared harder, my pulse beating faster. There was no mistaking that spectacular physique, or that horse.

Dominic.

What was he doing out of the palace at night, now riding like the wind? He'd said he'd had enemies . . .could he be in trouble?

I had no way of knowing what was wrong, but I intended to find out.

By the time I'd reached the stable, I'd convinced myself this was a terrible idea, yet I hadn't turned back. If there was something afoot, I needed to know about it. And if he was just going for a midnight ride to blow off some steam? What better time to catch him alone? Just the two of us...in the dark...maybe I could change his mind after all.

I squeezed my thighs together and hurried through the stable doors.

It was only then that it occurred to me I was still in my stupid ballgown. I ran the risk of losing Dominic altogether after just running here and quickly tacking her. But my corset was tighter than a hangman's noose, and it was going to be hard to mount Havoc, let alone let her have her head as we raced through the night.

Suck it up, Sienna. A little discomfort is nothing compared to either death or being the sex slave of someone like George. Neither of which will help you get to Jordan.

I shuddered and led Havoc out of her stable.

Timmy was sitting at the doors with another stable hand around the same age, and he jumped to his feet in surprise. "Miss Sienna. I didn't know you were riding tonight."

"Well, I am. And if I bring you a pastry tomorrow morning, will you keep it to yourself that you saw me?"

The other boy spoke up, brow wrinkled with concern. "Alright, but... You can't try to escape, Miss. It'll be on our heads."

Releasing a short laugh, I said, "Escape? Where would I go? I merely need to clear my mind. Timmy will tell you that I take Havoc out nearly every morning and I always return."

Timmy took in my gold gossamer gown, my updo, and the flowers woven into my hair along with the gold butterfly pin. I was always plainly dressed in the mornings, but I also knew I didn't have time to argue. Dominic was getting farther and farther ahead. I had a good chance of losing him if I didn't hurry.

"Do you want a pastry or not?" I asked.

"Make it two," Timmy said, casting a glance to his friend. "But if you don't come back—"

"I will. Now, open the stable doors."

"Don't you want a side-saddle, Miss?" the other boy asked.

"She don't use one," Timmy said. "But she don't usually look this pretty, either."

I wasn't sure whether to take that as a compliment or an insult.

"Don't you want me to help you mount her?" Timmy asked, giving me a dubious look. I suspected he doubted I could mount her myself dressed thusly.

"No, I'm going to walk her for now." I planned to take her through the same gate Dominic used, but I'd have to open the door to let us out.

I didn't wait to hear their protests, instead, turning left to get to the narrow gate. Dominic had left the door propped open, so I did the same. It took several attempts to mount Havoc from the ground, no step stool and in massive skirts. To my surprise, she stood perfectly still once I finally pulled my dress up to my waist with one hand and grabbed the edge of the saddle with the other and pulled myself up. The dress was full enough to completely cover my legs, as well as Havoc's rump.

Havoc was patient while I got situated, but she seemed to know when I was ready, because she took off without prompting. Then, as though she knew what our mission was, she headed in the direction Dominic had taken.

I was sure we'd lost him, but after Havoc sprinted for a good ten minutes, I could see horse and rider in the distance, the moonlight making the shiny adornments and buttons on his cloak shine.

The evening was cool and my dress was sleeveless, making me wish I'd at least taken one of the stable hands' outer garments. My skirts flapped as I rode hard, and the wind loosened the pins in my hair, sending it in a wild cascade down my back. But I was gaining on Dominic, who hadn't looked back once, so I wasn't about to slow down.

One thing was certain as his horse flew past the forest—Dominic was headed toward the eastern stone bridge...Werewolf Territory. When I was only a hundred yards behind him and the border several hundred feet more beyond that, he crested a small hill and disappeared out of sight.

I wasn't worried. I knew he'd appear again, if for no other reason, there was nowhere else for him to go except the forest on either side. Havoc slowed down as we crested the hill ourselves, and I knitted my brow when there was no sign of him. Not even on the other side of the river...

Unless he'd crossed the bridge. But surely he wouldn't do that. Would he?

Where the hell had he gone?

I shivered as a cold gust of wind washed over me, making my arms break out in goosebumps.

Maybe this hadn't been the best decision, after all.

I considered turning Havoc around and heading back to the castle, but before I could make a move, a horse bolted from the trees, coming straight for us. Havoc snorted, muscles quaking as terror shot through me like a knife.

Not Ares with Dominic on his back. It was Earl Anthony DuMont, and his face was filled with almost maniacal glee. How had I confused the two? At a distance, in the darkness, maybe combined with wishful thinking? Whatever the case, I'd made a critical error.

"Ah, you stupid bitch. Now, I've got you."

He kicked his horse's flanks hard, barreling straight at us, driving us toward the river... and the bridge.

I'd led us straight into a trap.

I could sense Havoc's panic as she tossed her head wildly and stomped her hooves in a furious beat. I needed to buy us some time. Time to come up with a plan. Time to calm my terrified horse.

Not an easy feat when my insides were knotted with terror.

Anthony yanked his horse to a sudden stop just a few yards in front of me, where it pawed the ground restlessly.

"Enough of these games, Earl Anthony," I managed through numb lips. "This isn't very gentlemanly of you to frighten a lady out for some evening air."

A sly grin spread across his face. "One could say you're not a lady."

I could only imagine what I looked like. Most of my hair had fallen down and I was astride the back of a horse, gown hitched high around my thighs. This wasn't how vampires of the court preferred their *ladies* to look. Or so they liked to pretend.

"In fact, I've found myself wondering far too often if you wouldn't be a little hellion once I have you on your back. Perhaps you'd scream for me?"

I tried to hide my fear, but he must have smelled it because he looked even more excited as he dismounted with a flourish.

He cocked his head and stared up at me, as if to say, "*Your move*", but I knew as well as he did, I was trapped. My only escape was the bridge behind me, which felt like almost certain suicide by werewolf, and my last resort.

There's one more option. Don't forget the river.

I didn't dare risk a glance to the roiling waters to test that idea. It was about thirty feet wide, but I had no idea how deep it was, and the icy water would only be survivable for a short time. Besides, what would stop him from following me in?

Anthony took a menacing step toward me and Havoc shuffled her feet, growing anxious.

"To be honest, I'd prefer if you fought me. I like it rough," he whispered, his smile downright evil.

It was all the encouragement I needed to make a move. As if she'd read my mind, Havoc reared back, striking her front legs wildly in the air. If we could get Anthony to step aside and hopefully spook his horse in the process, just maybe we could get enough of a head start that we could outrun them to the safety of the castle. Or at least get close enough where someone could hear me scream. I'd be punished for sneaking out at night, but that seemed like a small price, to avoid whatever Anthony had in store for me.

Anthony did take a step back, but as I urged Havoc to leap forward, he darted toward us, moving so fast, he was a blur. He managed to wrap his fist around a handful of my dress, still spread out on Havoc's backside, and gave a vicious jerk.

My feet flew from the stirrups and I tumbled off the back of my horse, hitting the ground in a bone-jarring fall.

Havoc snorted and whinnied as Anthony used the hem of my dress to drag me across the ground and toward the bridge.

"Boon! I want to use my boon!"

"You think I give a toss about your boon, girl?" he demanded with a snarl.

"The Duchess will punish you for—"

"And who will be alive to tell her that you tried to invoke it?"

Damn this bastard to hell.

"You're not permitted to touch me until after the Games!" I panted, kicking my legs furiously and scrabbling at the coarse grass for purchase.

"You think you're so clever, don't you?" he asked with a hard laugh. "Didn't Marguerite's antics teach you anything? If you're caught trying to escape, all bets are off. I can do what I please. I've got to be getting back to the palace, but I think we can have a little fun before I kill you and leave you in Werewolf Territory. The others will think you made a run for it, and got your just desserts. What a happy accident this has been."

I didn't even have time to consider his words as we reached the first of the cobblestones on the bridge.

Havoc let out a loud scream of protest, then charged Anthony as he started across the stone bridge with me in tow. She reared up on her hind legs again. Anthony let go of my dress, raising his arms over his head to protect himself. Blood pooled in my mouth as I tried to get to my feet, but I was tangled in the countless yards of fabric around my legs.

Havoc slammed her hooves to the ground, dangerously close to my ribs, but used her head and snapping teeth to force Anthony back several more feet and he tripped on a loose stone, tumbling ass over tea kettle.

Running on pure, terror-induced adrenaline, I finally managed to stand and broke into a sprint toward the trees on the south side of the clearing. I could still hear Havoc's hooves pounding against the stone bridge, and her furious snorts.

She was buying me time to escape. But at what cost?

I heard her scream of pain, dimly, as if through a fog, but even if I hadn't, I'd have felt it. A searing agony ripped through my throat. It was as if I'd been injured myself, and I knew Anthony had sunk his monstrous teeth into her.

"No!" I howled, knowing I should keep running but unable to stop myself from turning back.

A moment later, there was a second scream, only this time, it was that of a man.

I blinked, I spun and stared into the moonlit night as two figures grappled on the bridge.

"Where the fuck is she, you spineless bastard?"

SHANNON MAYER

Dominic's voice was an icy snap, jarring me from my confusion. I stumbled toward them, trying to speak, but finding my voice paralyzed with shock and fear.

He had a whimpering Anthony pinned on his back, a hand around his throat.

"I'll give you one last chance to reply before I tear your still-beating heart from your chest."

"She was trying to run away. I stopped her. You should be glad I didn't let those wolves tear the little slut to pieces," the Earl managed to hiss.

"H-he's lying," I called, finally finding my voice as I stumbled toward them. "I was out riding, and he cornered me and tried to drag me across the bridge."

Dominic turned toward me, and froze as he caught sight of me.

"Are you all right?" he demanded.

"I'm okay," I assured him, my heart skipping a beat at the raw emotion on his face. Moonlight skittered off a flash of silver as Anthony managed to yank a dagger from his boot.

"Look out!" I shouted, watching in horror as he drove it toward Dominic's heart. Heeding my warning, he turned at the last second, and Anthony's blade plunged into his thickly muscled shoulder.

The sound of bone cracking echoed through the night, as did Anthony's sobs. The hand that had previously wielded the dagger now hung by nothing but loose flesh, the bone snapped in two.

"You bastard! Your brother will have your head for this!" he sobbed, snot and tears running down his face. "That bitch doesn't deserve you!"

I did a double take. Jealousy laced Anthony's voice. Did Dominic even realize that was what was driving Anthony? Not desire for me, but desire for Dominic.

Dominic seemed not to notice. "Yes, I'm sure if there is anything left of you to find, he would. Because you're one of his, aren't you? A true loyalist? Let's see how he fairs with one less, shall we?"

Dominic closed his hand more tightly around Anthony's neck and the other man's eyes bulged.

"You think getting rid of me ends your troubles?" he croaked. "There are half a dozen more, and you'll never learn the identity of the others."

"Excellent. Then name them, or your death will be as slow and painful as I can make it," Dominic shot back, reaching for Anthony's uninjured arm menacingly.

"That's the beauty of it, isn't it?" Anthony replied with a choked laugh that bordered on hysterical. "I don't know. None of us do. Edmund wipes that piece of our memory after each meeting so we can never betray one another. It's a good plan, yes?"

"One you might've kept to yourself, because you're truly of no use to me at all now, are you?" Dominic ground out.

A second later, there was a curious gurgling sound and I turned away with a gasp. I knew it was over when the sound of Anthony's legs thrashing against the stone bridge went quiet. The plop of two pieces of Anthony hitting the water quickly followed. Dominic had beheaded him with his bare hands.

I was still shaking when I felt a hand on my shoulder.

"Sienna, it's all right. I . . . I need to know, did he hurt you?" Dominic asked through gritted teeth as he forced my chin up so he could meet my eyes.

I stared up at him, still reeling as he searched my face for the answer.

"Did he touch you?" he demanded more urgently.

"No...not in the way you mean," I managed, tugging my arm away as I heard a rattling wheeze and a low snort.

Damn me! Havoc was still alive.

I rushed toward the horse lying in the shadows and knelt beside her. Her breath sawed in and out of her lungs as a thick river of blood streamed from the wound on her neck.

"Aw, you sweet, sweet girl. You hero. You precious brave girl. Please don't leave me," I whispered, stroking her velvety muzzle, trying to give her some kind of comfort. Her eyes rolled wildly as her muscles strained and shook. "Can't you do something?" I begged, turning toward Dominic, barely able to see him through the blur of tears. "Please."

He strode toward us and laid a gentle hand on my shoulder, the fury in his eyes fading. "I'm sorry, Sienna. If it was just a bite...but this—" He broke off and gestured to the grisly gash. "I can put her out of her misery."

"No!" I threw myself in front of Havoc, shielding her head and neck with my body. "No...not yet."

I just couldn't bear it. Closing my eyes, I cuddled closer to her and burrowed my face against hers, cooing softly.

Please, gods, heal her. Please.

Acting on instinct, I laid my hand over the wound, and pressed. I could sense everything around me so keenly. The coppery scent of fresh blood as it coated my hand. The life force of the animal emanating from its body. Her fear.

Heal her.

Heal her.

A trembling thread of energy seemed to leap from my hand and I nearly pulled it away, but something made me still.

Heal her.

The thread thickened to a band and spread, pulsing from me into the beast that lay before me.

"Sienna?" Dominic muttered.

But I barely heard him as the energy leapt and expanded, consuming me.

Heal her!

And then, there was nothing but darkness.

Twenty-Three

Sienna

"Sienna?"

A low, melodic voice murmured my name, and I strained toward it through the tangle of cobwebs in my mind.

"Sienna, can you hear me?"

I tried to speak, but couldn't seem to get my tongue to work. When a warm hand closed over mine and squeezed, though, I managed to squeeze back.

"Thank the gods," the voice muttered.

Dominic.

I forced my eyelids open with what felt like a Herculean effort. It took a second for my blurred vision to clear, but when it did, I found him staring down at me, his face bone-white with worry.

"What happened?" I croaked. Images flashed through my mind, like fragments of a bad movie, but I couldn't seem to piece them together to make sense.

"We'll talk about that soon enough. How do you feel?"

I let my eyes drift shut, trying to assess. After a few long moments, I blew out a breath.

"Like hammered shit."

His hoarse laughter had my own lips twitching.

"Given that I wasn't sure if you were going to survive, I'll take it," he replied as he drew his hand away. "If you can manage to sit up a bit, I can give you a drink of water."

I groaned and shifted, scuttling back until I was propped against the headboard. I opened my eyes again as he held a cup to my lips. I took several, greedy gulps, and then nodded.

"Thank you."

He set the cup on a rickety table beside the bed.

"What hurts?" he asked, scanning my blanket-covered form from head to toe.

"Nothing." I shook my head. "I just feel like every single ounce of energy has been sapped from my body. I think when I—"

I let out a gasp and my eyes flew wide.

Anthony...the fight on the bridge...Havoc...

It all came back in a rush.

"My horse...is she—?"

Dominic's lean jaw flexed and he looked away. "She is alive." He shrugged his broad shoulders and scrubbed a hand over his face. "I don't understand it, but she's very much alive. In fact, when I went out to water her, the ungrateful harpy tried to bite my face off. How, Sienna?" He shook his head in awe. "How did you do it? She was dying."

I swallowed hard and tried to think back to the very moment it had happened. "I-I don't know, Dominic. I really wanted to save her. She willingly gave her life to protect me. I just kept thinking 'heal her'. The more I thought it, the more this weird feeling came over me. Like an energy coming from deep inside me that I didn't even know was there."

"And this has never happened to you before? You've never been able to heal anyone in the past?"

"Heal? No," I said firmly. "But there have been times..." I trailed off, thinking of my long-time affinity for animals, and how easily they seemed to take to me. "When Bee and I went to see the Hunters—"

"When you *what*?" he cut in, his expression incredulous. "Do you have a death wish, woman?"

I scowled at him and crossed my arms over my chest.

"I prefer the concerned, doting Dominic to the General, if you please," I shot back. "I'm feeling a little better, but certainly not up to arguing with you. Now, can you let me finish my story?"

He sniffed and waved a hand for me to continue, but he didn't look thrilled about it.

"*As I was saying*, Bee and I were trying to find out what happened to Holly, and we came upon the Hunters they had guarding the South border. There was a bit of a cock-up, we got too close, and long story short, one of them nearly ate us."

Dominic groaned and pressed his fingers to his temples. "I can't even believe what I'm hearing. You—" He broke off and sighed. "Forget it, go on."

"I don't know. I sort of just...willed it not to eat us. And it didn't. We ran out of there and didn't look back. But it's only ever been with animals. Never people. And nothing like what happened with Havoc."

His eyes searched my face as if there would be more answers tattooed on my skin. "I should've known there was something off when she let you ride her so easily. I figured it was just one of those rare connections, but this? This is *magic*, Sienna, of a kind I've never seen. The question is, how? Why? Your parents...they are both human?"

"Yes. I'm as sure as I can be they were, at least. They're both dead now."

I wracked my brain for some other explanation, and only then noticed my strange, unfamiliar surroundings.

"Where are we?" I asked, taking in the dark, wooden interior of the large room. A fire crackled cheerfully in the hearth nearby, and there were some other bare bones furnishings, but nothing like the quality of that in the palace.

"One of the hunting lodges in the forest on the northern grounds of the castle. I could hardly return with you unconscious and slung over the back of my horse without them assuming you tried to escape. Not to mention the fact that I'm covered in blood."

I winced as I took a gander at him. He wasn't kidding. His entire waistcoat was stained almost black with blood.

Anthony's blood.

The memory of Dominic killing him on the bridge resurfaced, and I shoved it away. I wasn't ready to think about that yet.

"Good point. But what about mine?"

SHANNON MAYER

I frowned and glanced down at my own clothes, realizing with a start that I was now dressed in a white, linen shirt that came to my knees, and nothing else.

"Did you..." I trailed off, my cheeks going hot.

"I did," he confirmed with a clipped nod as he looked away. "I was a perfect gentleman before you ask, and it was necessary. Your clothes were saturated and sticking to you. I couldn't tell what blood was yours, and what belonged to the horse or Anthony. I had to make sure you weren't wounded."

It made sense, but my whole body tingled at the realization that he'd seen me naked.

"I was pleasantly surprised to find you only had a small cut on your lip and some scrapes and scratches. Are you in pain now?" His fingers brushed along the edge of mine, almost as if he didn't realize he reached for me.

I shook my head. "No. A little sore from when Anthony dragged me off of Havoc's back, but other than that, I'm well. And my energy is steadily returning."

Dominic's face darkened. "Good. Maybe you can tell me what happened? Did he follow you?"

I bit my lip and winced as my teeth found the cut there. "Not exactly..."

His dark eyes narrowed. "Out with it," he demanded.

"I was following *him*," I mumbled miserably. "But to be fair, I thought he was you. I could've sworn I saw Ares and I thought maybe you were in trouble. You said something about enemies and—"

"What were you thinking? Godsdamn it! There are people here who would harm you. Anthony being only one of them. You can't just go gallivanting out alone at night." His words echoed through the cabin as he gained volume.

I glared at him, happy to channel my embarrassment into anger. "You're blaming this on me? He tricked me and then hunted me down like a hyena would a wounded gazelle, but *I'm* the problem here? If you don't want to see me hurt, then here's a fucking novel idea. Let me go! Help me get free of this awful place. Help all of us victims in this twisted game. Then I would be safe, and you'd be rid of me as you wish to be!"

He turned away with a snarl and speared a hand through his dark hair.

"It's not so easy, Sienna..."

"Tell me why it isn't then, stop keeping me in the dark," I demanded, desperate to know. Desperate for some answers.

His eyes were filled with banked fury as he shot to his feet and began to pace restlessly. "I can't," he replied in a hoarse whisper.

"Because of tradition?" I spat the word like it was a curse. "Misguided loyalty to your monster of a brother? *Why*, damn you?"

He reeled around and bent low to meet my gaze. "Because if I defy Edmund in any meaningful way, he will destroy them all. Everyone I love, Sienna. He will kill Will, my mother, our aunt. All of them. It might take a day, it might take a week, but he will have his revenge. Edmund doesn't believe in an eye for an eye, you see. If you take his eye, he takes your heart and devours it."

I swallowed hard and stared up at him, mind spinning. "Why do you put up with him, then? You're strong...stronger than he is. I watched you in the arena, sparring. You could've easily overtaken him—even I could see you were holding back. End him, Dominic. If he's dead, all the people you love will be free of danger."

"Don't you think I want to?" he demanded with a harsh laugh as he stood and paced the room. "I've dreamed of it every day for decades. But it's not just him. He has a small but fierce cabal of loyalists. He's set up a failsafe should anything happen to him. His death brings a cascade effect."

The last words he and Anthony had shared before his death on the stone bridge floated to the forefront of my mind. In my terror and confusion, I hadn't understood them. Now, though, it all made sense.

"If Edmund meets his end by foul play, or there is ever an attempted coup to put Will in power, Will's assassination would occur within hours," Dominic added gruffly.

I blinked, shaking my head in shock. "Which is why you agreed to be General and protect him..."

He inclined his head. "Exactly. What better way to ensure I would protect Edmund with my life, than the threat of death to those I love should harm come to him?"

"Can you not use those loyal to you and Will to stage a coordinated attack against Edmund's men? Hit them all at once and rid the palace of his influence so you can remove him from power?"

"It's possible. But I'd have to root them out, first. Which is what I was attempting to put into motion when you likely saw me riding out this evening."

"So it *was* you," I murmured softly. "I knew it!"

"Yes, well, apparently, Anthony knew it, too, which is why he must've followed me. He likely only stopped because he sensed you behind him. Anthony won't be an issue going forward. I've disposed of his body, and left no trace. But Edmund will wonder where he's gone, and he will have questions. We've got to make sure those questions lead to answers that don't include either of us."

"The stable boys...I spoke to both of them. Surely, he won't hurt them—"

"I will take care of it. In fact, I will take care of everything. We've got a good four hours before sunrise and, so long as we return you to the palace before the servants awaken, we should be fine." He took a step back and gestured at his filthy clothes. "I've got to step outside for a few moments, but have no fear, I won't be far. I have to meet with an ally now before he leaves the area. Once I return, I'm going to bathe and change clothes. Then, I'll put my mind to working out a believable tale, and a backup one, should we need it. For now, get some more rest so that your energy is restored upon our return. We'll both need our wits about us."

I had a million more questions that needed answering, but it was clear Dominic had enough on his plate, and already, my energy was waning.

I settled back against the pillow and let out a sigh.

"Be careful," I called softly after him as he strode out of the room, half-hoping he didn't hear me. Why did I even care if he was careful or not? So what if he had a reason for his support of Edmund and his twisted games? Lots of people rationalized lots of terrible behaviors. That didn't give them a pass.

An image of Will's easy smile and kind face flashed through my mind, and I squeezed my eyes closed. I thought of all the times Bee had gushed over his kindness, about how all the people loved him best of the brothers.

Not my problem. *None* of this was my problem. I needed to get some rest so I could figure out how this crazy turn of events would affect me and my future. Dominic might be the least awful of all the monsters here, but he was still a monster.

I tried to clear my mind of all the trauma and the strife, and focus on my breathing. Soon enough, exhaustion took its toll and I drifted away.

When I awoke next, the room was dark, save for the now dwindling fire and a crack of light beneath the doorway. I glanced out the window to see it was still full night, and the moon and stars had been blanketed by a thick cover of ominous clouds. They moved during the night, unlike the fake day time sky and clouds.

I'd been asleep then for maybe an hour, two at most.

I sat up gingerly and was relieved to note that the bone-deep weariness that had been hanging over me like a wet blanket had dissipated. In fact, I was feeling oddly energized. Restored, almost. Strange for such a short nap.

I swung my feet over the side of the bed and stood. No shaky legs, no pain or fatigue.

Excellent.

I made my way across the room and, when I reached the door, I tugged on it gently and peered into the next room.

It was a large living area with a settee and a table, and a rustic kitchen area with a wood burning stove tucked in the corner. Dominic clearly wasn't back from wherever he'd gone, so maybe I'd—

There was the distinct sound of water sloshing and I cocked my head. Where was it coming from?

A quick scan of the room revealed another open doorway next to the kitchen.

I didn't consciously make the decision to walk toward it...

Or through it...

Or down the short hallway.

And I certainly didn't intend to push the bathroom door open and peer inside.

But once I'd done it, there was no turning back. Not once I saw Dominic's naked back above the rim of the massive bathtub in the center of the room, bathed in golden candlelight.

I swallowed hard and let my eyes roam over his broad shoulders, and muscled arms. Lord, was he a specimen. My fingers itched with the need to reach out and touch him...

"I know you're there, Sienna," he muttered. "I can smell you. Go back to bed."

I willed myself to turn away. To leave and forget I'd ever been here. But I was frozen in place as surely as if my feet had been cemented to the spot.

"And if I don't?" I whispered.

"You will," he shot back without turning around. "You must. I'm not human, but I'm still only flesh and blood. It's been a trying night. My patience is thin and my self-control thinner. Get out of here."

I began to inch my way closer to the tub, trembling, breath coming in short gasps as each step revealed more of his magnificent body to me.

When I was only scant inches away, I slipped to my knees, on autopilot now.

"It will be a miracle if I make it through this mess alive," I murmured, slipping a hand into his chocolatey, damp curls. "If I'm going to die, I'd like to make a few more good memories to offset all of the awful ones I carry." I gave his hair a light tug and he growled low in his throat. "Surely, you would grant me that wish."

He turned his head, then, and captured my gaze. The need etched on his face stole my breath.

"I would give my right hand to do that, Sienna, but I won't give up my honor. Before the Games, we all make a vow not to defile the women—"

"I release you of that vow," I cut in.

"You cannot possibly, it is not your vow to release," he replied, his voice so rough it sounded as if he'd swallowed glass. "You aren't here of your own free will. You're here because you were taken. You aren't thinking clearly."

I rose unsteadily and moved to the side of the bathtub. "I know what I want, and I want you, Dominic. Here . . . now. My choice is my own. My consent my own."

I lifted my trembling fingers to the buttons of my shirt and began to unfasten them, one by one.

"Don't."

It was surely meant as a command, but came out like the desperate plea of a dying man. Despite his protests, though, his gaze was locked on my fingers as they worked. By the time I reached my belly button, every muscle in his body was tensed as he gripped the sides of the tub, white-knuckled.

I undid the last button and let the shirt slip from my shoulders into a heap on the floor.

Dominic's guttural groan rolled through me like an earthquake, starting at my toes and curling up to my already wet center where the sound seemed to pool and vibrate. His dark eyes swirled with heat and desire as I leaned toward him until my breasts brushed his forearm. Then, I pressed my lips to his ear. "If you will not touch me, then I will touch you."

He grunted and I pulled away, the power I held over him as heady of an elixir as his scent.

"Witch," he muttered, fangs gleaming in the candlelight.

"Monster," I replied, arching my back and making a show of tying my hair in a knot on the top of my head.

His fingers clenched and unclenched against the rim of the tub, and I let my gaze slide lower. Past his chest, past his trim stomach, past the muscular vee that made me want to trace it with my tongue.

"Sweet gods have mercy," I whispered.

I sucked in a breath as I took in the thick length of his cock, jutting proudly from between lean hips.

"You're killing me," he growled. "Go." As if he would take one last stand at sending me away.

"And I haven't even started," I managed, as I lifted one leg and slipped it into the warm water, on autopilot now.

"I will not be able to stop if you take this further," he warned.

I paused, understanding I was on a threshold I couldn't uncross.

Surely, this was a terrible idea. Tempting a vampire when I'd just so narrowly escaped another's clutches?

But as much as I wanted to lump Dominic in with the rest of them, he was different. I knew it in my bones. And, in this moment, I wanted nothing more than to feel him moving inside me, filling me up, making me forget...

I swung my other leg into the tub, straddling his hips, and sank down slowly, bracing myself on my knees. I stayed like that, poised above him, as I laid my hands on his bare chest.

"How much time do we have?" I whispered, my heart beating so loudly, I could hear it.

His lean throat worked as he tore his gaze from my breasts and looked into my eyes. "An hour. Maybe two."

"Then, I'd better get started."

TWENTY-FOUR

Dominic

HER WORDS MIGHT AS well have been wooden spikes of the dragon blood tree, because they brought me low just as surely.

If she hadn't even started yet, I was in for a world of hurt. Already, my cock wept for her, throbbing and pulsing against my belly, just inches away from where it ached to be. If that wasn't bad enough, the steam had only intensified her scent, heightening my need to taste her to a fever pitch.

I realized exactly how naive I was when she closed her fist around me with her silky soft hand, and then squeezed.

"Fuck!" I growled, instantly arching my hips toward her helplessly. If only I could close my hand over hers and work it up and down my aching shaft, it would give me some modicum of relief. Instead, I gritted my teeth, fangs exposed, as I held still, tensed like a coiled spring.

"You feel like velvet," she murmured, settling her sweet bottom against my thighs and studying my cock in her little hand.

It jerked and she tightened her grip, eliciting another groan from me.

Her golden honey eyes flew to mine and she wet her lips. Just the sight of her tongue had the blood roaring in my ears. And then?

"Can I...taste you?"

The rim of the tub groaned and squealed, the cast iron giving way and twisting under the pressure of my grip.

Deny her, a tiny voice inside my brain demanded. *She's asking...just refuse.*

But all I could do was watch, breath suspended, as she dipped her head forward, slid her ass back, and lowered her mouth to me.

Hot, wet heat enveloped the head of my cock, erasing any thought of refusal...erasing any thought at all.

Vampires were a highly sexual lot, and I'd been sucked off more times than I could possibly consider counting. But this? The tentative, subtle exploration, the gentle, torturous suction...It was unlike anything I'd ever felt.

I released my death grip on the bathtub and reached a hand toward her hair, stopping just before sinking my fingers in.

An impish light flashed in her eyes and she pulled my cock from her mouth with a pop.

"No touching, remember?"

Witch, indeed. I almost chuckled, but the desire fled as she lapped at the broad head of my cock again, and then drew me in deep. Deeper. So deep, I could feel the tender, soft flesh at the back of her throat. Her cheeks hollowed as she sucked, and the pressure in my balls built to the point of pain.

"Sienna," I groaned, shaking my head like a man possessed as I watched her. "Fuck, gods, please."

She turned her gaze on me once again and expelled me from her mouth.

"I need you inside me," she said breathlessly.

My tongue stuck to the roof of my mouth as she squirmed up my body and sealed her hips to mine. She didn't take me inside her, then. Instead, she nestled my thick cock against her seam and slid forward and back, slowly, at first, and then more quickly as her cheeks grew flushed. Killing me wasn't even close to accurate. This was pure torture to watch her climb the heights her body demanded.

"So good," she whispered, rolling her hips faster, clutching at my shoulders to steady herself. "You feel so damned good."

I tried to look away because the urge to take control—to grab her by the waist, lift her up and plunge my swollen cock into her, sweet, soft center—was so strong, I shook with it. But I could no more look away than stop the world from turning. She was magnificent. Head tossed back, hair loose from its constraints, now, streaming in a wild disarray around her shoulders, full breasts bouncing up and down, up and down—

"Dominic?"

It took a second for my brain to put it altogether. The new voice in the room. The oh-so-familiar Scottish brogue. Sienna must've finally heard it, too, because she froze, poised above me, eyes wide with shock.

"I'm sorry to interrupt, lass—you have no idea how sorry—but time is of the essence."

I leaned forward, wrapping my arms around Sienna and using my chest to shield her.

"What the fuck is it that couldn't wait, Loch?" I snarled, fury like a living, breathing beast inside me as I turned toward the doorway, and his grim expression was like a one-two punch.

I braced myself, but nothing could have prepared me for his words.

"I'm so sorry, Dominic. Your father is dead."

Which meant...

"Edmund is the king," I muttered.

Godsdamn.

TWENTY-FIVE

Sienna

KING STIRLING WAS DEAD. Edmund had taken the throne.

My mind was still reeling with the news.

"We're all going to die," I whispered the words under my breath as we raced across the fields, giving the horses the freedom to go as fast as they could.

Havoc and Ares were neck and neck, the mare pinning her ears every time he so much as looked at her.

I couldn't help glancing over at Dominic, leaned over the stallion's neck, body moving in perfect rhythm with his horse.

Damn, that had almost been me under him. If not for the whole, King is dead business.

I was doing my best not to think about naked Dominic, about the bathtub, about being interrupted. I was doing my best not to think about what would come next too.

"Chaos," Lochlin, Dominic's ally had said as we'd dressed. "The castle is in chaos. His death was not natural. The best I could hear was that he'd been speaking with his sister, when he suddenly keeled over the table, clutching at his throat."

That had stopped Dominic with just his pants on. "His throat, are you sure?"

Lochlin gave a slow nod. "Is it what I think?"

"Bloodworm," Dominic snapped. "Gods, we thought they'd all been eradicated! Edmund was in charge of . . ." He yanked his shirt on. "Edmund. It had to have been Edmund. He was the one who had the samples, who said there was no more bloodworms!"

"Explains the King's long decline," Lochlin said. "And the madness. Aren't the worms usually caught long before that? From our spies, we know it's been a long time since anyone died from them."

"Fuck. It won't even be seen as murder!" Dominic growled. "A natural occurrence, that's what Edmund will say, that it was an anomaly or a resurgence that couldn't have been seen. And he'll claim . . ."

Not that I didn't care about what had happened, I knew it would affect me seeing as I was trapped here. But I was trying to figure out how best to use this new twist in my fate.

I'd already planned to find a way to the werewolf territories, to get to Jordan. Maybe this was the moment I needed. Sooner than I'd thought, though.

Clean clothes, simple, worn, and very comfortable, surely not the fancy silks I'd been wearing for the games, had been laid out for me across the bed. My mind ticked over what was being laid in front of me, outside of the clothing.

Chaos. The games disrupted for what would be a royal funeral. Even I knew they wouldn't keep on with the Harvest Games—the vampires wanted to be seen as regal, as holding to traditions. Would the games start up again?

"Should I stay here? And stay hidden?" I asked quietly. Both men looked at me, but Dominic quickly shook his head.

"No. A girl missing from the games at this point would not go well. Though I understand why you'd want to hide."

Bugger. I was hoping he'd leave me behind, and I could explore my way to the werewolf territory. If I didn't use the bridge, surely I could slip through unnoticed.

There was no more discussion after that. The men prepared the horses, and without another word, we'd been off.

And now here we were, on our way back to the castle. To my prison.

As we drew close to the stables, the utter pandemonium was immediately apparent. People were rushing in all directions, both vampire and human. More disturbing though were the line ups in front of men with probes. One at a time, they took the probes and jammed them down people's throats until they vomited.

And no, there was no cleaning up of the probes before they were used again. Foul.

"Do not go near them," Dominic warned as he dismounted and offered me a hand. As if I needed any promptings to stay clear of the probing men. I leapt off on my own and he grimaced. "They will put a few bloodworms in others now, to make it seem like it's not just Father. To make it look like an outbreak."

How could he know that? Did he read minds now too?

"It is what I would do," he said, his voice laced with anger. "To throw off the scent of a murder I'd committed."

I shivered. How many murders had he committed exactly? I didn't want to ask that question, not right then, so instead I re-directed.

"Why didn't Lochlin come with us?" I asked.

"He's . . .not a vampire." Dominic shook his head. "He's one of our neighbors."

It took all I had not to suck in a sharp breath of understanding. I would bet every last stitch of clothing that he was a werewolf. A werewolf who'd been kind. Maybe a werewolf willing to help me find Jordan?

"Did he stay at the cabin?" I did what I could to keep the excitement out of my voice.

Dominic shot me a quick look, and did not answer my question. "Go to your room, lock the door and stay there until the Duchess calls for you." He moved to take my reins from me, but Havoc snaked her neck and snapped her teeth at him.

"I'll put her away, and do as you say," I tipped my head toward him as I did a slow curtsey, "General."

He grunted as if I'd punched him in the balls. "I have to go. Don't do anything foolish."

I stayed in the curtsey, head low so he couldn't see the deceit in my eyes. I knew that if he caught even a glimmer of what I was about to do, he wouldn't let me out of his sight.

"Never."

One of the stable boys was suddenly there, taking the reins of Ares, but he never made a move for Havoc. I slowly lifted my head.

Dominic was gone.

"Goodbye," I whispered, hating the strange lurch in my body. I didn't want this to be the last time I saw the General, but I knew that it was best for me that I go, while I still could.

I took Havoc back to her stall and tucked her in with some mash, warm water and a good amount of hay. I did not take off her saddle, just loosened the girth. I removed her bridle and set it on a hook outside the door.

I needed to be ready to move quickly as soon as I was ready,

Before the stable lad could ask me to remove the rest of her tack, I slipped out and headed toward my room. See, I *was* doing the first part of what Dominic had told me to do.

If I thought outside was chaos, it was nothing to the interior of the castle.

People were nearly running through the halls, their faces painted with worry. Even if I hadn't known what a tyrant Edmund would be, this reaction to the old king's death would say it all.

Everyone was afraid of what would come next.

I made it to my room and shut the door, locking it behind me.

"Oh!"

I spun to see Bee lifting her head from the bed. Her face was streaked with tears, and her eyes were terribly red and puffy.

"Bee, it's okay, I'm back."

Her crying didn't ease and fear shot through me. "What happened? Are you okay?"

"They took Will, they locked him up!" She wailed. "Everyone . . .everyone says he's going to die. Edmund will kill him to keep him from the throne."

She fell into my arms and I just held her. Thinking. Stupid, it was a stupid idea that was brewing, but it would give me some protection too. And maybe, just maybe it would save Will.

I gave her a squeeze and held her out at arm's length. "Bee, listen to me. Listen good. Where are they holding Will?"

"Just in his rooms for now, but—"

"Any guards?"

"No, everyone knows him. He'd never slip through, he has too much honor."

A crazy idea was forming, almost as wild as the one that had brought me here, believing I could outwit the Others, and bring Jordan home. "Okay, here's what's going to happen. I'll get him one of the General's cloaks. You get him to put it on, okay." I'd seen helmets in Dominic's room. I'd grab one of those too.

Bee was standing straighter now. "How am I going to—?"

"You tell the Duchess that you're bringing him cocoa. When you give him the cocoa, tell him to scale the wall with the cloak and helmet on, and meet me at the stable."

Her tears slowed. "What? Why would you do this?"

"Do you want him to live?" I asked as I stuffed a bag with additional clothes, a few coins and several of the fancier pieces of jewelry. I could use them to trade, I was sure of it.

"Wait, do you love him?"

"No." I slung the bag over my shoulder and looked at her. Really looked. She was still upset, but her face was pale. "I don't want him, not like that, Bee. He's important . . ." I did not want to tell her that saving him would not only give me a bargaining chip with the werewolves, but that I'd be saving Dominic's brother. A brother he loved.

"Go make the cocoa and meet me back here in five minutes."

I dropped the bag of supplies—if they could be called that—by the door and strode out, heading straight for the soldier's quarters. There was no hesitation as I made my way to Dominic's rooms. Not until I opened the door and saw a woman rifling through his desk. Her hair was brilliantly red, and I was sure I'd seen her on the training field. Her head snapped up and she bared her fangs for just a split second before she reined herself in.

"What are you doing here?"

"The General asked me to bring him a cloak, and a helmet," I said, dropping into a curtsey. "My apologies, I did not realize anyone would be here."

She straightened and strode past me. "I was never here. Understood?"

"Of course." Like I'd done with Dominic, I stayed in the curtsey, sweating, legs shaking, until she was well past.

I stood and hurried deeper into the room, grabbing a long cloak with a hood, and the helmet next to it. Pausing at the table, I scooped up two daggers and tucked them under the length of material. Maybe they weren't swords, but they were something.

I passed several vampires as I hurried back to my room, but none of them so much as looked at me. Their eyes were glazed, and they didn't look like they were all there.

So far, so good with my haphazard plan.

Bee was waiting in the room, a tray of cocoa and a bag at her feet. "I'm coming with you."

"Bee—"

"No. I love him. And I'm . . .I know that he won't ever love me, but I would die for him."

I blew out a quick breath. "The Duchess—"

"I am here, Sienna."

Jesus fucking Christ. I spun to see the Duchess standing in the shadows, near the door. "You're wanting to give me some gray hairs then?" I yelped, feeling my heart step up to double time.

"Why do you want to save Will, if you don't love him?" Her shrewd eyes were locked on me.

Time for some of the truth. "The General."

Her eyes softened. "So, it is for love. Just not love for my Will."

I closed my eyes. Was it love? It was something more than lust, stronger than friendship. Maybe it was love. I wanted to help him. "If Will isn't here, then he can't be killed."

"True. And if it was said that he stole two of the girls, then perhaps the General himself would hunt down his brother? That would buy us all time to find a way to dethrone the usurper who killed my brother."

A chill swept through me. "Are you reading my mind?"

Her smiled was wide. "I will have William to the stables in fifteen minutes. You girls be ready. Give me the cloak, the helmet and the cocoa."

We handed over our items, and she barely glanced at the daggers. The second she was gone, Bee and I were bolting from the room. "Here, this way!"

She dragged me toward a panel in the wall. With a single push on it, we slid through and then we were running through the castle, shoving our way past other servants until we were in the kitchens. Which were empty.

"Grab some food. Bread. Dried meats. Things that will hold." I said.

I was already snagging apples and a hunk of cheese and stuffing them into my bag. Bee grabbed a few things and then we were moving again, out the door, and to the stable.

The young boys were gone.

Were they getting worms stuffed into their throats? I could not save them all, I knew it.

"Hold my bag." I shoved it at Bee and grabbed two horses, dragged them out and began to saddle them.

I'd barely finished tightening the cinch when the Duchess swept in, blood across her face and dripping from her chin. "Girls. Take care of my nephew."

Will stumbled in after her.

Bee gasped. "Is he hurt?"

"Yes. You both will have to give him blood. Get him to the eastern forest. Ask for sanctuary from the werewolves. They may help you."

Other than the fact that Will was hurt, this was too good to be true. I helped him onto the bigger of the two horses, a deep chestnut stallion with a bright white blaze. Then helped Bee up onto the slightly smaller bay mare.

"Go," I said. "I'll catch you."

Bee took hold of Will's reins and led him out, then they took off at a gallop. Havoc would catch them easily.

"Why are you really doing this, Sienna," the Duchess asked.

"Because I have a friend who was taken by the werewolves. I won't leave him there," I said.

Her eyes widened. "You . . .manufactured being caught? Brought here to find your friend?"

I tipped my chin up. "No one catches me, unless I let them, my lady." And then for good measure, I winked as I slung my leg up over Havoc's saddle and urged her forward.

We had a chance. A chance. And for a chance to save Jordan, I would cast my luck to the wind and pray to whatever gods might still be listening.

TWENTY-SIX

Dominic

EDMUND PACED IN FRONT of me. "The funeral will be tomorrow, of course. And the coronation will immediately follow. And of course, the executions will begin once I take the throne."

Trying to act bored or unconcerned with a pronouncement like that was difficult. "And just who will you start with, Your Majesty?" I kept my tone light. "Teresa of Southwind? She's always fancied herself the next queen. Or perhaps Anthony DuMont? He's a royal pain in the ass."

Edmund gave a low chuckle. "I would start with every single one of the girls in the Harvest Games. A blood-letting like has not been seen for a thousand years. The people will love me for it. Think of it like a celebration, if you will. A return to the old days. Before we were neutered like we were nothing more than a pack of filthy dogs"

Holy . . .fuck.

"You can't be serious."

Edmund went on, as if I hadn't spoken. "And then, I will eliminate any competition for the throne. Not Teresa, she is of course far too removed from our bloodline. Anyone who has a legitimate claim to the throne of course. They will be on the front lines of the executioner's block." He gave me an appraising glance, watching to see if I understood he meant Will, without actually saying his name.

I clenched my jaw. How the hell was I going to get Will and Sienna out of this clusterfuck? Will, no doubt, was just waiting, like a lapdog in his rooms. Unknowing that his death was mere hours away. This was not the time to play the fool. This was the time for action.

But despite the flair of something more I'd seen in my younger brother, I still was unsure that he was capable.

My bigger concern was Sienna. I'd sent her to *her* rooms. To await me and now, death was coming for her. I could not stop my hand from drifting to the blade at my waist. Our heads were all on the chopping block. Would it matter if I killed Edmund now? He'd already decided on Will's death.

"And your bastard brother, what of him?" I asked softly.

Edmund smiled. "I suppose . . . I might have use of you for some time. Gathering people for me. Bringing them to the executioner. I won't bother with the Duchess unless she irritates me. Ha, so she will likely be dead before the end of the week. I think I will enjoy that the most."

I had to kill him, right then. My hand inched toward my sword. I'd be executed for killing the king, but Will would be alive. My aunt.

Sienna.

Closing my eyes, I could see her so clearly. Her skin in the candle light, slick with desire, her mouth parted. As far as a final memory worth remembering it was perhaps the best I could have had.

"Edmund, I don't think—"

There was a soft knock on the door.

"Enter," Edmund snapped.

The Duchess slipped in; her head bowed. "Your Majesty, I bring grave news." She lifted her chin slowly, the blood staining her face, and upper body shocking. I'd never seen her with so much as a hair out of place, never mind blood on her mouth.

Edmund took a step toward her. "What in the hell—?"

"I took Will some cocoa. He . . .threw me against the wall and escaped. I do believe that a guard tried to stop him. I would never think that boy could hurt me but . . ." She slid to the floor, her skirts pooling out around her.

Effortless, she looked graceful even in defeat.

Edmund stormed past her, shouting orders.

I went to her side, and she clutched at my shirt. "He escaped with Sienna and her maid. He's injured and likely assumed he would need them both to succeed."

Fear and rage ripped through me, and she winced as my hands tightened on her arms. "What?"

"Go after them on Edmund's behalf," her voice lowered further. "Hunt them down and save them all. You know how to get Edmund to send you after them. He has to believe you have reason to hate Will. Which . . .I think you could if you believed Sienna would let him drink from her, you could do just that."

It took all I had not to snap her arms.

"From outside the castle, you can rally . . . behind Will," she said. "You must."

She was talking about a full out war. The coup that had been building for years.

"You will be killed."

"I cannot leave. I have the girls here to try and protect," she whispered. "I know what he plans for them."

I let her go and stood, knowing there was nothing else. "Goodbye, Duchess."

Her smile was as soft as I'd ever seen it, but there were no more words between us. I left her there to go and find Edmund who was raging in the throne room.

"Two? He took two of the girls with him?"

Now was the time to play the gamble that my aunt had set up for me. A game of Blitzkrieg in real life. "Who did he take?"

Edmund spun. "Does it matter?"

My jaw ticked. "Yes. It rather does to me."

Edmund looked hard at me. "You wanted one of the girls this time." Not a question, but I answered it anyway.

"I did. And if Will took her, then I will hunt him down myself and gut him on my staff." I snarled. It took very little to imagine Will on top of her, taking her sweet body and drinking from her veins. The growl that slipped from me was not intended to be let loose.

My older brother sniffed. "He took a serving girl, and her charge. The one with the honey eyes."

I'd already known of course, but I let the growl turn into something else.

I tipped my head back and let the rage pour out of me. The primal bellow was picked up by the Hunters and they echoed my wildness. Instead of easing the fear and rage, I only felt it more deeply in my bones.

Sienna was *mine*.

Hands gripped into fists, I dropped to one knee. "Send me, my King. I will find them."

Silence met my words, and I stayed where I was, shaking. Fury holding me there.

"Excellent. A hunting party is exactly what we need."

Edmund's words had my head coming up. He was nodding, a look on his face I did not like.

"I will gather my horse, and a few more men—"

Horror cut through me. This was not...what I'd wanted. "What about the coronation? What about King Stirling's funeral?"

Fucking hell. If he came with me, Will was sure to die, and Sienna would be close behind. Or worse, Edmund would take her as his new pet. Which he could do as king.

No, I'd kill her myself before I let that happen.

"Ah, I believe all those official matters can wait for a hunt like this. I look forward to you killing our younger brother. It has been a dream of mine, I must say I never thought it would come to fruition." He smiled, and behind his eyes I saw the darkness, the absolute madness in him.

He clapped his hands. "Come now. The General is going to lead us on a hunt, to save his woman, and kill the usurper."

Dominic and Sienna's story isn't over...

Don't miss

HUNTED BY FATE

Alpha Territories #2
Coming in 2023

Sign up for release day emails by scanning the code below,
then come talk all things **Alpha Territories** in my fan group at
www.thelairofmayer.com

ALSO BY SHANNON MAYER

The Forty Proof Series
MIDLIFE BOUNTY HUNTER
MIDLIFE FAIRY HUNTER
MIDLIFE DEMON HUNTER
MIDLIFE GHOST HUNTER
MIDLIFE ZOMBIE HUNTER
MIDLIFE WITCH HUNTER
MIDLIFE MAGIC HUNTER
coming March 2023
MIDLIFE SOUL HUNTER

The Honey and Ice Series (with Kelly St. Clare)
A COURT OF HONEY AND ASH
A THRONE OF FEATHERS AND BONE
A CROWN OF PETALS AND ICE

World of Honey and Ice (with Kelly St. Clare)
THORN KISSED & SILVER CHAINS

FOR A COMPLETE BOOK LIST VISIT
www.shannonmayer.com

Lightning Source UK Ltd.
Milton Keynes UK
UKHW042221021122
411544UK00010B/205/J